MEDICAL THRILLER
A DR. BRYCE CHAPMAN NOVEL

DECEPTION

BRIAN
HARTMAN

"What is truth?" retorted Pilate.
John 18:38

"Half the truth is often a great lie."
Benjamin Franklin

To my colleagues and entire team in the Emergency Department. My interactions with you over the years have inspired so many of these characters and events. Keep fighting the good fight until we find ourselves off shift together, at which point it will be bolus, and titrate!

Chapter One

"Ma'am, do you know why I pulled you over today?" Officer Michael Jenkins had asked this question over a thousand times in his decade-long career with the Indianapolis Metro Police Department.

"I think I was going a little too fast," replied Destiny, a young, black college-aged driver.

"Yeah, I'd say. I clocked you at seventy-two. The speed limit on I-465 is only fifty-five. Where were you headed in such a rush?"

"Just headed home. It's been a long day at work. I had the radio on, windows down, and was focusing on relaxing rather than my speed. I'm sorry, officer." *And I was just keeping up with traffic, why did you single me out?*

"A long day? It's 9:00 a.m. Do you work nights?"

"Yes, I do. I work at a warehouse and it's non-stop. I've been working extra because school is about to start."

"Okay, let me go run your information and I'll get you on your way. Please slow down out here. There is a lot more traffic because of the road construction and we're seeing an increase in accidents. I want you to be safe."

"Yes sir, absolutely," said Destiny, relieved at the suggestion she may get away with only a warning.

Officer Jenkins retreated to his car parked along the right-hand shoulder of the road and waited for a break in traffic to open the door and sit inside. He used the laptop computer to run the license and registration for Destiny and found everything in order. A small icon showed she possessed a license to carry a handgun. He smiled. Another person who won't be a victim.

He navigated through the software to enter the citation information including date, time, location, and speed involved. He saved it in the system and printed a notice, before checking his mirrors and exiting the vehicle.

Destiny looked in her mirror and saw the officer returning, holding her documents along with a long, narrow sheet of paper. *What? I thought I was going to get a warning. I can't afford this!* She waited for the officer to approach her window and began pleading her case. "Sir, please don't give me a ticket; I can't afford it. I'm working two jobs to save for college which starts next month. I barely have enough for books as it is."

Officer Jenkins smiled at Destiny and said, "Relax, it's just a written warning. I was young once. You weren't driving recklessly; you were just driving too quickly. My job is to keep you safe, not fund the city budget." He handed her the documents and bid farewell, taking a step backward before turning toward his vehicle.

She breathed a sigh of relief and dropped her head to her chest. As she looked up for a last look at the officer, she screamed as he vanished; his image replaced by a car that missed her rear-view mirror by mere inches. The sound of the car striking the officer was instantly seared into her mind, bringing with it an overwhelming feeling of dread. She looked up and saw the officer thrown through the air, flipping several times before landing on the side of the road, motionless. The vehicle swerved back onto the roadway and continued down the road.

"Oh Jesus, don't let him die," she said as she jumped from her car and ran to his side. She had her phone out and called 9-1-1 to report the injury.

"9-1-1, what's your emergency?" asked the dispatcher with a tone of disinterest.

"I'm on the side of 465 and a police officer was just struck by a car. He's hurt really bad. You need to send help right away." Destiny's voice was a mix of screaming and crying. "The other car didn't stop. It was some sort of small, red SUV. You need to hurry; he hit his head and is not breathing well."

The operator's tone changed immediately as he asked a few more specific questions, trying to confirm where she was calling from. The enhanced 9-1-1 system communicated with her cell phone to provide location information, allowing the dispatcher to confirm her location quickly.

"Ma'am, I need you to help me assess the officer. Is he breathing?"

She looked at Officer Jenkins, the man who had treated her kindly and with compassion just two minutes prior. She saw him intermittently gasp for a breath, a gurgling sound coming with each respiratory effort. "A little. He's trying, but there's a weird noise when he tries. I think he puked, too."

"Listen, I need to you try to open his airway. Is he on his back or on his side?"

"He's on his side."

"Okay, good. I want you to place your hands behind the corner of his jaw and pull forward, but be careful to not move his neck much when you do this. It should pull his jaw forward and open his airway more. Can you do that?"

"I'll try," she said before tucking the phone between her shoulder and her cheek. She placed her hands on the officer's face and pulled forward, noting a bony crunch when she did so, but his breathing became less noisy.

"Okay, I did it. He sounds better, but I think he has a broken jaw."

The sound of tires crunching on gravel made Destiny look up, and she saw several cars pulling over to offer assistance. The faint sound of sirens gave her hope. *Just hang on, help is coming!*

Chapter Two

"Get your hands off me!" screamed the drunk patient in trauma bay two.

"Ma'am, relax. We're trying to help you. You fell and hit your head. You have a large wound that we need to repair and then get you to the CT scanner to make sure you don't have a skull fracture or a bleed in your brain." The nurse tried again to establish an IV, but the patient was too agitated and intoxicated to sit still for the procedure. "We're going to have to give you something to calm down so that we can take care of you. I'll be right back."

The nurse tracked down the Emergency Medicine physician at his workstation. "Hey Doc, the lady in trauma two could really use some Haldol or something. She won't let me put an IV in her and is pretty agitated. And I think she might be pregnant. She keeps screaming about 'us' and holding her abdomen."

Dr. Bryce Chapman pushed back from his keyboard and spun his chair around to face the nurse. "That lady is nuts. She's here all the time for alcohol related issues. Why can't people just get drunk at home while they're safely in bed?" He sighed and shrugged his shoulder. "She may have a head injury though, so I agree we should sedate her a bit and then get the IV and head CT. I'll add on a pregnancy test. Give her five milligrams of Haldol. That should buy us enough time to get our testing done and then some of the alcohol to wear off."

"Doc, sorry to interrupt, but they need you to answer the EMS line," said Paula, the ER secretary on duty for the day shift.

Bryce stood up and walked to the radio station next to Paula's desk. As he approached her desk, the sound of Christmas music rose above the noise of the busy department. "Do You Hear What I Hear" was sung by Bing Crosby with as much joy as Paula hoped to add to her life by listening to the music year round. "Hi, this is Dr. Bryce Chapman. Go ahead with your traffic."

"Doc, we're coming in with a trauma alert. A police officer was struck on the side of the road and sustained significant injuries. He has a head injury and is in respiratory distress. He has a flail chest on the right. We're a few minutes out. Do you want us to intubate?"

Bryce tried to control his growing anger and sadness for the officer while he listened to the report. "No, not if he's breathing. Just bag him with 100% oxygen and get him here in a hurry." He glanced at the tracking board on Paula's computer to find out which room was available. "We'll see you in trauma room three. Washington Memorial out."

He grabbed the microphone to make an overhead announcement in the ER. "Trauma One inbound, two minutes out. Have the rapid infuser set up and ready to go." He put down the mic and turned to Paula. "Page trauma surgery overhead to the ER stat, and find Thrasher. I'm going to need some help."

Bryce jogged back toward the trauma rooms to re-assess his drunk patient and prepare for the incoming police officer.

Chapter Three

B ryce could hear the intoxicated patient screaming at the staff before he even opened the door to the trauma rooms. Slurring profanity laced tirades, focused on volume rather than enunciation.

"What the hell wazzat? What did you just give me?"

"That was Haldol, my dear. In a few minutes you'll be resting much better," said her nurse, tossing the syringe and needle into the sharps container. "We gave it as an intramuscular injection, so it should take five or ten minutes to kick in. Once you're calmer, we'll put in an IV and get you to the CT scanner."

"Katie, thanks for being kind to her. I know she's here a lot for alcohol issues, but she may have actually hurt herself this time," said Bryce.

"No problem, Dr. Chapman. I figure if I'm nice to the drunks here, maybe I'll earn karma points to use when I'm the drunk, causing a scene somewhere else."

Bryce laughed and nodded his head. "There you go, nice attitude. Hey, we have a trauma coming in next door and we're going to need your help. Can you toss a line in her quickly before they get here?"

Katie agreed and turned back to the patient. "Let's hope the medicines are working because it's about to get busy in here. Is there any chance you're pregnant? You keep saying 'us' when you talk." She opened a cart and removed the IV supplies, laying them out next to the patient in her standard fashion. She laid the color-coded blood tubes in order and added a gray-topped tube for the alcohol level she wanted to run.

Doors opened behind her as members of the trauma team began to arrive. Respiratory therapists, lab technicians, additional nurses, and even a few doctors. They congregated outside trauma room three. Dr. Elisa Morales stood at the front of the group, easily six inches shorter than anyone else. She was the trauma surgeon on duty today and packs more intensity per square inch than any other doctor in the hospital. She was already dressed in a sterile gown and gloves, her mask equipped with a plastic shield to protect her eyes from any potential fluid exposure.

"Elisa, thanks for being here. I see we're still stocking the pediatric gowns for you," said Bryce with a smile. He turned around before she had a chance to glare at him. They were on much better terms now that their prior interaction had taken a new light.

In the next room over, Katie worked to place an IV catheter.

"Hold still, here comes the poke," she said, plunging the needle into the patient's antecubital fossa. There was an immediate return of blood into the needle hub, confirming placement in the vein. Katie used her index finger to flick the tab on the catheter, sliding it further inside the vein. She then retracted the needle and dropped it in the sharps container. She quickly drew the vials of blood and then secured the IV in place, leaving the tubes resting on the bed next to the patient's leg. While turning around to grab a sheet of stickers to label the blood, the doors burst open, and the chaos began.

"Patient is a thirty-nine-year-old police officer. He was struck by a car on the side of the interstate. He has agonal respirations, signs of a significant head injury, and a flail chest on the right. Blood pressure is sixty. We have two IVs established, and he's received a liter and a half of fluid. We decided to just load and go rather than try to intubate in the field."

Bryce surveyed the scene as the medics rolled him into the room. *Oh no, this is bad*. Pedestrian versus car at highway speeds is a difficult injury mechanism to survive. "Let's get him moved over to our cot. I want four units of blood hung on the rapid infuser immediately. Let's prepare to intubate and get a chest tube tray ready!" he shouted above the chaos.

While the respiratory therapist prepared equipment to place a breathing tube in the officer, Bryce bagged him to ventilate the patient. "Elisa, I think he needs a chest tube on the right. Can you make that happen?"

"Way ahead of you, ER. I've got a 36-French tube in my hand." She prepared the patient's right chest with chlorhexidine, a potent disinfectant, and then felt along the chest for the appropriate anatomic landmarks. "His chest is moving freely; he must have broken nearly every rib in multiple places. Get him on that vent now, ER. He needs positive pressure ventilation because his chest wall physiology is destroyed." She looked up at the head of the bed and saw Bryce had already passed the breathing tube into the airway, and was now confirming placement with his stethoscope on the chest. Elisa nodded her appreciation of Bryce's speed and skill and then sank her scalpel into Officer Jenkins' chest. Elisa made a two-inch incision over the fifth rib down to the muscle layer. She then traded the scalpel for a large pair of curved hemostats, which she placed in her left hand. She braced the handle against her ribs and leaned forward, popping through the muscles of the chest wall using the force of her entire body.

An immediate rush of air and blood soaked the front of her gown. "Well, at least I know I'm not in the abdomen. We wouldn't have that rush of air if I were below the diaphragm." She inserted the large bore chest tube and quickly sutured it in place. A nurse hooked it up to the vacuum collection system and blood poured out of the chest and into the device. "Let's autotransfuse that. He's going to need a lot of blood; may as well give him back his own, too," she said.

Bryce scanned the patient quickly, noting a sunken area in the right forehead. *He's got a depressed skull fracture.* Bryce imagined a fragment of skull pressing downward on the brain, decreasing the patient's chance of survival. Moving lower, he noted the pelvis to be unstable. "I think he has a significant pelvic injury, maybe a torn urethra, too. Do not put a Foley catheter in him," he instructed the nurses. The officer's right leg was bent in the middle of the thigh, indicating a significant femur fracture. He grabbed a sheet and, with the aid of a nurse, slid it under the patient's buttocks, then tied it in a knot to close the potential volume of the pelvis. Anything to help slow down the seemingly unlimited blood loss.

"Blood pressure is fifty! Heart rate is dropping!" shouted a nurse.

"Damn it," said Bryce quietly. "Start him on max dose Levophed. Where are we at with the blood? Elisa, can you drop in a trauma introducer? We need to give him blood as fast as we can."

He looked up at the head of the bed and saw Dr. Morales finishing up placing a large bore trauma catheter in the patient's right internal jugular vein. "Again, way ahead of you ER. This line is good. Move the rapid infuser to this line in his neck," she ordered. "Let's get X-ray in to shoot his chest and pelvis."

Bryce walked over to Elisa and whispered to her. "I don't think these injuries are survivable. He needs a neurosurgeon, trauma surgeon, interventional radiology, and an orthopedist. All at the same time. But he's not stable enough to go to the OR."

Elisa looked up at Bryce and nodded slowly but didn't speak. He saw her eyes were wet and a tear running down her cheek. "My father was a police officer."

Bryce felt something hit him in the back of the head and saw an IV start kit laying next to his foot. "What the–". He turned and saw more items coming over the curtain from the drunk lady in trauma bay two.

"Did you guys forget about me?" yelled the drunk patient. "I have been asking for a sandwich forever!"

"Ma'am, lay down and shut up. You are not going to throw things or bother our staff when we are dealing with a critically injured patient." The forceful words came from Dr. Peter Thrasher, the newest Emergency Medicine Physician in the group. He unlocked her bed and spun it around to face the wall, then took a sheet and wrapped it around her arms and chest before tying it in a knot. "We will not let you try to injure our staff. We'll be with you as soon as we can. Besides, no food for you until we get your testing back. You may have a significant head injury."

Peter entered bay three and scanned the room. "Woah, this sucks. What happened?"

"Car versus police officer. He's in terrible shape," said Bryce. "He's got blood infusing and should be nearly done with his fourth unit. We're hoping to get him to CT soon to look at his injuries. If he has a large epidural hematoma, we need to fix that at the same time you're fixing the rest of his problems," said Bryce, looking at Elisa.

She glanced at the patient on the bed. "If only it was a gunshot to the chest, or a stab wound to the abdomen. Something survivable. This poor guy has no chance."

"Blood pressure is seventy, Levophed is maxed out, the blood is in," called out a nurse.

"Okay team, if we don't get to CT now, we'll never make it. Let's roll," said Elisa to the room. She punctuated her speech by unlocking the bed and hooking the bedside monitor on the rail of the stretcher. Respiratory therapy continued delivering breaths while the nurses wheeled the officer down to CT.

Chapter Four

B ryce looked at Peter and said, "I have a bad feeling about this. Last time Elisa pushed a trauma patient to the CT scanner he coded on the table and died. She filleted him open and I had to go present the case to the Morbidity and Mortality with Tom Sharpe." The incident he was referring to involved a patient who Bryce evaluated after only having mild respiratory issues for several hours. Bryce felt he was stable and discharged him home before leaving on a trip to the Bahamas with his wife, Valerie.

"Oh yeah, I heard about that. Tom saw your patient as a bounce back, right? He came in as a trauma because he wrecked his car but really he was just severely septic and nearly arrested in the car. Didn't she do a bedside thoracotomy and laparotomy, only to find no traumatic injuries?" asked Peter.

Bryce nodded. "Exactly. She's like a top-of-the-line piece of mining equipment. It is capable of doing an outstanding job and achieving excellent results. You just gotta help it start in the right place."

Peter smiled at the reference. "I love mining references. Drilling, shafts, big loads. It's custom-made for my type of humor."

"Dr. Chapman, sorry to interrupt, but there are about twenty police officers out in the waiting room who want an update on your patient. What should I tell them? Do you want me to bring back the most senior one?" Jackie Sirico, the ED charge nurse, asked in a way that provided the answer that she thought was best, a sign of her experience as a nurse. She learned long ago to help direct the physician to answer her question in the correct manner.

"That's a good idea, thanks. And if his family arrives, bring them back immediately because I'm not sure he's going to survive this. It would also be nice to have consent for surgery if he needs it," said Bryce.

"Consent for procedures is so lame," said Peter. "You came to an ER for help, then we have to get written consent to actually help you. It's stupid. If someone shows up here for my help, I should have free rein to do what I think is best to help them. Signing a piece of paper only delays care and helps no one."

"I agree with you, buddy, but it's the system we operate in. Obviously, don't delay critical procedures while waiting on a signed consent, but if you have time, it's best to get them signed."

"Sometimes I wish I was more like a medical Spiderman. No, actually Batman. I just hang out in my mansion and wait for someone to get in trouble. Then I drive some badass bike or car to them, ignoring all traffic laws, and do whatever I can to help. Once done, I simply vanish into the night. That would be killer."

Bryce was ready to respond, but the trauma door swinging open interrupted him. Jackie walked through, followed by a tall, black, middle-aged police officer in full dress uniform. "Bryce, this is Captain Sammy Booker. He is the chief of IMPD and would like an update on your patient."

"Absolutely. Sir, I'm Bryce Chapman, Emergency Medicine physician," said Bryce as he extended a hand towards the chief. After a vigorous shake, he continued. "Officer Jenkins sustained severe injuries when the vehicle struck him. We have him sedated on a ventilator. His blood pressure is borderline despite four units of blood and high doses of medications to raise his pressure. He is currently in the CT scanner with our trauma team. Sir, I need to be honest with you. He is critically ill, and I am not sure he is going to survive this. Humans are not designed to be struck by vehicles."

The chief listened to what Bryce had to say and then shook his head back and forth slowly. "No, no, they are not. I trust your team is doing the best they can for Jenkins. That man has been on our force for over ten years. He is happily married with a few kids, and needs to pull through this for them. You know we haven't caught the person who hit him yet? As big as my department is, and we still haven't caught him."

Bryce could see the anguish in his eyes. "Sir, we are doing our best. Do you know if his wife is going to be here soon?"

"I just spoke with her. She's probably a few minutes away. She was at the mall with friends when she heard the news."

The doors burst open again and Officer Jenkins' bed flew through the gap, followed by several nurses. Dr. Morales was straddling his chest, doing CPR.
"What happened?" asked Bryce.

"We finished the scans and as we moved him back to the bed, his heart rate dropped and then went to zero," said Dr. Morales.

Bryce watched her CPR technique, impressed with the depth of compression she produced, despite her slight frame. "Elisa, you need to open him up and see if there's anything fixable."

She flipped her head to get her hair out of her eyes and stared directly at him. "ER, this guy is toast. Blunt traumatic arrest has about a zero percent survivability rate. Add in his head injury, the number of broken bones I saw in the CT scanner, blood in the chest, and it's just not going to be survivable. We might keep him alive a bit longer as an organ donor if he's made that decision."

Bryce looked at the Chief of Police and then back to Elisa, who continued chest compressions. "Elisa, we need to try."

She bowed her head and exhaled deeply, then jumped off the bed. "Fine, get me a surgical tray. We're going in. I want to cross-clamp his aorta in thirty seconds."

Peter stepped to the bed and began deep rhythmic chest compressions while Elisa opened the surgical instrument tray.

"Thrasher, get the hell out of my way when my scalpel gets close to you. Once I've clamped the aorta, continue open cardiac massage." She plunged her scalpel in to the officer's chest just left of the sternum and pulled it quickly toward the armpit. Peter leaned back and lifted his hands to avoid a traumatic manicure at the hands of an irritated trauma surgeon. Elisa dropped the scalpel onto the surgical tray and picked up the thick scissors. She cut through the muscle between the ribs and then inserted the rib spreader device. She twisted it quickly, widening the gap between the ribs so she could fit her petite hands in further. Once spread, she grabbed the vascular clamp and reached halfway into the chest of Office Jenkins, feeling for the thick-walled aorta and placing a clamp around it. Once satisfied with her positioning, she closed the clamp. This blocked blood flow from reaching the lower two-thirds of his body and focused flow to his coronary arteries and brain. With any luck, this would allow his heart to beat again, and then she could repair the injuries below the clamp and release it before the organs suffered irreparable harm.

Bryce reached into the chest cavity and began internal cardiac massage on the officer. He had gowned and gloved in anticipation of the need and stood ready when Elisa removed her sharp instruments. "Two more units of blood and a milligram of epinephrine!" he shouted to anyone who had a free hand to help.

"No, no more blood," said Elisa as she stared into the chest.

"What?" asked Bryce. "He's hemorrhaging from everywhere. He needs blood immediately!"

"Save it for the next person. His aorta is essentially transected. It's almost cut in half, Bryce. That is not a survivable injury. We need to let him go."

A scream from the doorway startled the medical team, who had been looking at the patient, and just heard Dr. Morales give a sobering prognosis.

"Michael!" she screamed again, pushing past the team to approach his bedside.

"This is the patient's wife. She arrived a minute ago and wanted to see him immediately," said the triage nurse.

Bryce continued compressing the heart and glanced at Elisa before addressing the patient's wife. "Ma'am, I'm Dr. Bryce Chapman. I'm the ER doctor taking care of your husband. He has sustained catastrophic injuries from the accident today. I'm sorry to tell you this, but we cannot save him." He removed his hands from the patient's heart and stepped back, removing his gown and gloves as a single unit.

The officer's wife screamed a loud denial at Bryce and fell to her knees next to her husband. She grasped one of his hands in hers. "Don't you say that to me," she moaned. "Mike, you promised me you'd be home tonight. You promised me you'd be careful out there." Her speech eroded into tearful, body-shaking sobs. No one spoke for a few minutes until her sobbing slowed and her breathing recovered.

Elisa walked over and knelt down next to her. She placed an arm on her shoulders and spoke softly. "I'm Dr. Morales, the trauma surgeon who tried to help your husband. If it's any consolation, I can assure you that he felt no pain from this injury. I am very sorry for your loss." The officer's wife nodded, but did not reply. Elisa stood, walked past Bryce and Peter, and headed toward the door. She paused before exiting and in a hushed voice she said, "You know Bryce, just a few months ago you said I did too much and hacked your patient apart. Now today you demanded I do the same thing again despite there being no chance of saving him. I felt like I was doing a thoracotomy on my dad. Thanks." She turned and pushed the door open, angling her body to squeeze through the opening before it had the chance to fully open.

Chief Booker thanked Bryce, Peter, and the rest of the team for their efforts. He then walked behind the officer's widow and placed a hand on her shoulder. "The department will come together as a family and walk with you through this."

Chapter Five

B ryce and Peter excused themselves from the room and walked back to the physician's work area. "Paula, can you call the coroner for me?" said Bryce before slumping down into his chair.

Peter sat down next to him, put his hands behind his head, and leaned back.

"Life isn't fair, you know?" said Bryce. "That guy worked to help people and keep them safe, and he gets killed for it. Do we even know who hit him?"

"I heard it was a hit and run," said Paula. "They have a description of the car, but haven't found it yet."

"Oh man, that's going to be even harder for the family to accept. I hope they find the guy," said Bryce. He opened the officer's chart and began documenting the details of the visit. He was halfway done with the task when Paula interrupted him.

"Dr. Chapman, the coroner's investigator is on the line."

"Is it Ashley?"

Paula nodded and gave him a motherly expression. "You be nice to her. She's just doing her job."

"Poorly, she's just doing her job poorly, you mean," said Bryce as he picked up the handset and pressed the button near the blinking light. "Hi, this is Dr. Bryce Chapman."

"Hi, Ashley Saxon, coroner's office. Are you calling about Officer Jenkins?"

"Yes, I am. Are you already aware and on your way?" he asked.

"Sure am. An officer informed us a few minutes ago. I'll be there in about ten. What room is he in?"

"He's in ER trauma bay three. See you soon." He hung up the line and looked over at Peter. "This is the same investigator who signed off on my patient a few months ago. They claimed he had cystic fibrosis, and that's why he died of multi-drug resistant pseudomonas, despite him having zero history of pulmonary infections and no significant hospital contact to pick up a bug like that.

"That's not cool, man. Did they at least test him for it?" asked Peter.

"No, they said they didn't need to. Young guy died of a bug like that and since his father had cystic fibrosis they called it a done deal. So stupid." Bryce did not reveal the part where he and his orthopedic friend Graham Kelly broke into a sperm bank to get a sample and tested it for CF. It's a great story, one he was quite proud of, but it would only lead to further questions. What did he do with the information once he had it? Admit that he used it to help prove Clay murdered Kent and then enact his retribution through a pressure washer? Why didn't he go to the police with that information? Bryce liked Peter and was getting to know him much better, but that was a story best saved for another day.

Bryce picked up his portable phone and dialed the nurse taking care of the officer. "It's Chapman. Can you let me know when the coroner investigator arrives? I want to talk to her."

He only had to wait fifteen minutes before he was notified of her arrival.

"Ashley? Hey, it's Bryce. We talked on the phone."

"Yeah, I remember you from the last case we had together," she said without looking up. "Why do we only talk when a patient of yours dies?"

Bryce could feel the coldness in her words. "Well, you are the coroner's investigator. When would you like me to call you when it's not work related? That seems inappropriate, actually."

Ashley looked up at him and gave a quick sigh. "Whatever. This case will not be very difficult at least. We will decline the body, as there is no question as to the cause of death. But because he's a city employee, we will need to run a toxicology panel on him per our standard protocol. I should have those results by tomorrow. Will you sign the death certificate?"

"Of course. It's just a shame. He didn't deserve to die," said Bryce.

"That is something we can both agree on. Let me just grab a sticker for this last tube of blood I'll be on my way." She picked up a sheet of patient labels and attached one to the gray-topped tube before dropping it in the evidence bag.

A nurse broke into their conversation. "Dr. Chapman, the CT tech asked for you to look at the images on the drunk lady from room two. She's on the scanner now."

Bryce excused himself and walked down the hallway toward the CT scanner. He knocked on the control room door and entered.

"Hey doc, figured you'd want to see this. She's got a big bleed with some shift," said the tech, pointing at the monitor.

Bryce looked at the monitor and gave a low whistle as the tech scanned through the images on his drunken patient, whom Peter had tied to the bed, whom had a large bleed in her skull, but outside of the brain. The subdural hematoma had both bright white and darker gray components, suggesting it was at least partially chronic. The blood was causing increased pressure in the skull that was pushing on the brain. "I'd better call neurosurgery. If we don't get this drained soon, she may not be able to come back and keep causing us problems."

The techs laughed in response. "Are you really sure you need to call neurosurgery, then?"

Don't tempt me. "Yeah, I guess we should. Now that you guys documented she has an emergency medical condition, you sort of tied my hands. When she comes back because home rehab facility can't stand her anymore, I'll blame you all for it." He looked through the glass in the control room and saw the patient resting comfortably on the table. Or adequately sedated thanks to the Haldol. Either way, she had stopped screaming and throwing things at staff, which was an improvement.

Bryce exited the room with a smile on his face. The CT department was chronically understaffed and overworked. Their machine was running twenty-four hours a day thanks to the complexity of patient conditions and the 'no-miss' culture that exists with emergency care. Gone are the days when a delayed diagnosis was considered a reasonable risk to avoid advanced imaging on nearly every patient. If there was a two percent risk of appendicitis, that meant only one in fifty patients had it. So forty-nine patients avoid the harm of radiation for no benefit, while the one appendicitis patient will get worse and return and undergo testing at that point. This delayed diagnosis is rarely significant if the patient returned appropriately, but delayed diagnosis is frequently the basis of lawsuits. So now everyone gets the CT scan at the first visit. Bryce had never received an award for saving a patient from the dangers of ionizing radiation, only penalties for missing a diagnosis. Striving for the lowest possible first visit missed diagnosis rate has led to massive overutilization of resources, health care expenditure and overworked employees. But for this moment, it was time to laugh with the team.

"Paula, I need neurosurgery paged for the lady in room two."

She turned to look at Bryce, but stopped short and grabbed her right calf muscle. "Okay, I'll get them paged right away, doc."

"Are you Okay?" he asked. "Did you hurt your leg?"

"I must have. It's been bothering me for two days but I can't think of what I did. If I sit still and take ibuprofen, it's tolerable. But it sure hurts when I try to walk on it."

"Well, let me know if you want me to look at it," said Bryce before sitting back down at his workstation and updating charts.

"Dr. Chapman, what did the CT scan show on that lady?" asked Emily Baldwin, Peter Thrasher's scribe and former girlfriend.

"She is actually sick this time. She has an acute on chronic subdural hematoma causing some midline shift, and will need to go to the operating room fairly soon."

"Will she have bur holes and a drain placed?"

"Yes, exactly. Good job. Sometimes I forget you're not a medical student. You certainly have picked up enough knowledge, as a scribe, to play the part," he said.

"Well, I have been applying for a few years but haven't gotten in anywhere yet. I'm considering going to the Caribbean for school, but it's so expensive and I don't have that kind of money."

"Emily, let's go. There's a new abdominal pain patient waiting to be seen," said Dr. Peter Thrasher. "We can talk about subdurals later."

"No thanks, I have a pretty good grasp on them already, I think. And besides, the only thing you can teach me is how to choose a better boyfriend." She said the last sentence quieter; just loud enough for him to hear as they exited the physician's work area.

Chapter Six

J ackie Cirico entered the department just before 3:00 p.m., earlier than her usual start time of 7:00 p.m. She usually works the night shift and functions as charge nurse for the department, handling patient flow and managing staff as needed. But not today.

"Hey Jackie, I saw you on the schedule earlier. What are you doing here while the sun's up?" asked a fellow nurse.

"I know, right? Now that the hospital gave us the extra staff on our shifts, I'm not as stressed as I had been. I'm actually able to take some time off. I switched a shift and am covering today to bank up time for my vacation and I'm doing usual duties today, not even in charge."

"Oh, that's great," said her colleague. "Where are you going to go?"

"I have no idea, but I know it will not be Indiana. I want a beach, some rum, and a lounge chair. Maybe an umbrella, if it gets too hot."

"For you, or your drink?"

"Both." Jackie winked at her friend as she passed by, headed to the time clock. She swiped her badge to begin her shift and then tracked down the assignment sheet to find where she will be working. *Hallway two, not bad. No trauma, not the psych unit, I'll take it.*

"Hey Jackie, you're here early. Are you working or checking in as a patient?" asked Dr. Tom Sharpe, one of the senior attending physicians in the ER group.

She laughed and turned to look at him. She held her badge out and pulled on the leg of her scrub pants. "What do you think?"

"Honestly, it's hard to tell. Seems like a lot of our staff work when they're sicker than some patients."

"Ain't that the truth? I have worked with an IV in place, getting fluids between patients. It's hard to muster up compassion when you feel worse than the patient you're coddling and bringing a turkey sandwich," she said. "See you out there."

Dr. Sharpe has worked at Washington Memorial for a few years longer than Bryce. They first met when Bryce was a medical student rotating through the ER while Tom was a resident. They bonded well that month and have grown close over the years. Tom had even driven down to North Carolina recently to help Bryce recover a lost memory card. A Duke student had found it while on vacation in the Bahamas and was using the footage to extort Bryce for half a million dollars. That memory card held valuable footage that helped clear Bryce's assault charge in the Bahamas. Had they not recovered it and shown it to Niles Proffit, the CEO of the private-equity company who owned the hospital, Bryce would likely be unemployed today. It also contained some sensitive bedroom scenes between Bryce and Val, something they both wished to keep private.

Tom entered the physician's workspace and saw Peter talking to Emily as they worked on patient charts together. Bryce was on the phone with a consultant.

"Hey Tom, you missed a crazy morning. Absolutely tragic, my man," said Peter.

"I saw it on the news. Glad you and Bryce were working instead of me. Who responded from the trauma team?"

"Elisa Morales. She was here right when the officer arrived. Bryce asked her to do a thoracotomy and clamp the aorta, but she wasn't happy about it. The guy was toast no matter what we tried to do. You don't get hit by a car on the interstate and walk away from that."

"Wait, this time Elisa did not want to do a thoracotomy and Bryce asked her to? What is this, opposite day?" asked Tom, his head cocked sideways in confusion. Just a few months ago, Elisa had been called to the ER for a presumed trauma patient. The guy had wrecked his car and presented nearly dead, but Tom believed a medical illness had led to the accident and accounted for his critically ill appearance. Elisa had continued in the trauma mindset and opened his chest and eventually his abdomen before realizing he probably was just a sick medical patient who wrecked his car. Ultimately, the patient died from an overwhelming infection, and that led to a malpractice case involving Bryce, who had evaluated the patient on the first visit a few days prior, Tom Sharpe, and Elisa Morales.

"It must be. The worst part, though, is that apparently her father was a police officer. She said it felt like she was doing a thoracotomy on her father and walked away pissed after Bryce pronounced him."

Tom sat down in his chair and exhaled deeply. "Oh man, that's terrible. Sounds like this case affected everyone. Do they know who hit him?"

"Not yet. They have a vehicle description but it hasn't been located. I'm sure they will soon. You don't hit a guy at sixty miles an hour and not leave significant damage to the vehicle. All he's doing, by running, is making it worse for himself. The entire city is going to descend upon him."

"I'm going to hit the bathroom. Be back in a few," said Emily, closing her MacBook Pro. Peter waved and turned back to his computer.

Tom leaned over and whispered to Peter. "Hey, what's the deal with you two now? I know you broke up, but aren't you still living together? Is that getting weird?"

"It's a lot better this week. We moved her into an apartment a few days ago. Had to find a furnished one, since she really has nothing other than clothing and a car. It feels weird to not have someone at home, though."

"I bet. How long were you guys together?" asked Tom.

"A little over two years. She wanted to get married, I did not. She says I broke up with her, but really she ended it when I said I didn't want to get married. So yeah, I guess you could say my decision broke us up, but I would have been fine to keep dating her. She's pretty fun to have around most of the time."

A long tone from the EMS line interrupted their conversation, followed by a static filled report from a paramedic. "We're a few minutes out with a woman in her late teens. She was checking out at Walmart when suddenly she lost her vision. She's not able to appreciate light, but has no other neurologic defects. Do you want us to make this a stroke alert?"

Bryce walked over to the radio and replied, "This is Dr. Chapman. Do not make her a stroke alert, just check in like usual. I'll see her when she gets here. Washington Memorial out."

"Sudden bilateral vision loss in a teenage girl? Do you want her in psych?" asked Jackie, who had overheard the call.

"You're right that it's probably psychogenic blindness, but let's save those rooms for the suicidal and others who are at risk to themselves or others. She can just be in a standard bed. Is there room in your hallway?" he asked with a smile.

"I'm not sure. You'll have to ask the charge nurse," replied Jackie, waving her hand dismissively as she turned and walked away.

Bryce laughed as he replaced the handset back on the radio. He walked back and saw an oversized pink zebra-striped lunch bag sitting next to Peter.

"Hey Thrasher, I forgot to compliment you on your lunch box. It matches your long hair very well. Honestly, though, I always pictured you with more of a refined modern taste. Like a black bag with brushed nickel clasps or something."

"Whatever, that bag belongs to Emily. Since she moved out, she brings an entire buffet with her every day. I don't know how she fits it all in."

"Fits what in, Peter?" asked Emily as she rounded the corner. "Are you trying to spread lies about your bedroom prowess? Because I'd be happy to clear that up right now."

The four turned toward Paula, who had exploded in laughter. She had her eyes closed and shook her head back and forth, her palm raised up in a sign of apology. "Sorry, that was too much to hold inside. Maybe I need to turn up my music so I can't hear you all."

Bryce glanced at Peter and saw his face was nearly an identical color as Emily's lunch bag. "I think they need me somewhere else, I'll show myself out," he said as he backed out of of the physician work area. He started toward the trauma rooms when he saw a young woman being wheeled past on an ambulance stretcher. She had her eyes wide open and staring straight ahead.

"Doc, this is the patient we called in about. She can't see anything. We're headed to room twenty-three," said the paramedic.

"Okay, I'll follow you there. Her nurse will be in soon."

Bryce helped the medics transfer the patient over to the cot, the whole time watching her eyes for any sign of recognition of events in her vision. He saw none.

"This is Mackenzie Hearst. She called us from Walmart about fifteen minutes ago. She was in the checkout line and when she went to pay for her groceries, she lost her vision. Both eyes at the same time. Previously healthy, had nothing like this happen before. Her neuro exam is normal except for her loss of vision. Vitals are normal." The medic finished his report and wished the patient good luck.

Bryce introduced himself and sat down on the stool next to her bed. Mackenzie scanned around the room, looking for the source of the sound.

"What happened today, Mackenzie?"

Her phone buzzed in her lap. She quickly pressed a button on the side to stop the vibration. "I don't know. It was a pretty normal day. I was on my way to a park to do some filming and remembered I had to stop for a few props. I went into Walmart, and when I got to the register, I suddenly couldn't see anything."

"Filming? Props? Are you an actress?" he asked.

"Sort of. I'm an Instagram influencer and Youtuber. Do you know if anyone has called my parents yet?"

"I don't believe so. Do you want us to reach out to them for you?"

"Oh, that would be wonderful, thank you. Let them know I'm here, but I'm fine. My dad is Charlie Hearst. I can give you his number."

"Charlie Hearst? As in Hearst Family Ford?"

"Yep, that's him. And Honda, Subaru, Toyota, Chevy and I think a few others. I can't remember."

Bryce raised his eyes in appreciation. Charlie Hearst ran the largest car dealership empire in the state and had money oozing out of every pore in his body. "Ah yes, I've bought a few cars from him. I'm curious. What do you drive?"

"Audi!" she said enthusiastically. "That's the one I forgot. He has an Audi dealership too. I drive a red R8."

"Mackenzie, what are you feeling right now? Any weakness? Numbness? Any symptoms at all other than blindness?"

"No, I really do feel fine. I just wish I could see," she said. Her phone buzzed again, and she quickly silenced it.

Bryce spent a few minutes doing a detailed neuro exam and confirmed her only symptom was lack of vision in both eyes. The door opened and Jackie entered the room to begin her assessment. He brought her up to speed on the history and requested an IV before excusing himself from the room.

"Tom, my blind patient is here and is so eerily calm about the fact she can't see. I mean zero emotions about it. I would be fearful and pleading for answers. Asking if this was going to be permanent. She's just sitting there pleasantly talking and asking me to call her parents. I guess she's some sort of online celebrity."

"Wait, is she the daughter of the car dealer guy? Hearst?" asked Emily.

"Yes, she is. Do you know her?" said Bryce.

"Not really, but I've followed her on-line for over a year. Her Instagram posts are insane. She's in a new country every month. She also posts a lot of videos and likes to film while she drives. She puts the phone in a cradle, I guess on the dash or windshield, and just rambles about nothing. But it's so captivating."

Bryce sat down on the counter next to his computer. *I'm getting a bad feeling about this.*

"Hey guys, I think they found the car that hit the officer!" announced Paula. "Someone saw a small red car with significant front-end damage parked and called it in. I hope they catch the guy. He can't be too far away."

Peter pulled out his phone and searched Twitter for stories about the officer. He found a few posts with pictures of a small red car with heavy damage to the front passenger side. "Oh man, that's not a Maserati, but it's still a nice car. Looks like an Audi R8. Well, it used to be."

"Can you tell where the picture was taken?" asked Bryce.

"It looks like it's in a Walmart parking lot, but I'm not sure what side of town. Do you think—" Peter stopped talking mid-sentence when he looked up and saw Bryce was no longer there.

Chapter Seven

B ryce opened the door to Mackenzie's room as Jackie was placing the IV. "Ma'am, I wanted to ask you a few more questions about your condition. Oh, and Jackie, draw a gray top tube also if you can." Jackie looked up and nodded before reaching behind her to a drawer containing several types of blood collection tubes.

"Mackenzie, I think what you are experiencing is not true blindness, but a psychiatric side effect of a traumatic event that has happened. I have an app on my phone that I'd like to have you look at. It has a series of black and white lines, something very basic for the eye to follow." He pulled out his phone and opened the application, revealing a repeating video stream of alternating black and white vertical lines marching across the screen. This is a test of a visual reflex that tests the eyes' ability to track moving objects. "If you have a problem with the eye itself, the nerves or your brain, your eyes will not move when you look at this."

He held it about a foot in front of her eyes and started the animation. He noted the quick back-and-forth movements of her eyes, showing her brain was perceiving the image and reacting according to the natural reflex associated with moving images. Bryce nodded and put his phone away before sitting down again.

"Mackenzie, tell me exactly what happened today. Did you see something that upset you? Were you involved in an accident?"

She didn't look at him, but slowly shook her head no. Her emotions quickly tore through the physical denial of her head shake as her face tightened, eyes closed, and tears filled her eyes. Her breathing became rapid and irregular and eroded into audible sobs.

"Mackenzie, in order to get your sight back, you need to be honest with us. Were you in an accident today? Is it possible you may have hit someone with your car?"

Again, she did not respond, but the intensity of her emotional reaction increased two-fold.

Jackie placed her hand on Mackenzie's shoulder and talked in as motherly a voice as Bryce had ever heard her use. "Look honey, accidents happen. That's why they're called accidents. People can understand accidents. But they have no patience for deceit or dishonesty. You need to tell Dr. Chapman what happened if you want to get better. Your body is hurting and to deal with that pain, your brain has stopped allowing your eyes to work. You need to tell us what happened."

Mackenzie nodded, took a deep breath, and began speaking in a quiet monotone. "It was a normal day, just like always. I was headed to a park to film a few videos for a new sponsor and I realized I had forgotten the items I was going to use, so I had to make a stop at Walmart. On the way there, I was practicing what I was going to say. I had my phone in the cradle and wasn't even holding it. I may as well have been talking to a friend sitting in the car next to me."

Bryce listened silently, nodding along with her story.

"I saw the sign for my exit and drifted over for the off ramp. That's when I heard a loud bang and felt my car shudder, like I hit something. I had no idea what it was. I assumed it was a deer, because I hit one before and it sounded exactly the same. My car was still driveable, so I continued to Walmart and parked. When I watched the video, I saw the police car in my window. I panicked. I didn't know what to do, so I just got out of my car and started walking. Eventually, I wound up in a checkout lane and that's when I lost my vision."

"Do you remember exactly what you did at the register just before you lost your vision? Often something triggers the brain to shut off the input from the eyes. If we can identify what it was, that may help your sight come back," he said.

"I had just reached for my phone to pay with it. I glanced down at the screen and saw an Instagram notification. Then... nothing."

"So it may have been looking at your phone that triggered your blindness. What was the last thing you had done with your phone before the checkout lane?"

"It was in my car watching the video. I nearly vomited when I saw what happened and deleted the video immediately. Then, I put my phone away."

Jackie looked at Bryce, her face showing a mix of anger and sadness over the situation. A police officer dead and a young girl's life ruined over something avoidable.

"Mackenzie, I can assure you that your brain and eyes are just fine. Your vision loss is because of the psychological trauma you experienced because of this accident. By opening up and talking about it I think your vision will return shortly. Let me call your parents to let them know where you are." He looked at Jackie and continued. "Can you get her something to drink?"

"Sure, I'll be right back," said Jackie, following Bryce out of the room.

"When you bring the drink back, hold it out of her central vision so she'll need to use her peripheral vision to see the cup. I have a feeling she'll have no problem taking it from your hand. If she does, try to be amazed and happy that her vision seems to be returning. Hopefully that will give her psyche a way to restore her vision and still save face."

Bryce went back to the physician workstation to share the news with his partners. "I think I know who hit the officer," he said, turning multiple heads in his direction. "My nineteen-year-old factitious blindness patient hit something while filming a video for Instagram. This is going to get ugly. I need to call her dad and get them here to be with her."

He picked up the phone and dialed the number listed on Mackenzie's demographic page. Her father answered on the second ring.

"Charlie Hearst, what can I do for ya?" The southern accent reminded Bryce of a trip he took to Dallas, Texas a few years back.

"Sir, my name is Bryce Chapman. I'm an ER doctor at Washington Memorial. Your daughter, Mackenzie, is here with us. She's okay, but is asking for you and her mother to come be with her."

"Mackenzie is in the hospital? What in the hell happened? Is she hurt?"

"No, she's fine, physically. But I believe she may have been the one who struck the police officer that was killed earlier this morning. She's struggling emotionally, and that led to temporary blindness."

"She's blind? You're telling me my daughter is blind?" he said, his voice loud enough through the earpiece to make Peter turn his head toward the call.

"I believe it's temporary. There is every sign her eyes and brain are normal, and that this is a temporary condition due to psychological stress. I suspect by the time you arrive, she will see just fine."

"Lord, I hope so. Her mother was fixin' to get ready, anyway. I reckon we'll be there in thirty minutes. Thanks for callin' doc." Charlie Hearst cut off the call abruptly.

Bryce slowly replaced the handset while laughing. "I think I just talked to Yosemite Sam," he said, meeting Peter's gaze.

Peter broke into a wide smile. "I loved that guy. Thanks for seeing that patient for us, Bryce. This way, they'll only have to subpoena you instead of all of us when this goes to trial. We'll cover your shifts."

Bryce sighed and dipped his head forward. "Great, just what I needed. My life was finally settling down, too. This shouldn't be that complicated, though. She admitted hitting the officer and there's video footage of it. Well, there was until she deleted it."

"Yeah, well, Yosemite Sam probably has some kick-ass lawyers. This may not be as easy as you think," warned Tom. "And nothing is ever truly deleted. I'm sure the file can be easily recovered."

Bryce was in his last hour of shift, the time when docs rarely pick up another patient and instead focus on wrapping up their existing ones. "Guys, I'm going to head upstairs and see how Clay is doing. I'll be back soon. Paula, please call me when Mackenzie Hearst's parents arrive." He pulled his stethoscope off his neck and laid it next to his computer, then headed toward the elevators. He passed several uniformed police officers grouped together and talking to each other quietly. *What a sad day.*

Chapter Eight

B ryce pushed the button to summon an elevator upstairs to the inpatient units. It was time to pay a visit to Clay, the paramedic who sustained a significant injury while helping Bryce do some outdoor chores a just a few weeks ago. *I've been dodging you since I gave you the correct antibiotic, but it's time we had a chat.*

He exited the elevator and walked to the nurse's station where Clay's nurse was entering a note in the electronic medical record system. "How is Clay doing?"

"Oh, hi, Dr. Chapman; I'm glad you came by," she said. "He has been asking to see you every shift for as long as I can remember. He'll be glad to see you. His wound is improving quickly. The drainage is decreasing, and he hasn't had a fever for several days now. Dr. Morales hopes to get him out of the ICU later this evening. It's a good thing you thought to change his antibiotics around. No one expected it to be that nasty of bacteria."

"I just had a hunch," he said. "Do you have anything you need to do in the room? I was hoping for some private time with Clay to chat for a bit. I was the one who caused the injury and want to apologize."

"Nope, I'm all done. He's had his medications and the vitals will update remotely every thirty minutes. Take all the time you need," she said.

Bryce thanked her and rapped his knuckles on the glass door before stepping through. He nearly had the door slid closed before Clay began yelling at him.

"You bastard! This is not what we agreed to!" The words were yelled with as much force as he could muster without using his accessory muscles, still sore from the deep wound he suffered. Bryce had closed the door before Clay had spoken the second sentence. He looked at the nurse and saw her face never looked up from her phone.

"Be quiet, man! You can't say things like that. We need to talk."

"Screw that. I've got nothing to say to you. I'm supposed to be dead right now, yet here I am. Improving every day," said Clay. "You lied to me."

Bryce pulled a chair up next to the bed and sat down. He let out a deep sigh as his body relaxed into the chair, as if releasing a heavy burden. "You're right, I did. After you killed two people. Want to keep making statements on morality?"

"Well, you nearly cut me in half with your pressure washer loaded with bacteria. I don't think you have any room to talk, either."

"That's a bit dramatic, Clay. I didn't nearly cut you in half. In fact, I used one of the lowest pressure nozzles. I wanted to limit the damage but still get the point across. Frankly, I was shocked the wound was as big as it was. Can you imagine if I had used the zero-degree nozzle?" Bryce's eyes widened at the thought.

"If water can dig the Grand Canyon, then certainly it can cut through skin. And what point did you want me to get?"

Bryce paused and look at Clay for a moment before continuing. "Don't mess with me, my family, my friends, or my patients. That's a red line that I'm not going to let anyone cross again. You killed Kent Carpenter. You–"

"He deserved to die," said Clay, cutting Bryce off mid-sentence.

"Maybe he did, but you did it in a way that caused problems for many more people. I'm getting sued by his family, and so are Tom Sharpe and Elisa Morales. That and a few other things led me to drink heavily, which pissed off Val enough to leave with the kids. I nearly killed myself in a moment of drunken stupidity."

Clay turned his head and looked out the window. After a few seconds, he said, "Sorry about all that, Doc." He turned back toward Bryce. "After what happened with David Lewis, I tried to be more indirect in my approach to solving problems. David was too up close and personal, and that made me worry about being discovered. I thought inducing a fatal medical illness would be a better way to do it," said Clay.

"Considering you killed the wrong David Lewis, I think it's easy to improve on your first attempt. But you clearly didn't consider all the downstream consequences of your actions."

"I just figured he'd get sick and die. That strain of bacteria from Eleanor is brutal. Why did you give me the correct antibiotic, anyway? After what I did, I don't deserve to be alive. Now I have to deal with this awful wound, probably never work again, have a guilty conscience and live in constant pain. This is worse than death."

Bryce paused before asking another question. "You know, I never thought to ask before now. How many more have there been?"

Clay looked away and sighed. "Just a few more. But I guarantee all of them deserved to die."

Bryce shook his head and dropped his gaze to his lap. "Do you believe in God, Clay? In Heaven and Hell?"

"Absolutely. Most people that served on a battlefield do."

"Were you prepared to face judgment after killing two people and committing suicide?"

Again, Clay took a moment before responding. "No, I guess I wasn't. That's not exactly a good resume to bring before St. Peter, is it?"

"Nope. I wanted you to think you were killing yourself. To admit to yourself that your prior actions warranted death as punishment. How else could you truly prove remorse for what you did? But if it took death to prove your remorse, how would that help anything? How could we turn that into a positive? You'd be gone and the opportunity wasted."

"What are you talking about? Turned into a positive how?"

"Clay, you killed the wrong person and nearly ruined my life when you killed Kent. But like I told you, I think deep down you're a decent guy. You can still do a lot of good in this world. What are the consequences of your past actions that you wish you could change right now?"

"That's easy," he said. "Get rid of the lawsuit for you, help Kent's kids, and do something for the family of David Lewis."

Bryce smiled and nodded. "Perfect. And I want to see you redeemed and also assuage my guilt over the wound I caused you. I have a plan that I think can accomplish all of that and more."

Clay looked at him and motioned to continue.

"This is difficult because I can't just go to the lawyer and say 'I know Kent was murdered and how it was done', because that will implicate you as the murderer and me as the one who assaulted you.

I also can't say he didn't have cystic fibrosis with certainty because that would implicate me in the theft of the semen sample."

"Right, it's getting complicated," said Clay.

"What we need is money, and a lot of it."

"Do you have a secret fortune stashed somewhere?"

"No, but my insurance company does," said Bryce with a smile.

"What do you mean?"

"I mean, you sue me in civil court for damages over this injury. Valerie and I have a rather robust personal liability umbrella policy. I convince the insurance company to settle, and you get millions of dollars. We pass some of that to the Carpenter family, some of it to the family or in memory of David Lewis, and you have enough left to get by on. Plus, you still have your disability income and pension."

"Isn't that basically insurance fraud?" asked Clay.

"Is it? I don't know. I mean, I injured you on my property. You have legitimate wounds and will have rehabilitation expenses, and your future earnings have been affected. Is there a law that says we can't still be friends and I can't advise you on what to do with the money you won in a lawsuit?"

"Who knows man, I'm just a paramedic."

"Look, we're talking about all of this because you killed two people, and I sent you to the ICU with a huge laceration from a pressure washer. Is insurance fraud really what's making you nervous right now?"

Clay chuckled a few times. "Good point. Okay, I'm game. We have legal representation through the firehouse. I'll talk to them and see what they think about it. I'm sure they can come to the hospital to chat."

"Actually, you may need to plan a different meeting location. I talked to Elisa, and she thinks you'll be ready for a rehab facility in another day or two. At this point, it's just wound care and getting you stronger. The infection is doing much better. You'll have to have a PICC line though, because the antibiotic is only available intravenously."

"Good, I am sick of being stuck here. At least at rehab I can move around a bit and get off my ass," said Clay, swatting the bed rail to emphasize his point.

Chapter Nine

"Daddy, are you busy?" Destiny's voice cracked a bit, and the pitch was higher than normal.

"Baby, what's going on? Are you okay? Shouldn't you be home by now?"

"I know. Something happened. Did you see the news about the officer hit by a car?"

"I did, why?"

"Because I was right next to him, Daddy." She lost control of her emotions and broke down crying. She squatted down to her knees and closed her eyes. "It's my fault. I was speeding, and he pulled me over on 465. He was so kind and only gave me a warning. But as was walking back to his car, another person swerved and smashed into him. It happened right next to my door. I saw and heard everything."

"Oh my gosh baby girl, where are you at? I'll be right there."

Destiny told her father where she was and hung up the phone. She wiped the tears away and slowly stood up. Looking around, she saw at least ten marked police cars, several more unmarked cars, and a fire truck. Two news helicopters circled above her head.

"Miss, do you mind if I take your statement? Are you the driver of the car that Officer Jenkins had pulled over?" The words came from a female officer standing next to her Destiny's vehicle.

"Yes, I am. What do you need to know?"

"Why did he pull you over?"

"I was driving too fast. I had just gotten off work and was on my way home to sleep. I wasn't paying attention to how fast I was going. The officer was so polite; he said he just wanted me to be safe and gave me a written warning."

"Did you get a look at the vehicle who struck him?"

"It was red, I know that. It seemed like a small SUV of some sort, but I'm not good with cars."

"And what did it do after it struck him?"

"It jerked back onto the road quickly, like the driver pulled hard on the wheel."

"Did you happen to get a look at the driver or the license plate?"

"No, I didn't. I was more focused on the poor officer and trying to get to him to help." Destiny began crying. "There was nothing I could do. I helped him breathe better, but I felt so useless. And if I hadn't been speeding, he wouldn't have been standing there."

"Ma'am, it doesn't work that way. We are out here every day. If he had given you a ticket, that would have taken longer and he wouldn't have been standing there. If you had been going faster or slower, you would have stopped in a different location and the car would not have struck him. This isn't your fault. It's the fault of the driver who left their lane and struck him."

Destiny nodded but continued to sob. "What do I need to do now?"

"I have your contact information and will follow-up if we need anything else from you. You're free to go."

"Okay, thank you. I'm so sorry about what happened. He was so kind to me, even though I was breaking the law."

"He was one of the good guys, that's for sure," said the officer. "And ma'am, I suggest you see a counselor to discuss what happened today. Post-traumatic stress disorder is real. Let's not make this worse than it has to be."

"Destiny!"

The shout came from behind a group of officers. She turned to see her father walking quickly toward her.

"Daddy!" The two hugged tightly and rocked back and forth slowly.

"Are you okay?" he asked.

"Yeah, I'm fine. Just shook up. Every time I close my eyes, I see the car hit him. The lady who took my statement said I should see a counselor about PTSD."

"We'll find you somcone, no question about that. Sorry it took a bit to get here; traffic is bad everywhere. I had a friend drop me off on the other side of the road and I hopped over the barrier. Let me see if we can get you out of here."

Her father walked over to the closest officer and had a quick conversation before returning.

"They said we can leave, but to be careful with all the people around. Are your keys in it?"

Destiny nodded and walked toward the passenger side of her car. She sat in the seat and closed her eyes as her father navigated the car through the emergency vehicles and onto the road.

Chapter Ten

B ryce returned to the ER to check on Mackenzie and her vision before leaving the hospital. He was nearly at her room when a voice called to him from the hallway.

"Excuse me, Dr. Chapman? Can I have a word with you?" The request came from a plainclothes detective who had a gun and badge visible on his belt.

"I guess. What's this about?" asked Bryce.

"Thank you. I'm Detective Gregory Stephenson of the Indianapolis Metropolitan Police Department. I'm here about the accident today that took the life of Officer Jenkins. You are treating Mackenzie Hearst, the young woman believed to have hit him. Is that correct?"

"That's correct, I am. She's doing fine and should be able to be discharged soon. I did not find any injuries, and she's feeling much better."

"That's good news, I suppose," said Detective Stephenson. "No sense making this tragedy any worse than it already is. Did you get the sense that she was impaired in any way during your visit? Any chance she was drinking alcohol or on drugs?"

Bryce shook his head and looked at the floor. "Detective, I'd really like to help you out and answer these questions, but the doctor-patient relationship is privileged. I cannot legally divulge what we talked about without her consent. You know that."

"Even if that information was relevant to a potential criminal investigation?" said the detective. "Because I can guarantee there is going to be a criminal investigation into this."

"Yes. The only time I can violate the privacy rule is if I believe someone is in immediate danger and not betraying the confidence would lead to harm of the patient or a third party. I can't see that applying here, can you?"

The detective adjusted his posture and rested his right hand on his belt, just behind the grip of his handgun. "Doctor, my colleague is dead, and it seems you have information about what led to that. Are you seriously going to stonewall the department here?"

"I told you, I really want to help. Truly I do. But I can get sued for violating her privacy. I could lose my license," said Bryce.

Detective Stephenson raised his hands in frustration and then crossed his arms across his chest. He let out a long sigh and looked both ways down the hallway before continuing. "Let's try this a different way. One case I'm investigating is the theft of a sperm sample from a local cryogenics lab. Coincidentally, the sample belonged to a person who just so happened to have been one of your patients. And his family is suing you for malpractice, isn't that correct?"

Bryce felt his heart race. His palms were instantly wet, and his breathing quickened. *Holy crap! He knows about the sperm bank. If he knows about that, it won't take much to figure out I thought my patient was murdered. And then to guess that I blamed Clay for it and slashed him with a pressure washer.*

"Kent Carpenter? Yes, I am involved in a malpractice case regarding his care. It's a complicated scenario that I'm hoping to settle out of court." Bryce leaned against the wall and tried to get his breathing under control.

"I see. Well, it's been a back burner case for me, you know? Someone steals a dead guy's semen from a business that sustains no damage? A bit strange, but I don't really see the harm in it. Of course I'll investigate it because I hate to see a crime go unsolved, but it's not something I'm going to spend a lot of time on at this very moment." He paused and then flashed a quick smile. "Sorry, I got sidetracked there. Let's get back to the current issue. Did Mackenzie Hearst give any indication why she left her lane and struck Officer Jenkins?"

Ugh. Do I break confidentiality to keep the detective off my back about the sperm bank robbery and its ultimate connection to Clay's crimes? Yeah, probably.

"I'll say this. She is an Instagram celebrity who likes to record videos on her phone while she drives. Does that give you something to go on?" It was true, and it was also not breaking confidentiality yet.

"That's easy enough to tell, doc. I found that out in fifteen seconds when they told me her name. You're going to have to do better than that," said the detective.

"Look, it's all I can do right now. I really need to think about this a bit more. Do you have a card or something that I can keep and call you later? This all just happened."

"I know, doc, I was just talking to Jenkins yesterday." The detective held Bryce's gaze after finishing his statement. Bryce turned away first. "This case won't take very long. We have her for hitting him. What we don't know is what caused her to do it. Here's my card.

Call me if you think of anything useful for our investigation. Oh, and can I get your cell number in case I have questions about the other cases I'm working?"

Bryce shared his number and slipped the card into his scrub top. "I'm sorry for the loss of your fellow officer. My team did everything we could for him. I'm going to go check on my patient now. Have a good day."

He left the detective standing in the hallway as he knocked and then entered Mackenzie's room. He saw three new people in the room. The first was standing in the corner. A tall, thin man in his late fifties wearing a black cowboy hat. The next appeared to be his wife, the mother of Mackenzie. She was sitting next to the bed and rubbing her daughter's arm. The third person was a slightly overweight, balding man in a well-tailored suit. He sat in the opposite corner, typing on a laptop.

"Hi Mackenzie, how are you feeling? Is your vision improving?" asked Bryce.

"Yes, it is. Thank you. The nurse brought me some water a while ago, and it's been improving steadily since then. I think it's pretty much normal now," said Mackenzie.

"Oh great, I thought it would be soon. Glad to hear." Bryce did a quick test of her visual fields, moving a light in all four quadrants of each eye, which she could see without issue. "It looks like your symptoms have resolved. As I said before, I think this was your mind's way of dealing with the stress of what happened today. I think when you tried to use your phone to pay, it triggered the memory of watching that video you were recording when you struck the officer and your psyche couldn't handle it. Now that you've had some time to process it, your vision has returned. There's not much for us to do at this point, so I'll get your discharge papers ready. I'm sorry this happened, Mackenzie."

Bryce smiled at those in the room and turned to leave.

"Well, hang on there, doc." The Texan drawl was identical to the one Bryce heard on the phone earlier. "You leave any quicker and you'll catch up to yesterday." The tall man in a cowboy hat leaned forward with an outstretched hand. "I'm Charlie Hearst, and this is my wife Marybeth. We're Mackenzie's parents."

Bryce returned the handshake. "Thank you so much for coming. She will certainly need your support moving forward. This is going to be quite an ordeal for your family, I'm afraid."

"Indeed. That's what I wanted to talk to you about. Why did you mention a video? Mackenzie wasn't recording a video. She said she just sneezed, and that pulled her arm which caused the car to swerve. Isn't that right, honey?"

Mackenzie looked at Bryce and then back to her father. "Yes, Daddy, it is. My allergies were acting up today and I had been sneezing. My exit was coming up and I could feel the sneeze about to happen. When it did, my eyes closed and my arm jerked. Next thing I knew, I heard a thump but didn't know what happened. I thought I hit a deer. I'm not sure what happened at Walmart with my vision, but I'm glad it returned."

You've got to be kidding me. She changed her story! "That's not what you told me when you arrived here. You told me you were recording a video and looked into the camera for emphasis. Jackie, your nurse was here when you said it. I already have that written in my note. What's going on here?"

"Doc, are you calling my daughter a liar?" said Charlie Hearst, stepping forward toward Bryce. "Do you have any idea who I am? I will not let some damn ER doctor tarnish my baby girl's reputation. I suggest you edit your note to reflect what actually happened. It was an accident brought on by allergies and a sneeze. That's it."

Bryce looked at all three Hearsts. The only one to return his gaze was the father. "Sir, I can't falsify the medical record. That's fraud."

"Look son, don't go diggin' up more snakes than you can kill. You hear me?"

"Honestly, I have no idea what that means, but I think we're done here. I don't like the tone of this conversation. Mackenzie, I'll get your discharge paperwork ready."

"Vincent, can you remind the doctor about privacy laws?" said Charlie Hearst.

The man in the suit looked up from his laptop and gave a weak smile. "Of course, sir. My name is Vincent Leoni and I represent the Hearst family. Of course, we would never tell you what to document in your chart, that is your independent decision to make. However, I should remind you what they said in this room is privileged under the doctor-patient privacy laws, as well as attorney-client privilege, since I'm here and representing the family."

Bryce had heard enough. Once a patient encounter descended into talks of lawyers, it was usually time to end the visit. "Yeah, got it," he said before walking out and closing the door behind him. He scanned the hallway, but the detective had already left. He removed the card from his scrub pocket and snapped a picture with his phone. *I have a feeling I'm going to need to talk to you soon.*

He tracked down Jackie and updated her on what happened. "I just spoke with the parents of Mackenzie, the girl who struck the officer. I think they convinced her to change her story and now claim she wasn't recording a video. They said she has bad allergies and just sneezed, which caused her to hit him."

Jackie couldn't hold back a laugh. "You're joking. A sneeze?"

"Nope. She just told me a new story. They even have a lawyer that reminded me I can't tell anyone what she told me because doctor-patient information is privileged. Her dad suggested rather strongly that I not document in my note what she told us the first time. I don't like where this is going. I think I need to talk to the hospital attorney."

"Well, I don't care about any of that. but I'm not charting any of it. I don't have time for court appearances. Not going to lie, just not going to say anything. Honesty is always the best policy, right?" said Jackie.

Bryce considered the recent events involving Kent, Clay, sperm banks, memory cards, and more. "Sometimes, yes."

Chapter Eleven

B ryce left the hospital after the emotionally charged shift and climbed into his GMC Yukon for the drive home. He initiated a call to Valerie before pulling forward out of his space.

"Hey Bryce, are you leaving the hospital?" she asked.

"Yes, leaving now. It was a heck of a day. I'll tell you about it when I get home."

"Okay, but we're not there right now. Why don't you meet us at the park? It's a gorgeous day and the kids have too much energy. I brought balls, frisbees, and anything else I could think to have them run after."

Bryce whipped his head left as he passed a panel van, thinking he saw someone familiar. "No, it couldn't be," he said.

"What's that? What couldn't be what?"

"Hang on," he said as he looked in his rear-view mirror. The van hadn't moved. Bryce continued along the long row of cars and made two quick left turns to head back in the same direction. He passed behind the van and saw the driver's seat was empty. "I thought I saw Tony sitting in a van as I pulled out. I'm coming back around to check out the van. Let me call you back."

"No! Don't hang up the phone. What are you going to do if it's him?" asked Valerie, the concern evidence in her voice.

"No idea. I don't even know why he'd be here. I'm coming up on the van now." Bryce slowed down and stopped in front of it. He could see no one inside the vehicle. "I'm going to get out and take a quick look."

"Bryce, I don't like this. He's a big guy, and he's had a head injury. Who knows what he's capable of?"

Tony Proffit is the man who aggressively pursued Valerie on their trip to the Bahamas. He and his drunken friends had surrounded her inside Thunderball Grotto and made inappropriate advances that caused Bryce to intervene. Unfortunately, that led to a physical altercation, which left Tony's face smashed against a rock. His anger escalated, encouraged by his alcohol level and friends who were with him, and he chased Bryce back toward the boat. He took a shortcut and became trapped under water, causing him to drown. This is when Valerie and Bryce turned from victims to heroes as they successfully resuscitated their attacker, restoring a pulse before flying him out to the hospital on a country music star's private sea plane. It turned out that Tony was also the son of the man whose company owns Washington Memorial Hospital.

"I agree with all of that. I'll be careful. And besides, I doubt he could catch me in a foot race. Plus, we have armed security at the hospital." He exited his SUV and left the door open with the engine running. He walked up to the van and peered inside, finding no one there. Tinted rear windows made it difficult to examine the back, but the cargo area seemed empty from what he could tell. "Val, there's no one inside. I must have been hallucinating. I'll meet you at the park in fifteen minutes. Love you."

Bryce walked back to his SUV and looked in the rear seat and cargo area, just to make sure no one sneaked in while he left the door open. Satisfied he was alone, he climbed back in and drove away.

Tony listened for Bryce's SUV to pull forward and then stood up from behind the truck he had been squatting next to. "Good to see you again, Dr. Chapman," he said. He watched Bryce exit the hospital parking lot and noted the time before climbing back into the van. Tony wrote the make and model of the other cars in the doctor's parking spaces and their license plates. He smiled at the Honda Civic parked next to a Maserati. The dichotomy amused him, as did the stickers advocating 'Make Love Not War' and an Apple logo in the rear window. He opened a cooler and removed a sandwich and a beer, then leaned the seat back a bit and took a large bite before chasing it down with a swallow of beer.

What kind of doc drives a Honda Civic? I'm more curious than anything, and I have nowhere to be for weeks. Come on out, let Tony have a look at you.

Three hours later, he saw a young woman walking out toward the employee parking lot. She looked different from the others who had come out in the past few hours. She was younger and dressed in khaki pants and a black polo shirt rather than scrubs. He watched her approach the Maserati and give it her middle finger before turning and unlocking the Civic. She quickly backed out of the parking space and headed for the parking lot exit.

Well, this could be interesting.

He sat up and started the van's engine while tossing the contents of his lap into the passenger seat and pulled out to follow the Civic. He didn't have long to follow as she soon turned into a local restaurant known for advertising chicken wings and cold beer.

Tony watched her park and then enter the restaurant, carrying her purse and a small folded piece of paper. After waiting a few minutes, he followed her inside.

"Hi sir, table for one? Or are you meeting someone today?" asked the young hostess stationed just inside the door.

Tony scanned the room and saw the woman sitting alone at the bar. He turned his attention back to the hostess and replied. "Just me, for now. Can I take a seat in the bar?"

"Sure. The bar is open seating. You can sit anywhere you'd like," said the hostess, gesturing toward the open tables with her arm.

Tony walked toward the woman and sat at a table behind her. The bartender poured a Stella Artois into a pint glass and placed it in front of her. He watched her take a drink and then lift the folded piece of paper and stare at it. From the closer vantage point, he could see it was actually an envelope. She tapped it on the bar and then ripped an end off of it before pulling a piece of paper out. The woman scanned the words quickly and then leaned back quickly in her chair before ripping the letter in half from top to bottom. She crumpled the pieces up and dropped them next to her beer glass before putting her head on her arms and crying. One deep sob caused her arm to hit the wad of paper and knock it onto the ground.

Tony stood up and retrieved the paper. He put his hand on the woman's back and said softly, "Excuse me, miss? I think you dropped this."

She sat up and turned her head to look at who was speaking to her. Tony flashed a weak smile, framed with as much compassion as he could put into his face. She wiped her eyes with her right hand and then waved him off dismissively. "You can just throw it away. Or maybe I should, like I have my life these last few years."

Why don't you tell me all about it, my dear?

"Do you mind if I join you? It appears you could use some cheering up. My name's Tony."

"I guess, sure. I'm Emily," she said while adjusting herself in her seat. "You sort of caught me at a bad time, sorry."

"Hey, no need to apologize. I just wanted a drink but had no one to share it with. You seem down and look like you need to talk something out. Maybe we can help each other."

Emily took in his appearance more fully now that she was upright. He appeared to be about thirty years old and ruggedly handsome, with straight white teeth and a decent tan.

"So what do you want to talk about?" she asked.

"I'm just drifting through with no particular destination in mind. You are the one that seems to be dealing with something at the moment. Why don't we talk about what that paper said?"

Emily sighed and took another drink of her beer before responding. "It's just another rejection letter. The most recent one in a long string of them."

"Sorry to hear that. What are you being rejected from?"

"Medical school. I've been applying for two years and haven't had any success. I'm about to give up and try to find something else to do."

"Wow, you want to be a doctor? That's pretty amazing," said Tony, feigning interest. "Do you work in healthcare right now?"

"I'm a scribe in the Emergency Department at Washington Memorial. I actually just finished a shift there."

"A scribe? What's that?"

"I follow a doctor around and document the chart for them. The charting requirements have become so onerous that they pay us to do the charting for them so they can focus on actually treating patients."

"Ah, I bet you see a lot of interesting things then." Tony flagged down the bartender and ordered a Stella Artois.

"You like Stella?" asked Emily.

"Sure do. I fell in love with it when I visited Belgium. There's just something about sipping one while examining diamonds in Antwerp. Really caps off the whole Belgian experience."

Emily raised her eyebrows and took another look at her new acquaintance. This time, she noticed the Omega watch on his left wrist, adorned with diamonds on the face and a tight leather band. "What is it you do again?"

Tony smiled back at her. "It sounds cliché, but I do whatever I want. My father actually owns the hospital you work at. I travel around and check out his investments to look for any major issues that need to be addressed. It's like the show Undercover Boss; no one knows who I am, so it's perfect."

"That must be pretty fun. So you don't have a set schedule or a boss?"

"No. I just tell my dad a few things once in a while to make him think I'm truly investigating his businesses. In reality, I like to spend my time traveling the world and living life to its fullest."

"That sounds exactly like the retirement I always pictured after my clinical career was over." She looked down at the crumpled paper and sighed again. "But, it looks like that may never happen now." She stared straight ahead, focusing on nothing, and took another large drink of her beer. After pausing a few moments, she turned and smiled at Tony while placing her hand on his left forearm. "Will you excuse me for a moment? I'll be right back." She picked up her purse and headed toward the bathroom.

Tony leaned back in the bar stool and smiled. A few seconds later the bartender delivered the drink along with a compliment.

"Pretty smooth buddy. One of the best entrances I've seen in years."

Tony made a fist and bumped the bartender across the wooden counter.

"Thanks. She's an interesting girl. We'll see where this leads."

"And pretty hot, too. I've seen her in here a few times before, but usually with a muscular doctor. I wonder if something changed with them."

Tony nodded to the bartender and stared in on his beer.

I bet he drives a Maserati. Probably knows Bryce too.

Emily returned a bit later and appeared much more put together. Her hair was back in place, and she now smelled faintly of vanilla. She slid into her seat from the left, causing it to slide toward him a bit.

"Sorry about that. Where were we?"

"I was just going to offer to buy the next round. Or do you have somewhere you need to be later?"

"Nope, I'm off for the next two days. I had planned to go for a run and then binge a few hours of Netflix before crying myself to sleep."

"I bet we could find something more fun than that. What do you think? To new friends?" Tony raised his glass and held it out in front of Emily. She raised her glass and clinked it into his.

Tony snapped his fingers to get the bartender's attention and then raised up two fingers before pointing down at the glasses of beer.

The bartender nodded and gave Tony a mischievous grin.

Chapter Twelve

Tony woke to the sound of a toilet flushing. He opened his eyes and then scooted backward in bed so he was sitting up against the headboard. The next sound was the sink running, followed by the bathroom door opening.

"Good morning. Did you sleep well?"

Emily nodded her head as she exited the bathroom and slowly walked over to him.

"Did you forget to pack pajamas again?" asked Tony.

"Why do I need them? They would just slow down our pre-breakfast workout." She climbed onto the bed, straddling him. She put her hands on his chest, causing him to jump backward and grab her wrists.

"Hey, that's freezing! Didn't you dry your hands?"

Emily laughed and pulled her arms behind her back, turning Tony's grasp into a hug. "Sorry, I couldn't find a towel. I figured as hot as you are, I'd just dry them on you."

"You seem like you are in a better mood lately. I know we just met, but I like seeing you happy."

She smiled and twisted around on top of Tony before leaning back against his chest. She took his hands and placed once on her stomach and one on her hip. "I am very happy right now. Maybe that rejection letter was a good thing. If I hadn't broken down at the restaurant, you may not have come over to cheer me up."

Oh, I would have found another way to meet you. I needed to find someone who works with Bryce Chapman and doesn't have much to lose.

"Tell me about it. This has been my best business trip in years."

"How long are you planning to be in town?"

"A few more days. I actually wanted to check out the Emergency Department. They had a problem recently with a review committee and my dad wanted me to see what I thought about it. The problem is, I sort of know one doctor who works there."

"Really? Which one?"

"Bryce Chapman."

"That guy?" Emily made a grunting sound before continuing. "He is so full of himself. Everyone loves him and it makes him walk around like he's the second coming of Christ. How do you know him?"

Tony took a deep breath in, his muscular chest expanding and raising Emily up as if she were weightless. "Have you ever been to the Bahamas?"

"Oh, my gosh! You're the guy who drowned!" said Emily, sitting up and twisting around to face Tony. "I thought you seemed familiar, but I couldn't place it."

"Yep, that's me. In the flesh."

"Wow, I saw the video. I can't believe you're alive. You are lucky Bryce and his wife were able to bring you back."

"Lucky? I wouldn't have drowned if it wasn't for them. I was having a killer time with my friends on Swan Cay and then my life changed in an instant. That bastard kicked me into a wall while we were snorkeling Thunderball Grotto, and then I let my anger get the best of me. The sad thing is, I don't even remember it. The last thing I remember is being on the island and then waking up in the hospital in Nassau. My friends filled me in on the details, and of course I also watched the video."

Emily rolled over and laid on her side next to him. She put her hand on his chest and traced the outlines of his muscles. "That must have been awful. How do you feel now?"

"I feel okay most days. But I have what they called an anoxic brain injury. It's like having a stroke in your entire brain. I'm a lot better than I was, but I'm at risk of getting worse with future head injuries. Also, alcohol slows me down a lot quicker than it used to. It's also left me with a bit of an impulse control problem."

"Like you can't control your anger?"

"Yeah, that is part of it. But there's a better part as well."

"What's the good part of a lack of impulse control?"

"I have a hard time controlling my desire for pleasure, too." He grinned and rolled to face her. "Would you like to see another demonstration?"

"No, but I'd love to feel one," she replied as she pulled a pillow over her eyes.

Tony slipped out of bed without waking Emily and took a quick shower. He had the coffee nearly finished before she rolled over and cuddled up to the empty place next to her in bed.

"Hey, where'd you go?" she asked without opening her eyes.

"I'm making coffee. Check out is in half an hour and I need to get to the hospital."

"Is there anything you're looking for in particular? I've been there a few months and understand how it operates."

Tony brought over two cups of coffee and sat down next to her in bed. "I don't even know. My dad thinks Bryce is some sort of hero for saving me that day. I'd love to find something about the ER that makes him want to fire everyone. Let Bryce Chapman see what it's like to have your life ripped out from under you."

Emily opened her lips to respond, but hesitated and took a sip of coffee instead.

"What is it?" asked Tony. "You looked like you were about to say something."

"I don't know; I barely know you. It's hard to open up completely."

"Barely know me? We've known each other several times just in the last twenty-four hours," Tony said with a grin. "You can tell me whatever you want; I won't judge."

Emily took another sip of coffee and then glanced sideways at him. "What if I told you I'm trying to get the ER shut down?"

Tony laughed and shook his head. "That would be hilarious. That's just as good as getting Chapman fired. How would you do that?"

Emily put her coffee down and sat cross-legged on the bed. She splayed her hands out toward Tony and explained. "Okay, so every hospital has to undergo a review by an oversight body from time to time. The one that Washington Memorial uses is called the Quality Control Commission. They review various things, and they change every year. Usually it's stuff like looking for charting deficiencies, unsafe protocols, expired products, stuff like that."

"Okay, I'm following."

"If they find something, they mark a deficiency and plan to come back for a repeat visit. If there is a major violation that is not remedied, they can force a temporary closure of the unit in question while they bring it into compliance."

"And you've been sabotaging the reviews?"

Emily nodded with her whole body, causing the bed to move up and down with her excitement. Tony's eyes followed the movement closely.

"Hey, pay attention!" said Emily, laughing and swatting his shoulder. "I have been putting expired products out when the reviewers show up and even took it to the next level this last time."

"What did you do?"

"I left a dead rat in the nutrition room." Emily burst out laughing after delivering that line. "You should have heard the scream of the reviewer when she walked in there. We never know when they're coming back, so I keep another rat and more expired items in my lunch bag."

Tony grinned at the story and at how happy Emily appeared in the moment. "Why are you doing this? How does it benefit you?"

"Well, this is awkward, but here goes. I have been dating one of the doctors, Peter Thrasher. He used to do locums, and we'd travel around to a new place every few months. But he really likes it here and signed on as a full-time doc in the department. He kept saying how awesome all the docs are in the ER and stayed to work with them."

"Locums? Is that where people take temporary jobs? And you didn't want to stay here?"

"Yeah, we'd move a few times a year. And no, I didn't want to stay here, are you kidding me? In Indiana? There's an entire country to explore. We'd worked in Florida, Oregon, Texas, and a few other places. Why stop in Indiana, of all places? Then Peter broke up with me, the bastard. I figured if I could get the department closed, maybe he would take me back and we could keep traveling around."

"So, you're wanting to get back together with Peter?" said Tony, the disappointment clear in his voice.

"Well, I was. But that was before I met you." She reached out to touch his cheek and blew him a kiss. "You're so much more than Peter ever was. Besides, I've given up on being a doctor. It's obvious the medical schools don't want me."

"Well, I think they're missing out. You're smart and competent. You'd make a brilliant doctor."

"Thanks, I appreciate that. But how do I seem for girlfriend material?"

"Top shelf for sure. Maybe you can travel the world with me instead of traveling the country with Peter?"

"Oh, I would love that."

"Well, let's plan on it then. But first, maybe we try to get the ER shut down?"

Emily raised her hands above her head for a double high-five. "Deal!"

Tony completed the high-five and then dropped his hands behind her shoulders and pulled her in close.

Chapter Thirteen

B ryce removed his scrubs and put on a T-shirt and shorts before exiting his car and walking toward his family.

"Thanks for changing. We don't like hospital germs," said Valerie once he was close enough to hear. His children, Hannah and Noah, came running up and gave him a hug. "Hey kids, are you having fun out here with Mom today?"

"Yep!" said Noah. "I've been practicing for my soccer game. Watch how hard I can kick it now." He picked up the soccer ball and placed it on a small clump of grass elevated several inches above the surrounding blades. He took about twenty steps backward and then ran as fast as his little legs would go. When he got to the ball, he nearly stopped before swinging his leg and kicking it with his toe as hard as he could. The ball had a few seconds of air time and traveled a short distance before the long grass slowed it to a halt.

"Wow, great job buddy! But remember, we're working on kicking with the laces or inside of the foot."

"I know, but I wanted to show you my super strong kick. I'm going to score a goal next game with it."

Bryce patted his son on the head and pulled him in for a hug. "We could use a few goals out of you. Last game didn't go so well."

Hannah was sitting near her mother on a blanket, holding a small white flower up by her head. Bryce looked up and saw Valerie had three of them tucked into her hair. He leaned over and took the flower from Hannah and wove the stem into her hair, so the flower stayed just above her ear. "There you go, you look just as beautiful as mommy."

The two most important women in his life smiled at each other and then at him. Bryce had nearly lost his family a few months ago when his drinking and depression about recent events had soured his demeanor to the point Valerie took the kids to her parents' house in Destin, Florida. After a drunken night that included nearly over-dosing on sleeping pills, Bryce had rededicated himself to his family and to personal improvement. He still had not had a sip of alcohol since that night and continued to see a counselor at his church for other self-improvement help. *I like this a lot better than how it was a month ago. This is perfect.* He leaned back on the blanket next to Hannah and rubbed her back, before a soccer ball struck him on the left side of his chest.

"Dad, I used the laces on that one!" shouted an excited Noah from twenty feet away.

Bryce made an exaggerated effort to rub his chest and pretend to be in pain. "I could tell, man, you had a lot of power on it!"

"Hey coach, do you think the game will go better Saturday than it did last week?" asked Val.

"How can it not? How many goals did we give up? Twenty? I wanted to make them run a lap for each goal they allowed, but I didn't want to have to spend all the time tying shoelaces and yelling at them to stop playing with the grass."

"Oh, relax," said Valerie, laughing at her husband. "This is an under-six league. They're just out to have fun."

"Easy for you to say. You didn't play competitive soccer. I want to win every time I step onto the field."

"Should I tell you that every time we get into a pool?" Valerie was a Division I swimmer at Indiana University and had the arm definition to prove it. "You need to redefine winning. It's not always about beating someone. Sometimes it's just about having the team grow. It will click for them one of these days." She paused a moment to let her comment sink in. "Are you about ready to go home? A package came today, and I'd like your help to set it up."

"Set what up? What did you order?"

She grinned like a boy who just got his first BB gun. "A 3D printer. I'm going to make all sorts of crazy stuff and may even start selling some of it."

"Oh, that's pretty sweet. I can't wait to see what you can do with that. I mean, a degree in mechanical engineering should give you a bit of a head start in 3D design and manufacturing, right?"

"Let's hope so. I hope to find some products I can sell on-line to scratch the entrepreneurial itch I'm feeling. Let's head out. Oh, and the kids said they wanted to ride with you while I take the scenic way home and maybe walk around the park for a bit."

"We did?" asked Hannah. "When?"

Bryce picked her up and put her on his shoulders. "She could just tell by how happy you guys were to see your dad. Mom deserves some time alone for a bit. It's good for mommies to get a break once in a while." He leaned over and kissed Valerie on the lips while Hannah leaned down and hugged her head. "See you at home. I'll come up with something for dinner and let you know when it should be done."

"Sounds perfect. Thanks, Bryce." She waved goodbye and then stretched out on the blanket. "I may need to rest up a bit before my fresh air walk."

Bryce took the kids home and spent some time reading and playing games with them before starting on dinner. He sent Val a text with a thirty-minute warning of when dinner would be on the table.

She arrived just as he pulled the pasta out of the oven.

"Oh, that smells wonderful. What did you make?"

"The Chapman special—baked ziti and garlic bread. I figured I'd choose something we wouldn't have to fight the kids to eat. I opened a bottle of pinot for you; it's on the table."

Once dinner ended, the kids ran upstairs to play in their toy room and Bryce sat down on the couch with Val. "Today was insane. I took care of that officer who was struck on the side of the road. His aorta was nearly torn in half, and he had a severe head injury. Fortunately, he probably never even saw it coming. He went straight from doing a job he loved to Heaven."

"I saw that on the news; sorry you had to deal with that," said Val. "I always get nervous when I see people stopped on the side of the road. It seems no one pays attention anymore. Texting and driving used to be the problem. Now I swear people are just watching YouTube or TikTok the whole time."

"Funny you say that. The girl who hit him was recording a video when it happened. At least she had the phone in a cradle on the windshield, but it distracted her enough that she swerved toward the exit early and hit him. Well, that was her story before her parents arrived. Once they got to the hospital, she changed her story to say it was a violent sneeze that made her jerk the wheel."

"A sneeze? That's ridiculous. The prosecutor can just look at your chart, right?"

"That's just it; I don't think so. They even had a lawyer there who reminded me that doctor-patient conversations are privileged and I can't reveal what she said without her permission. It doesn't help that they are absolutely loaded and can probably hire a hundred attorneys without blinking an eye."

Valerie pulled Bryce in for a hug. "I'm sorry, honey. Why does this stuff always happen to you? Aren't there more people at the hospital who can bear some of these burdens for you?"

"It's just how it shakes out. We see the patients we see and that's it." He leaned into her and rested his head on her lap.

"I also saw Clay today."

"Yeah? How is he doing? Was this the first time you'd seen him since you gave him the correct antibiotic?"

"Yep. He was pretty pissed when I walked in. But we talked for about twenty minutes and I think he's on board with my plan. He's eager to get out of the hospital and start rehab. I knew deep down he was a good guy. He just screwed up in a bad way."

"What if he screws up again and takes you out?"

"He wouldn't do that. He's a proud man who values his reputation. If he takes me out, they'll nail him for three murders. Besides, he feels bad about the consequences of what he did and wants to do what he can to make it right. He truly thought he was giving up his life when he injected the contents of that syringe. He didn't know it was really the antibiotic that would save his life."

Valerie sat her wineglass down and rubbed his chest with her left hand. "I hope you're right, but I'm still nervous."

"So am I, babe," he said.

Chapter Fourteen

The Emergency Department's monthly administrative meeting starts at 9am on the first Monday of each month. It is typically attended by the nursing managers, director, the physician department chair, pharmacy, and anyone else who had an item to bring to the committee.

"Thank you all for coming," said Dr. Ashford Tate, the Chairman of the Department of Emergency Medicine and the administrative head of the physician group who staffs the department. "As you know, we expect to have our site visit by the Quality Control Commission this week. We never know the exact time they are coming, but this is the last week of our evaluation window. Check all supplies to ensure they are in date, and have all food labeled with names and dates in all fridges, even the employee lounges. If a reviewer asks you a question and you're not sure of the correct answer, please refer them to a director or manager. You're not required to answer. Just tell them you are busy doing patient care and don't wish to be interrupted."

"I hate these people," said Jackie. "Such a waste of time. Do we have to buy them lunch again this year?"

"Probably. You know how it works. It's a necessary evil that we have to get through in order to serve our patients. Last time we got dinged on charting and even a dead mouse in the nutrition room, so please be careful this week. They can randomly pull charts to review while they are here. If you see anything out of place, either fix it or call a manager to deal with it."

"A rat, actually. It wasn't a mouse; it was a rat," said Peter.

"Right, thanks. A rat," said Ash, rolling his eyes.

"Bunch of hacks. They couldn't cut it at the bedside, so they went into administration where they now wield all the power. Too many poor performance reviews to stay employed at the beside? No problem! We'll hire you to tell everyone else what they're doing wrong. Welcome aboard!" Jackie's displeasure was as obvious from her words as it was her body language.

Ash smiled at Jackie. *Preach it, sister.* "While I agree with you, I'd like to say that I can still move some meat at the bedside, even though I'm an administrator."

Jackie's face softened, and she turned toward Ash. "I'm sorry. I didn't mean to imply anything about you. It's just that I hate the administrative nonsense they keep throwing at us. I just want to care for patients."

"I completely understand. I went into administration to shield our docs from a bulk of it." He looked back at the rest of the room. "Anyway, let's be on the lookout this week for the reviewers and spread the word when they arrive at the hospital."

The rest of the meeting consisted of presentations on patient satisfaction, introduction of new staff, updates on protocols, and other standard agenda items. Ash adjourned the meeting and then stepped across the hall into his office.

Sitting on his desk was a yellow post-it note that read 'Lorena McCarthy called, she'd like to speak with you', followed by a phone number. He pushed his door closed, then fell backward into his chair. *First QCC, now a malpractice attorney. What a day.*

He dialed the number and Lorena picked up on the first ring. Her Irish accent bringing an ironic smile to Ash's face. Like when you're in front a firing squad and one shooter reminds you of a person you used to date.

"Dr. Tate, hello. Thank you for calling me back so quickly. As you know, I formally sued Drs. Chapman, Sharpe, and Morales. As a courtesy, I'd like to give you plenty of notice to arrange the depositions. I know taking two of your doctors for an entire day could disrupt your scheduling. I'd like to get it done in the next month if possible. These poor children are distraught without their father. Having this ordeal behind them would allow them to start the healing process."

Oh, spare me. You could not care less about the kids, other than their use as props in front of a jury. "That's very considerate of you. I'll talk to Bryce and Tom and see what dates work best. Do you have an email I can send it to?"

"I do, but I'd prefer a phone call. Email is so," she let the word fade into silence before continuing. "Admissible. I much prefer phone calls for most of my work. That and meals. Nothing like a tax-deductible meal that also counts as billable hours."

"Okay, I'll call you when I have something to share."

"Thanks, and any update on Dr. Chapman's theory about this being a murder? I'd be interested in hearing about that if there's anything to share."

"No, I don't. He has shared nothing else with me about that."

She clicked her tongue before replying. "Pity, that. It was a fascinating theory that could have ended this lawsuit. I'll guess I'll wait to hear from you."

He ended the call and then placed one to Bryce.

"Hey Ash, what's up?" asked Bryce. The sound of children playing in the background brought a smile to Ash's face.

"I just got a call from Lorena McCarthy. She wants to set a time to depose you and Tom regarding Kent Carpenter. She also asked about the murder theory. Do you have any more information on that? Last I heard, you thought someone murdered him, and were looking into a DNA test to see if he truly had cystic fibrosis. Did anything come of it?"

There was a brief pause, and then Bryce answered. "No, I wish. I struck out on that search. I'll talk to Tom and try to get some dates together. We'd like to do it on the same day for a little moral support."

"Or shared suffering," offered Ash. "Okay, let me know. Enjoy the day with your family, Bryce. Sorry to bug you with this."

"No problem at all. I appreciate you fielding the brunt of this stuff for us while I play dad."

After ending the call, Ash looked at the pictures on his desk. Three frames filled with photos of his wife, two children and his grandkids. Just twenty years ago, he had been in the park playing with his kids while someone else bore the administrative burden for him and his partners. His wife had died a few years ago, but the memories remained strong. *You're welcome, Bryce.*

Chapter Fifteen

Harriet Bonner pulled into the Starbucks lot and sneaked her car past the long line at the drive through. She exited the rental car and rushed inside the business.

"That's mine; thank you," she said to the barista behind the counter as she picked up the cup with her name on it. *How many Harriets order coffee with an app at 7:00 a.m.?* She turned around and exited the store, lifting her cup in a salute to the driver of the car she had walked in front of last time. It had not moved an inch since she passed by the first time.

She set her cup in the holder and glanced at her watch. *Ten minutes until I can drink that.* She pulled up the navigation app on her phone and entered Washington Memorial Hospital. The app told her it was going to take twelve minutes to arrive.

"We'll see about that," she said, as she backed out of the space and left the parking lot. Eleven minutes later, she shifted into park and turned off the car. She picked up her coffee and took a large sip. "Perfect temperature. Ten minutes after I pick it up, every time. That sort of reproducible result is only possible with proper training and supervision. Kudos to Starbucks' management. Now let's see if this hospital learned anything from our last visit."

She opened her email app and composed a message to the Emergency Department manager.

> Good morning. The Quality Control Commission will be in your department at 8am for our second site visit. Please be prepared to discuss your action plan for the deficiencies documented on the prior visit. I will see you soon.

> Harriet Bonner, MSN, RN, CNE, TCRN, CHSA

Harriet glanced at her watch. 7:20am. She took another sip of coffee and sent a text to the other person on her team.

> Cecil, I am headed in. Let me know when you're close and I'll have someone bring you inside.

She glanced in the mirror and then applied another layer of lipstick and a spray of perfume before shouldering her laptop bag and exiting the car. Her high heels kept her speed to a minimum as she entered the front lobby of the Emergency Department.

A registration clerk sat at the triage desk and Harriet walked directly toward her.

"Good morning, my name is Harriet Bonner. I'm with the Quality Control Commission and am here to conduct a site visit. Can you let your management know that I am here?"

The clerk nodded and walked through a door to find someone in management. Harriet watched her walk away and smiled. *Leaving the triage desk unattended in an Emergency Department. We'll have to talk about that.*

She turned around and leaned back against the counter to wait. Glancing around the room, she saw a nurse kneeling next to a small child who was actively vomiting. The nurse held a plastic basin in her hands, trying to catch as much of the vomit as she could.

She isn't even wearing gloves. I'm so glad I elevated beyond bedside nursing. Harriet turned away from the scene and tried to take a sip of coffee, but stopped at the last second. She shook her head quickly to clear the image of the child vomiting, and let out a long sigh before she could take a drink.

"Hi, Harriet?" said a voice from behind her.

Harriet turned around and saw a woman standing next to the registration clerk.

"Actually, it's Ms. Bonner. And who are you?"

"I'm Diane Hopkins, director of Washington Memorial Emergency Department. We weren't expecting you until 8:00 a.m."

"Good morning, Diane. Nice to meet you," said Harriet, smiling. "I like to be early if I can. The earlier we get started, the earlier we can get done, right?"

"I suppose that's true. We are just finishing our shift changeover, so once that's done, I'll come back and we can get started."

"No need, Diane. I don't mind coming back now. I remember what shift change was like," said Harriet.

Diane formed a thin smile. "Oh, please call me Mrs. Hopkins. And I'll be back once the day shift settles in. My first responsibility is patient care; then I can move on to administrative concerns. I'm sure you can understand." She glanced at her watch. "It'll probably be another thirty minutes. See you then."

Harriet watched her turn and walk back through the door leading to the department. *Well played, Mrs. Hopkins. Exactly what I would have done in your position. You'd make a fine reviewer.* Harriet took another sip of her coffee and searched for an open chair. She found the farthest one from the vomiting child and took a seat. She typed out a quick text before opening up her laptop.

> Cecil, ED manager is a bit of a firebrand. Should be fun.

Diane Hopkins rushed back to the core of the Emergency Department and made an announcement over the nursing communication system. "Attention, the QCC review team is here for a site visit today. In the next fifteen minutes, I need everyone to perform their sweeps for expired medications and supplies, remove all personal items from patient care areas, and anything else that may be flagged. If you have any concerns, let me know immediately." She posted a message on the internal Facebook group to inform staff who would come in later and followed it up with an email.

Harriet looked over at the nurse kneeling next to the vomiting child. Diane's voice came through her communication device, loud enough to be heard across the room. She successfully stifled a laugh and continued typing on her laptop; her wide smile was the only sign she had heard the announcement.

Her phone vibrated, and a message from Cecil displayed on the screen.

Parking now, be there in a few.

Dr. Cecil Digby walked through the double doors of Washington Memorial Hospital and stopped just inside the automatic doors. He fidgeted with the buttons on his blazer, checking to make sure they were lined up appropriately.

"Cecil, I'm over here," said Harriet, lifting her coffee cup in the air.

He nodded his head in her direction and claimed a seat across from her.

"Good morning, Ms. Bonner. How was your night?"

"Cecil! What a thing to ask a woman!"

His polite smile morphed into a look of surprise and embarrassment as his eyes darted to the floor. "I'm sorry. I meant nothing by it. You had a late flight and had to be up early."

Harriet laughed loudly, her arm trying to balance the coffee as her stout frame jiggled with movement. "Lighten up. I'm just messing with you. I got to bed around midnight and then up again at five-thirty."

"Oh, sorry to hear it. You're probably dragging."

"Not at all. I feel like a kid on Christmas morning. I love these reviews. Especially if it's a second visit because of citations found last time. Everyone is so on edge. One more serious violation and the department can be shut down entirely."

"That's one of the reasons I quit practicing medicine. The administrative burden was too much for me to handle. I couldn't stand people reviewing my work and judging how good of a doctor I was. Plus the constant changes in guidelines with mandated compliance."

"So you became part of the administrative burden instead?"

"I needed to pay off my school debt and still feed my family. I could have worked for an insurance company reviewing claims, worked for a malpractice attorney, or this."

"So, are you happy with your decision?"

"No. I should have been a dentist."

Harriet let loose another round of intense laughter that was still settling down when the ED manager returned to the lobby.

"Okay, we are ready to get started." She looked at Cecil and held out her hand. "Hi, I'm Diane Hopkins, the Director for Washington Memorial Hospital Emergency Department."

"Pleased to meet you. I'm Dr. Cecil Digby. I am a former ER doctor and will be assisting Ms. Bonner on the site visit today."

"Wonderful. Glad to have you, Dr. Digby. Where would you like to start?"

"Please, call me Cecil," he said, smiling pleasantly at Diane.

Harriet stood and gathered her things together. She tried to grab her laptop with her right hand, but the coffee cup was in the way. She held it out toward Diane, who stared at her for a moment before suddenly reaching out and taking it from Harriet's hand.

"Oh, sorry. I didn't know you needed me to hold that," said Diane.

"Actually, you can just throw it away. I'm finished with it, thanks. I'd like to start with random chart audits, if that's okay with everyone else?"

Cecil nodded and stood up, falling in line behind the two women as the group headed into the department.

Chapter Sixteen

B ryce heard the clicking sound of a shod horse coming down the hallway and looked up to see what was making the noise. He saw Diane Hopkins leading a man and a woman dressed in business attire into the core of the department. Each one held a laptop slung over their shoulder and a black folder with the letters 'QCC' embroidered into the imitation leather.

"Here comes QCC," said Paula under her breath.

"You mean Q-U-A-C-C, or QUACC, a bunch of quack hacks. They spend their days telling us we can't have drinks on the counter in front of our workstation and then tell their family how much they are improving patient care."

Paula laughed but composed herself as the team marched past her workstation.

"Let's start with chart review," said Harriet. "I'd like to take a look at your restraint documentation. Can you get me a list of the patients who had restraints ordered on them in the last three months?"

Diane led them into her office and performed a search of the medical record system for the patients requested. When it finished, she spun her monitor around for the QCC team to view.

"Wow, almost three hundred patients. You guys sure use restraints a lot here," said Harriet with a disapproving frown.

"Well, any time a patient is not allowed out of bed due to overdose or psych concerns, we place an order for a restraint. Seclusion counts as a restraint," said Diane.

"I know that," said Harriet as she scanned the list. "Show me that one," she said, pointing at the chart of a thirteen-year-old patient.

"Ugh, I hated dealing with pediatric psych patients. So much manipulation and even worse insight than the adult patients. I don't miss that at all," said Cecil.

"So a pediatric patient aged thirteen needs restraint orders every two hours. Can you pull up the orders tab and we'll see when they were done?"

Diane complied and quickly saw the times were off. She kept a neutral face while swearing profusely internally.

Harriet clicked her tongue and began writing in her notebook. "I see most of these orders were written after the fact and timed for earlier than they were written. Each of those is a violation."

"It's not possible to work in a busy department and place a new order for the same thing to continue happening at exactly the right moment. Our nurses remind the doctors, but they are not immediately available to enter orders all the time," said Diane.

"I'm not here to tell you how to run your department. I'm just here to see if you are doing it correctly," said Harriet, smiling back at Diane.

The team continued chart review for another hour, focusing on such important patient care items as whether the indication for a Foley catheter was documented and whether patients who underwent sedation had been NPO for an appropriate time prior to sedation.

"This isn't an outpatient surgery center," protested Diane. "We can't schedule our sedations and procedures. If someone falls and dislocates their shoulder right after leaving Burger King, we just deal with it right then. Leaving the shoulder out of joint causes more harm than the risk of sedation with a full stomach."

"Again, we don't write the rules. We're just here to see that they're followed. It is perfectly acceptable to sedate a patient who has not been NPO for six hours, it just needs to be documented that it was an emergent situation. Nearly twenty-five percent of your charts do not document that exemption," said Cecil. "That's an enormous risk of aspiration events and other significant complications."

"No, it's not," said Diane. "The risk doesn't change at all. This isn't about patient care, it's about whether they checked a box in a chart. The risk is what it is. You are trying to grade us on whether we crossed our Ts and dotted our Is. How about focusing on our patient outcomes instead?"

Harriet laughed out loud. "Wouldn't that be nice? But that's not how it works. We improve outcomes through these back-end compliance reviews. We simply assume patient outcomes improve through our constant focus on process improvement."

Diane fumed and needed to step out for a moment. "Excuse me, I'll be back in a minute." She exited her office and pulled the door closed.

"Hey, how's it going in there?" asked Jackie.

"Well, I walked out rather than punching them in their faces, so I guess it could be worse."

Jackie hugged her boss and friend. "So glad it's you talking to them rather than me. I still would have walked out, but with a pretty sore hand. Don't worry, we've gone over every inch of this department. Everything is in shape. They'll be out of our hair for two years after this week."

"I sure hope so. Quick bathroom break and then I'm diving back in. Wish me luck."

Bryce exited room twenty-six, near the back of the department, and nearly bumped into a large zebra-striped lunch box carried by Emily Baldwin.

"Hey, sorry. Didn't see you coming, Emily. Are you guys working today?"

"No, I left something here that I needed to grab." She lifted the lunch box as she spoke.

"Ah, gotcha. Well, have a great day," said Bryce, heading back to the physician work area.

The QCC team reviewed several more charts and then suddenly Harriet closed her notebook and slid it back into her laptop bag.

"I think that's enough chart review for one day. I don't know how you bedside nurses do it. I can't even stand charting for one hour, let alone a whole shift," said Harriet.

"It does get tedious. It seems like we have little time for patient care anymore because of the ever-increasing charting requirements that are added each year." Diane stared at Harriet, who simply returned a smile but said nothing.

Cecil shifted awkwardly in his chair and then stood up. "Right, well, can we move to the tour portion?"

"Great idea, Cecil."

"Thanks," he said. "I read that last time there was an issue with expired products and even a dead rat found on the walk-through." He said the last comment with a cringe on his face.

"Unfortunately, yes. That rat was unexpected, but we have not seen another one since, and have had professional exterminators in the building every week. Rats completely gross me out. I'd probably vomit if one ran across the room." Her body experienced a brief shiver at the thought of a rat in the room. "We solved the issue with expired products by educating staff on first-in-first-out stocking practices and weekly audits of expiration dates for items that are used in patient care."

"Well, I'm glad to see our oversight has led to positive changes around here," said Harriet as she raised a hand to high-five Cecil. "Let's start in the stockroom. Diane, can you take us there?"

Diane led the group to the stockroom, centered between two long hallways full of patient rooms. Inside was a wire rack system with hundreds of different containers, each full of dozens of items.

"You go through this area weekly?" asked Harriet, raising her eyebrows at Diane.

"We have a staff member assigned to do it, yes."

"I'm impressed. Good job." Harriet slowly walked down the first aisle as Cecil poked through a few plastic containers with his pen, moving items and checking the dates on them.

Diane moved down the next aisle in a final check and quickly inhaled when she saw what was on the floor. *You've got to be kidding me! Again?*

She quickly knelt down and picked up a rat off the floor. She held it by the tail, suspending its lifeless body toward the ground.

"Everything seems in order over here. We'll check out the other half next," said Harriet, walking back toward the divider between the rows.

Diane had mere seconds until Harriet rounded the corner and saw her holding a dead rat.

"Looks like more of the same on this side," she said, taking in the equipment lining this aisle. Harriet looked at Diane, who was adjusting the collar on her blouse in an agitated manner. "Everything okay?"

Diane looked up quickly. "What? Yes, I'm fine. Just feeling a bit off suddenly. I'm going to need a moment. Please, continue to look around and I'll be right back."

She walked out of the room and made a beeline to the soiled utility closet. She saw Jackie and motioned for her to follow.

"What's up?" asked Jackie as she closed the door behind her.

Diane pulled her blouse over her head and whispered intently with her eyes closed, "Get it off of me!"

Jackie looked at her boss's exposed bra and saw a leg and tail sticking out of the right cup. She quickly reached in and pulled it out before throwing it in the sink containing an industrial garbage disposal and flipping the switch.

Diane elbowed Jackie aside, leaned over the sink, and emptied the contents of her stomach into the sink.

"Oh my gosh, are you okay? Why did you have a rat in your bra?" asked Jackie, confused whether to laugh or scream.

Diane held a finger up and retched a few more times before regaining her composure. She spit into the sink and grabbed a paper towel to wipe her face. "I found it on the floor of the supply room. I was there with the QCC team looking for expired products. No one saw it but me, so I picked it up and had to hide it somewhere." She groaned loudly. "Why couldn't I have worn pants with pockets or a white coat today? I didn't have anywhere else to hide that disgusting thing."

"And I thought I sacrificed for this department. I'll never doubt your dedication again, Diane."

The director put her blouse back on and adjusted it to fit properly. She turned to Jackie and asked, "How do I look?"

"Not bad for a lady who just tried to nurse a rat."

"Hilarious. If you tell anyone about this, I'll promote you and force you to deal with the administration instead of me."

Jackie pulled her fingers across her lips as if she were closing a zipper. "You're secret is safe with me. But why was the rat cold? It should have been room temperature if it was dead."

"Good point. I was too mortified to consider it at the time. I don't know why, but it was definitely chilled. QCC is still in the supply closet. I need to get back to them. Thanks for the assist, Jackie."

Diane walked back to the supply closet and found Harriet and Cecil looking bored and engaged in idle chit-chat.

"There you are. Is everything okay?" asked Harriet.

"Yes, sorry. A GI bug I guess," said Diane.

"While you were gone, we found a few expired items." Cecil displayed several IV catheters in his hand and pointed to the expiration date on them. "These expired over a year ago and were mixed with the other supplies."

"Let me see those," said Diane. She took the catheters and examined the packages before taking another one from the shelf and comparing them.

"We don't even use these. Look, the expired ones are completely different from all the rest of the ones we use."

"Did you switch vendors recently?" asked Harriet.

"No, we've used the same product for years. I have no idea why this is in here, but it's not one of ours," said Diane defensively.

"Interesting. So you're saying you have no way of ensuring your supply chain?" said Harriet.

Diane hesitated before replying. "No, that's not what I'm saying. I don't have an explanation for it other than to say those do not belong to the Emergency Department."

"We'll have to discuss this later. Let's check out a few patient rooms and then break for lunch. What did you order for us?"

"Cheesecake factory salads and sandwiches. I hope that's okay."

"It'll do," said Harriet as she walked out of the supply room. "Come on Cecil, let's check out some rooms."

Harriet walked down the hallway and stopped in front of room twenty-three. "I loved Michael Jordan. Let's start with this room."

She knocked and entered the room, finding it already occupied by an elderly patient and her daughter, who was sitting in the corner. "Excuse me, we are with the Quality Control Commission and are conducting a site visit. We'll only be in the room a few moments."

Cecil and Harriet examined the equipment and looked inside every drawer and cabinet. Harriet pulled open the drawer with IV supplies and clicked her tongue, drawing Diane's attention. "You don't use these in the Emergency Department, eh?" She was holding another expired catheter she had just found in the supply drawer.

Diane sighed and shook her head. *What was going on here?*

An hour later, the review was complete, and Dianne led the team back to the conference room for lunch.

Harriet filled her plate with food and summarized their visit between bites. "Honestly Diane, the review wasn't too bad. I'm glad we didn't find any rats this time. That would have been a health code issue besides a patient care problem. The expired products won't get you a serious violation, but will require an action plan for remediation."

Diane listened but did not respond. She did, however, adjust her blouse and suppress a wave of nausea.

Cecil pointed to the food. "Are you not going to eat?"

Diane shook her head. "No, thanks. I'm fasting until dinner today."

Harriet chuckled and finished her bite before responding. "Fasting? I don't understand that. Give me my food and keep me happy. No one wants to be around me when I'm hangry."

Cecil picked up his cup and took a sip while making eye contact with Diane. He winked and hid a nod in the motion of taking a drink.

After the meal, Diane escorted the review team through the department toward the front lobby. They were saying their goodbyes when a piercing scream echoed through the department.

Everyone who heard the scream stopped what they were doing and rushed to investigate the source, including the QCC team. A second, quieter scream followed shortly thereafter, and it came from a nurse standing by the pneumatic tube station used to send supplies throughout the hospital.

She was pointing at something on the floor. "Rat!" she said. "I opened a tube thinking it was the antibiotics for my patient, and a rat fell out."

Diane's face tightened and turned a few shades darker. She heard a clicking sound next to hear and knew Harriet was about to say words she didn't want to hear.

"Well, would you look at that? Cecil, good thing we hadn't left yet."

Cecil leaned down and flicked the rat with his pen, causing it to flip over, but it made no spontaneous movement. "I think it's dead."

Harriet looked at Diane and shook her head. "I need to talk to my superiors about this. We'll be in touch in the coming weeks. My recommendation, if you want to stay open, is hire an exterminator who can actually do the job, and do it quickly."

She snapped her fingers and pointed toward the exit. "Come on Cecil, we need to get out of here." She looked back at Diane one more time and said, "careful where you walk."

Chapter Seventeen

"Are you sure you want to do this?" asked Destiny's father as he parked the car outside the police station.

She nodded in the back seat. "I want his family to know even in his last moments, he was kind. I also want to apologize for making him stand there in the first place."

"I am so proud of you, Destiny," said her mother. "This wasn't your fault, but you still are trying to do what you can to make it easier."

Destiny exhaled deeply and then pulled the handle on her door. "Okay, let's go."

They held hands as they walked inside the reception area. A reception desk was straight ahead, down a short hallway lined with chairs. Sitting in a chair on the right was a well-dressed man with a familiar face.

"Hello Reverend, thank you for coming today," said Destiny's mom as she hugged him deeply.

"No problem at all. My job is to help my flock through any struggle they find themselves in."

The group continued down the hall.

"Hi, may I help you?" asked an officer stationed behind the desk.

"Yes, we're here to meet Mrs. Jenkins. This is Destiny," said her father, putting his arm around his daughter's shoulder.

"Ah, yes. Thank you for coming. His wife, Courtney, is in the conference room down the hall. Her sister is with her, along with our staff counselor."

The officer led them down a short hallway and pushed open the door to the conference room.

"Ma'am, this is Destiny and her family," she said before standing aside and letting the group pass her. She then pulled the door closed and returned to her post.

Her sister flanked Officer Jenkins' wife to her right, and the department counselor on her left. Destiny walked over and extended a hand to introduce herself. Her right-handed handshake was accepted, and then Courtney stepped forward and embraced Destiny with her left arm. The two let go of their hands and held each other as they both sobbed. The counselor slid a box of tissues down the table toward them. It bumped into large spiral notebook.

After a few moments, Courtney leaned back and looked at Destiny. "Thank you so much for coming here and meeting with me. I want you to know that I don't blame you for what happened."

This brought another round of tears that coalesced into a wave of emotion through her body. Courtney held her firmly until Destiny could compose herself. The two separated and took their seats at the table.

"As the wife of a police officer, I always had a fear of receiving the call that I did." Courtney looked at her sister before continuing. "It's not something we talked about very often, but Mike always knew there was a possibility he would not be coming home."

"That day started like any other. He got up early and made a pot of coffee, drinking one cup and putting as much as he could into a thermos to take with him in the car. He had only been on duty a few hours when it happened." She looked at Destiny with a soft expression. "Can you tell me everything you remember about my husband? Yours are the last memories of him that anyone has, and I want them to be mine as well."

Destiny blew her nose and wiped her eyes, all sense of pride eroded by the flood of emotions she had already experienced.

"Well, honestly, the first time I saw him was when he was behind me with his lights on. I was terrified because I knew I was speeding, and had never been pulled over before. I didn't have any money to pay for the ticket since I was saving for college expenses. Sorry to say this, but I was mad at him."

Courtney laughed and wiped away a tear. "It's funny you say that. Mike used to tell me all the time about how mad people would get when he enforced the law. He didn't take it personally."

"Really, though, I was mad at myself more. I was being stupid and didn't realize how dumb it was until his lights came on. But, I pulled over and got out my license and registration. When he got to my car, I was trying to be polite and not cry in front of him."

"Dear, you should have. He was a sucker for actual tears. Especially if it was just speeding."

"No, I didn't even need to cry. He asked me where I was going so fast and I explained I was just trying to get home after my night shift. We talked about how I was saving for college and I really couldn't afford a ticket."

"Let me guess, he said he wasn't interested in giving you a ticket to fund the city budget, but he just wanted you to be safe?"

Destiny nodded. "That's almost exactly what he said. He mentioned all the construction and how it was leading to more accidents. Then he went back to his car with my information and then came back with a piece of paper. I thought I was getting a ticket and started pleading my case again. He told me to relax; it was just a warning. He told me to have a good day and then turned to walk back to his car." She paused and closed her eyes, trying to imagine anything other than the officer flying through the air after the car struck him. "That's when the car hit him. I'm not even sure he saw it coming. I like to think he didn't."

"I know, me too. You also got out of your car and tried to help him, right?"

"Yes ma'am, I did. I called 9-1-1 and ran to see how badly he was hurt. All I could do was hold his head and try to keep his mouth open." She looked down at the table before continuing. "I'm so sorry there wasn't anything else I could do."

"Honey, there's nothing anyone could have done. As soon as it hit him, his fate was decided. I believe Jesus caught him before he even hit the ground."

Courtney's sister leaned over and offered a hug, then added between sobs. "I do too, sis."

The group listened as Courtney shared a few stories of Michael Jenkins' life before the meeting naturally drew to a close.

"Destiny, thank you so much for coming to meet me today. I appreciate you sharing my husband's last moments with us. It means a lot to know that he was the man we knew him to be, even up to his last moments here on earth. I wish the girl who killed him had the kind of character that you do." She looked at Destiny's father and then mother. "You two have done a great job raising her into a strong and confident woman. Please keep reassuring her that this wasn't her fault, and that my husband would want her to be as successful as she can be."

Courtney picked up the spiral notebook and flipped through it until she found the correct page. She sighed and put her finger on it before laying the notebook on the table. "Michael and I would always start a game of some sort before he left for a shift. We would finish it as soon as he got home safely. That day it was tic-tac-toe. Looks like I'll have to wait a while before I can finish it with him."

The reverend spoke softly. "Would you all mind if I said a quick prayer before we ended the meeting?"

Everyone nodded before he offered a soulful prayer requesting healing for all, and a celebration for Michael in Heaven.

The group stood and hugged goodbyes before Destiny's family and minister walked out together.

Chapter Eighteen

"**H**oney, it's about to start!" yelled Valerie from the family room. She heard six footsteps in rapid cadence fly down the stairs. Bryce and Hannah rounded the corner first and headed around the end of the couch. Noah suddenly appeared in mid-air, sailing over the back of the couch and landing next to Val, directly in the spot Hannah was aiming for.

"I won!" cheered Noah excitedly.

Hannah crossed her arms and stuck her lower lip out. "No fair, you cheated. I wanted to sit next to mom."

"Come here, sweetie," said Val, picking Hannah up and setting her on her lap. "You get the best seat of all." Hannah looked at Noah and stuck her tongue out at him.

"Let's be quiet. I want to hear what they have to say," said Bryce.

The TV displayed the image of a podium inside of a conference room at the police headquarters. Several uniformed officers stood next to the podium with somber looks on their faces. The officers on the left side adjusted their position to allow their chief Sammy Booker to squeeze past. His large frame made it somewhat difficult. He stepped up to the podium and pulled the microphone higher toward his mouth.

"Good afternoon. I am Sammy Booker, Chief of the Indianapolis Metropolitan Police Department. I called this press conference to share the sad news of the passing of one of our own. Officer Michael Jenkins, a ten-year veteran with the department, was struck and killed on the side of the road this morning. He was conducting a routine traffic stop when another vehicle swerved out of the passenger lane and struck him while he was talking to the driver. They transported him to Washington Memorial Hospital, where he was pronounced dead."

The chief paused and wiped his eyes before continuing. "Officer Jenkins leaves behind his wife and three children. Our department is setting up a fundraiser for the family and we will post information about this later as it becomes available. The members of our department courageously serves the citizens of Indianapolis every day, in so many ways. Officer Jenkins was killed while enforcing traffic laws, likely by someone who was not paying attention behind the wheel. All we ask is that you put down your damn phone and pay attention. Distracted driving can end your life or someone else's. It's not worth it. Send the text later. Make the call on speakerphone. But for the love of God, please keep your eyes on the road."

He continued on for a few minutes, discussing Officer Jenkins' history with the department, including several awards given to him by the community. After another plea to avoid distracted driving, the chief opened the conference up to questions.

The first question came from a faceless voice behind the camera. "Sir, there are reports circulating online that the officer was struck by a car registered to Mackenzie Hearst. Is she the one believed to have killed the officer?"

"We are aware of those reports, and our detectives are investigating the accident. I am not prepared to comment on any suspects at this time."

A second reporter's shouted question rose above the others. "What charges could we see in response to this accident?"

The chief turned to address it. "Any official charges would need to be coordinated with the prosecutor's office. But I can see the possibility of reckless homicide, depending on what led to the driver leaving the traffic lane. Distracted driving sure sounds reckless, doesn't it?" The chief raised his hands to quiet the reporters shouting questions at him. "I'm going to end the conference now. I want to express our deepest condolences to the family of Officer Michael Jenkins. The department is here for you and we will walk through this together. The men and women of this department consider ourselves to be aunts and uncles to your children. Michael Jenkins was our brother, and will be remembered as such. Thank you."

Chapter Nineteen

The next day, the chief was sitting in his office when a report on the news caught his attention.

"You have got to be shitting me," screamed Chief Booker. The reporter on the television paid no attention to his outburst and continued reading the story to the camera.

"Our experts tell us that an alcohol level of 320 would cause a person to be severely impaired and, if not a frequent drinker, potentially even unconscious. Any person able to function with an alcohol level of 320 has drank heavily for quite some time. The question is, why would an officer be on duty with an alcohol level that high? These and other questions into the death of Officer Michael Jenkins continue."

"He didn't drink, you jackasses!" The chief turned off the television and threw the remote into a chair next to his desk. "Linda!" he yelled out his door, "get me the coroner!"

His secretary stepped into his office and nodded. "Yes, sir. What should I tell him this is about?"

"He just accused Jenkins of being an alcoholic and drunk on duty. I want to know how he came to that conclusion."

Linda offered a weak smile before returning to her desk to track down the coroner.

A few minutes later she returned to the doorway. "Sir, I have the coroner on hold for you."

"Thanks, Linda. Would you mind shutting my door?"

Linda pulled the door shut gently and sat back down at her desk a few feet outside the Chief's office. She was close enough to be useful, but also close enough to hear phone calls through a closed door.

The chief stared at the blinking red light on his phone. *You'd better have a good reason for trashing the character of my fallen officer.*

He picked up the handset and smashed the button to connect the call. "This is Chief Booker."

"Hi, this is Zac Pullard. You wanted to speak with me?"

"You're damn right I did. I just saw a news report where they claimed Officer Jenkins was an alcoholic and heavily intoxicated when she killed him. Where do you think they got that idea?"

"That's on the news already? We haven't released our final report yet."

"Well, someone got a whiff of the preliminary report, and now it's all over the news. How did you conclude he was drunk?"

"His alcohol level was .32. That's four times the legal limit," said the coroner.

"Don't you think I know that? I've been a cop for twenty-five years! You don't need to tell me about my job."

"What else can I help you with, chief?"

"Jenkins did not drink alcohol. There is no chance he had an alcohol level of 320. You screwed up and are tarnishing the memory of my fallen officer."

The coroner replied with a raised voice of his own. "We checked the sample repeatedly. We checked the machine repeatedly. It gave us the same number within a point or two. I stand by the work my team does. And trust me, I don't need to be told how to do my job either."

"Apparently you do. This is the last straw, Zac. We're going to clear Jenkins' name and then I'm coming after you." He slammed the handset back into the cradle and then continued to stare at the phone. *We'll figure this out, Jenkins, I promise you.*

Chapter Twenty

"Hey, did you see the news about that police officer struck by the Hearst girl?" asked Valerie as soon as Bryce walked in the door.

"No, what happened?"

"The coroner released their preliminary report today, and it said the cop was drunk. Alcohol level over three hundred, nearly four times the legal limit. That's crazy."

"What? How is that possible? The driver struck him after drifting onto the shoulder. His alcohol level would have nothing to do with that. And from what I can remember from the chart, he was only a social drinker."

"Well, some people are good at hiding their problem, I guess. It doesn't mean the girl who hit him is any less at fault, but it puts a stain on his legacy that he was working while drunk."

Bryce shook his head. *It didn't make sense. Why would the officer be drunk at work? I certainly smelled nothing on him during the resuscitation.*

Bryce's phone vibrated on the counter. The screen showed a blocked caller ID. He chose to answer rather than deal with a voice mail later.

"Doctor Chapman?" said the caller.

"This is he. Who is this?"

"Hey doc, it's Detective Stephenson from IMPD. Did you hear about the coroner's report? It said Jenkins was intoxicated at the time she struck him."

"Just did actually. I think it's ridiculous. Was he known to drink excessively?"

"No, he was not. I spoke with his wife. She said he may have a beer on the weekend but nothing significant. I know enough about alcohol levels to know someone without a significant tolerance could not be doing his job at a level of three hundred."

"You're absolutely correct, detective. How did the coroner conclude that?" asked Bryce.

"They ran an alcohol level on blood obtained from the hospital. They confirmed it had his name on the label and the investigator herself collected it from the room. I talked to the investigator who claimed they even ran it again after recalibrating their device. Same result."

"It's hard to argue with those results, but I still don't believe he was drunk. How can I help you, detective?"

"I need to understand how blood is drawn and stored. How secure is the chain of custody when a patient has labs drawn? Is it possible this was someone else's blood?"

"It's probably easiest if we meet at the hospital and I can show you how it works. I'll have our lab director join us. But can't you just run a DNA test on the sample to prove it isn't his blood?"

"I'll meet you whenever, doc. Just tell me when. We are asking for the DNA test to be run, but it's going to take a week or two since they don't do them locally. We need to get this story corrected soon before the public assumes it's truth and stores it in their permanent memory."

"Okay, I work tomorrow. I'll get in touch with Alani, our lab director, and ask her to meet us in the ER. Does noon work for you?"

"Yes it does, thanks, doc. See you then.

Chapter Twenty-One

"Val, I still can't figure out the police officer's alcohol level."

"What do you mean? I thought it was four times the legal limit. What is there to figure out?"

"That's just it. The report said it was, but I don't believe it. He did not smell intoxicated and his family denied any history of drinking. What if this is another case of the coroner's office botching an investigation? This one could have serious implications for the public. The entire IMPD force is pissed off at how the case was handled, and I'm smack in the middle of it because I treated both of them."

"Aren't you the one always telling me not to under-estimate someone's ability to mess things up?"

Bryce nodded. "Yeah, but usually I'm referring to people other than myself."

"What did you mess up here?"

"Nothing. But I always feel like it's my fault because I was involved."

"I've told you to stop doing that. You take your job too personally," said Val.

"I can't do it any other way. I've tried to be disinterested. It just makes me feel like an uncaring jerk. I'll just deal with the emotional baggage like I always do."

"Well, I'll help you as best I can, you know that. But maybe you should talk to one of your partners about the medical side of the situation."

Bryce smacked her thigh gently and rocked forward and out of the couch. "Good idea. In fact, I should head in for my shift, anyway. I'll see you guys tonight."

Bryce arrived at the ER and quickly tracked down his partner, Tom.

"Hey, you got a minute?" he asked.

"Sure, just closing out my shift, but I have a few minutes. What's up?" said Tom.

"I was thinking about the officer's blood alcohol level. I don't think the result is accurate. His wife said he didn't drink at all. I hate to call out the coroner again and just pour more gasoline on this fire. I wanted your opinion before I started ruffling feathers."

"Well, we see lab errors all the time, right? Someone's hemoglobin is diluted down from their fluids running in, sodium is elevated for the same reason, potassium is elevated from hemolysis," said Tom.

"You're right. I guess it could have been a lab error. I'll call Ashley Saxon and try to ask nicely."

"Good luck, man, but your history with her will not make it easy."

Tom was right. Ashley was the investigator assigned to Kent Carpenter's death, and convinced the coroner to sign off on Kent having had cystic fibrosis, despite no genetic testing to prove it or medical history of frequent pulmonary infections to support it. Bryce and his orthopedic surgery friend Graham Kelly had to break into a sperm bank and steal a sample from Kent to test the DNA for cystic fibrosis. As Bryce suspected, Kent did not have CF. But he could not bring that information back to the coroner since he got it illegally. It also helped convince him that Kent was murdered and to look for the person who killed him. It didn't take a great mental leap to assume Bryce had put Clay in the hospital after learning this information. And they can't have that. Both would likely go to prison.

Bryce searched his phone and found the number for Ashley Saxon. He initiated the call and hoped for a pleasant interaction.

"Saxon." Bryce heard the deflated tone in her voice, the pitch falling as if in a sigh.

"Hi Ashley, this is Dr. Bryce Chapman from Washington Memorial. How are you today?" *Maybe we can get along today?*

"I know who you are. What do you need?" *Okay, business as usual then.*

"Sorry to keep calling you about situations like these, but I'm having trouble with the blood alcohol level of Michael Jenkins. His family said he didn't drink at all, and the woman he had pulled over said she didn't smell alcohol on him, nor did he seem intoxicated. Is it possible that the blood you tested was from someone else? Or that your machine had an error?"

"You just don't stop, do you? Last time you didn't want to believe your patient had cystic fibrosis, now you want me to change our findings to show the officer wasn't blindingly drunk when he was killed? Look, I didn't want that reported either, but what am I supposed to do when the machine gives me that result three times in a row? I even recalibrated it after the initial abnormal reading. I ran it off the gray top tube we collected at the hospital. Sorry doc, the value is correct."

"Then is it possible the blood was from someone else? Maybe we can accept that the value the machine gave is correct, but it was an incorrect sample. Say, from a different patient who actually was drunk."

"I collected the blood myself. The labels on the vials all say Michael Jenkins. What do you think?"

Bryce didn't have an answer. Well, he did, but not one that would help move the conversation forward. It had to be an error. But how?

"Okay, well, thank you for walking me through it. I'll let you know if I come up with anything. IMPD is pretty pissed about their slain officer reportedly being drunk. No one believes it."

"I know. We're catching plenty of heat on this end. But it is what it is. Data doesn't lie."

Bryce ended the call and considered the situation further. When a data point doesn't fit the overall picture, it's important to step back and look at everything from the very beginning. Was there something not identified? Is the current basis incorrect?

He dialed the number for the detective next to find a different angle.

"Stephenson," came the curt reply.

"Hey sir, it's Bryce Chapman. Do you have a moment to speak?"

"Yes. In fact, I'm just parking here at the hospital. I'll find you in a few minutes and we'll do this in person."

Bryce ended the call and shivered. "Not a fan of hearing police are coming to talk to me about something, even if we're both on the same side."

"Better get used to it. Just a part of life in the ER," said Tom.

Yeah, but most ER docs didn't just slice a guy open with a pressure washer after breaking and entering a private business. "Knowing it and feeling it are different," said Bryce.

He picked up the phone and called down to the lab. He asked for Alani and did not have long to wait.

"Hello, this is Alani Kahele. How can I help you?"

"Hey Alani, it's Bryce Chapman. Can I ask another favor?"

"Sure Bryce. Your favors are usually for someone else's benefit, anyway. What's up?"

"There's a detective here investigating the death of the officer on the side of the road. Are you able to come to the ER and talk us through what could give a false positive on a blood alcohol sample?"

"Yes, I'll be right up."

"Dr. Chapman? Is this a good time?"

Bryce turned to see Detective Stephenson standing by the secretary's desk, looking toward the physician's work area. He stood and walked over to greet him.

"Yes, my shift doesn't start for fifteen minutes. Thanks for coming in."

"Of course. What have you found out?"

"I talked with the coroner investigator who came here and collected the samples. She collected the vials of blood, confirmed the labels, and even recalibrated the machine. She is confident the result is accurate."

"She is, huh? Well, I'm confident she's wrong. I just can't prove it," said the detective.

"Can you explain what happens when a patient gets a blood draw to evaluate for impaired driving? Who handles that blood and where does it go?" asked Bryce.

"If it is to be used as evidence, we need to determine the chain of custody," said the detective. "Medical personnel collect the sample after the suspect gives consent, or by a warrant signed by a judge. Once obtained, it's labeled and then handed to the police officer, who places it in a sealed evidence bag and it's transported to our crime lab for analysis. The technician who processes the sample breaks the seal and logs the specimen in, confirms the identification, and then runs the test."

"So at no time is the blood ever out of sight of someone, at least until it's in a sealed evidence bag?" asked Bryce.

"That's correct. This way, there is always someone who can testify where the sample was, and that no one tampered with it."

"I wonder if the coroner investigator did the same thing? I didn't question her when she said she collected the sample herself. Maybe I'll follow up and see what she says."

Bryce saw Alani walking down the hallway toward them and smiled broadly.

"Thanks for coming so quickly, Alani. Detective Stephenson, this is Alani Kahele. She runs the lab here at Washington Memorial. If anyone can sort out something with a lab result, it's her."

Alani helped to connect the pieces with Bryce's patient Kent Carpenter. She realized the multi-drug-resistant bacteria that killed Kent was only found on one other patient, Eleanor Livingstone.

This helped Bryce investigate who was in contact with her and eventually determine the paramedic Clay Turner committed the murder.

"I'll do my best. What is the concern?" she asked.

"Ma'am, I believe there was an error with the blood sample collected on Officer Jenkins. The coroner's report stated his alcohol level was 320, but I think they got it wrong. How could that have happened?"

"Well, there are plenty of ways that a result can be invalid. The machine may not have been calibrated or there could have been something on the machine already it detected. Maybe the wrong tube was used to store the blood. Sometimes it's even the wrong patient. I've had a few pregnant men over the years. It seems funny at first, until you realize that is just the most obvious example of an incorrect patient identifier being on a tube. There's really no way to tell on other blood work or a urinalysis, unless the result is wildly different from a recent value we have in the system. We are constantly looking for ways to ensure our samples are collected and identified properly. The problem is, it's a process full of humans."

"And humans make errors," added Bryce.

Alani nodded her agreement.

"The coroner investigator said she collected the blood from the patient herself. Assuming that's true, what else could cause an elevated level? What if she used an alcohol wipe on the skin before obtaining the sample?" asked Detective Stephenson.

Alani shook her head. "The purpose of the alcohol wipe is to decontaminate the skin and reduce risk of the blood draw causing an infection. It would be unusual to worry about that in a person who was deceased. Plus, the isopropyl alcohol of the wipe does not cause an elevated ethyl alcohol level. I think the best bet to challenge the level is to look at the chain of custody and try to prove it's not his blood. Is it possible she collected the wrong patient's blood?"

"I suppose anything is possible, but it would be pretty unlikely," said Bryce. "It was clear who she was there to see. But now that you mention it, there was another lady in the trauma room that day. She is one of our frequent fliers and was quite drunk at that visit. She had fallen and struck her head. Peter Thrasher actually tied her down to the bed because she was trying to get up and was throwing things to get attention. We didn't have staff available to watch her since we were all helping Officer Jenkins."

"You tied a patient to the bed?" asked Detective Stephenson with raised eyebrows.

"It was the only choice we had. She was on the monitor and was safe the entire time. It's a soft restraint to keep her safe while we attended to your colleague," said Bryce.

"I'll just pretend that stuff doesn't happen here. Truth be told, we have to restrain violent and psychotic patients in unique ways from time to time ourselves." The detective typed a few sentences on his phone and then put it back in his pocket.

"Aren't you supposed to write notes in a small spiral-bound notebook?" asked Alani.

The detective smiled. "That's how we did it when I started. Now, I use a smart phone backed up immediately to a cloud storage system. You do not know how annoying it is when someone spills coffee on your notebook, or you leave it in the bathroom. Now, if I lose my phone, I just flash the new one with my old content. Plus, we can share notes in real-time with other members of the force and do global keyword searches. Such a better way to do things."

"Okay, so where do we go from here?" asked Bryce.

"I'm going to talk to Ashley Saxon," said Stephenson. "I want to know exactly what she did and how she did it. Is there anything else you can tell me about the patient in the other room?"

Bryce chuckled at the coincidence he was about to reveal. "Yeah. She was pregnant."

"I'll review her blood collection history and see what I can find out," said Alani. "Bryce, I'll call you if anything stands out."

After the group went their separate ways, Bryce sat down to prepare for the beginning of his shift.

Chapter Twenty-Two

"Hey, the Hearst family press conference is about to start," said Tom.

Bryce looked up from his computer and turned toward Tom's workstation, where he had the local news broadcast playing. The camera angle showed a podium setup in what appeared to be a conference room of an attorney's office. Dark mahogany shelving lined the walls behind the podium, filled with books that likely hadn't been opened in years.

A few seconds later, the Hearst family attorney stepped to the lectern and laid out a few pieces of paper. He looked around the room and settled his gaze on the news camera in the center of the audience. "Hello, I am Vincent Leoni, founding partner of the law firm Leoni and Womack. My firm represents Charlie Hearst and his family in all legal matters. As you know, Mackenzie Hearst was involved in a tragic accident that caused the death of Officer Michael Jenkins of the Indianapolis Metropolitan Police Department. We all extend our condolences to the family of Officer Jenkins and will keep them in our prayers." He looked down at the podium and adjusted the papers in front of him.

"Mackenzie Hearst has an exemplary driving record, having never even received a speeding citation. She is active in the community and volunteers her time mentoring teens at the Boys and Girls Club of Indianapolis. Together with her family foundation, she has helped build parks, sponsor school sporting events, provide scholarships to inner-city children, and so much more. It devastated her that her allergies have led to this unfortunate situation. She experienced a severe fit of sneezing, brought on by her seasonal allergies, and this lead to her car swerving slightly out of the traffic lane and striking Officer Jenkins. It is unclear why the officer was so close to the lane, though from footage it appears the car he had pulled over stopped much too close to traffic. As to why Officer Jenkins approached on the driver's side rather than the passenger side, unfortunately we can only speculate, though recent evidence may provide insight. It is also not standard practice to stand so close to traffic when interviewing a person on the side of the road."

Vincent Leoni looked up from his papers and stared into the camera. "We believe the coroner's report provides that answer. Officer Jenkins' blood alcohol level was 0.32, or exactly four times the legal limit to operate a motor vehicle. I am not intending to smear the memory of Officer Jenkins, but this is relevant when considering the entire situation. We will have more information as the details unfold. Thank you all for coming today. I ask that you allow the Hearst family privacy as they deal with this tragedy on their end. Please direct any questions you may have to my law office."

The lawyer stepped away from the podium and the feed cut back to the news anchor sitting at his desk. Tom Sharpe closed the browser window and turned to Bryce. "Wow, this is going to get interesting. What are you going to do, Bryce? I mean, she's lying, right? Wasn't she filming a video when she struck the officer?"

I have no idea what the hell I'm going to do, Tom. Why can't the job just involve treating disease and not social issues? He took a breath, but paused a moment before answering out loud. "I documented in my chart what she told me the first time. I also documented that she changed her story. No doubt the city will try to subpoena the chart, and since I do not know how that works, I didn't want to leave anything left unsaid. The courts can figure it out." The truth was Bryce had told several colleagues and nurses that Mackenzie had changed her story. It was part of working in an ER. Stories are told and they share they share patient histories among staff. Everyone is involved in the treatment team and HIPAA does not apply. But this was going to be different. This is expanding outside patient care and the ER. Could there be a HIPAA violation claim made if the first story leaked?

A HIPPA complaint could cost me my job along with $50,000. Bryce shook his head and looked down at the floor.

"Cheer up Bryce. We've got your back," said Tom.

"I appreciate that. Really, I do. I can't imagine working at a place where docs just punched a clock and went home. I wouldn't make it through all of this non-sense if I didn't have you, Peter, Ash, and everyone else on my side."

"Don't forget your ortho buddy and, of course, your wife. Val's a tough lady and you have no bigger cheerleader than her," said Tom.

"You're exactly right. I'd be lost without her." Bryce stared past Tom and thought back to the low of his depression a few months ago. His confidence had eroded to the point he was doubting himself as a physician and his alcohol intake accelerated to the point of abuse.

Val called him out on it and took the children to her parents' house in Destin, Florida to remove them from his behavior. This led to a night of severe depression and alcohol consumption that nearly resulted in him committing suicide.

"Hey, you in there?" asked Tom.

Bryce shook his head and refocused to the present. "Yeah, sorry. Just thinking about life a bit."

"Well, if you're done, I'd like to get out of here. Can I tell you what I have left?"

"Sure, lay it on me," said Bryce, sitting next to Tom and grabbing a sticky note.

Chapter
Twenty-Three

Vincent Leoni entered his personal code into the keypad outside the gated entrance to the Hearst estate and then waited for the gates to open. "How are you going to get out of this one, Tex?" he said to himself. "Money? Threats? Disappearance?" Once the gates had opened wide enough, he sighed and drove the car down the quarter mile tree-lined driveway toward the massive home.

He pulled three-quarters of the way around the large ornamental fountain and parked against a detached garage. As soon as he exited, the musty smell of a Cuban cigar signaled Charlie Hearst was somewhere outside.

Vincent saw a vague outline of a man sitting in a chair on the porch. A bright, reddish-yellow glow illuminated Charlie's face before it vanished into a cloud of smoke.

"Good evening, Vincent. Care for a cigar?"

"No, thank you. I still don't smoke." He pulled a chair several feet back and sat down slightly upwind from his employer. *How are you going to screw my life up tonight, Charlie?*

"Tonight is about circling the wagons, do you understand?"

"Oh, I understand. I just don't agree."

"What does that mean?"

"It means this is wrong, Charlie, and you know it. It's a shame the officer lost his life, and it's a shame your daughter caused it. But we both know this wasn't a sneeze. She wasn't paying attention and killed that officer."

"Well, the poor drunken bastard shouldn't have been standing so close to the road," said Charlie.

"I don't believe for a moment he was drunk. Everything I'm hearing through the grapevine is that the officer was a stand-up guy. Didn't really drink, and wouldn't even be on his feet with a level of 320, let alone driving a squad car and giving out written warnings."

"Well, I guess we're just lucky the coroner released the report the way they did, aren't we?"

Vincent stared at Charlie, waiting for him to continue. He quickly lost patience. "Was it luck? Or was this another example of you using your wealth to create luck?"

Charlie coughed deeply and then adjusted himself in the chair. "What's that phrase you blood suckers like to throw around? Plausible something-or-other?"

"Plausible deniability?"

"Yeah, that's the one. Look Vincent, don't go squattin' on your spurs, you hear? We need to all be singing the same song if we're going to keep my baby out of jail."

"I will not work against you, sir, you know that."

"Damn right you won't. Your daughter wouldn't be alive right now if I hadn't done what I did."

"I know that, and I think about it every day. But you also know where I stand on the whole situation. Yes, you saved her, but you also brought those events into our lives. If you hadn't started working with—"

"Hey! Enough of that!" Charlie cut in, stopping his lawyer from finishing the statement. He lowered his voice to a whisper, but maintained the intensity. "You do not talk about that around my family, do you understand?"

Vincent sighed audibly. *Your crimes nearly caused my daughter to die, and now I am covering for yours? Smuggling and gang retribution is one thing, but covering up for the death of a police officer is something entirely different.* He allowed a few minutes to pass before responding.

"Like I said, I am on your team and will do what you want; I just wish it was being handled differently."

"If you ever decide to go shine someone else's boots, make sure you are prepared to pay off the rest of what you owe me. I reckon it's just under a million right now." Charlie tossed the cigar down on the rocks behind his chair before walking through the front door. He left it open, and Vincent followed a few moments later.

Charlie Hearst walked through his marble tiled foyer and entered his library. Mackenzie and Marybeth sat close together and leaned toward each other in hushed conversation.

"There're my two pretty ladies. What are y'all discussin'?

Mackenzie sat upright and gave a quick glance to her mother before answering. "Daddy, I don't want to do this. It was my fault I hit that officer. I wasn't paying attention and everyone knows it. His family deserves an end to this ordeal. I'll face whatever consequences I have to."

Charlie walked over to his daughter and ran his hand through her hair. "I love your heart, child. So full of goodness." He pulled his hand away and started pacing the room. "Unfortunately, we planted that seed at the press conference. Vincent over there told the entire world that you had an awful sneeze because of allergies. If we change now, it will be obvious we were lying. It will destroy our reputation. Who would buy a car from the family who killed a cop and lied about it?"

"But I don't sell cars, Daddy. Why do I have to reap the harvest of a field I didn't plant? This was all your idea."

"My idea? It wasn't my damn car that flattened the cop. That was you!" He slammed his hand down on the back of a chair. "All I did was work to protect you and your future. I hate to say it, but that means more to me than how one person died. He's dead no matter what. Why ruin your life too? We can make a large donation to his family. Pay their house off. Pay for college for their kids. They'll be fine."

Mackenzie brought her knees up to her chest, buried her face between them, and began to cry.

Marybeth moved over and wrapped her arms around her daughter. "Charlie, money can't solve everything. You better know what you're doing here, because we only get one shot at this." She pointed at her daughter's back while she said the last phrase.

"We are going to burn them all down. Drunken police officer. Stupid girl who broke the law and then parked too close to the traffic lanes, starting this whole thing. By the time we're done spinnin', it will sound like the officer was lyin' down in the middle of the road when poor Mackenzie came upon him."

"Charlie, you can't put this on the girl the officer pulled over. It's not her fault," said Marybeth.

"The hell it ain't. If she hadn't been speeding, the officer wouldn't have pulled her over. He would be at home eatin' biscuits and gravy with his family." Charlie looked at his attorney who was sitting quietly in the corner. "Vincent, I want to know everything about this Doctor Chapman and the girl who Jenkins had pulled over. We need Chapman to get his mind right about what Mackenzie told him in the ER before we got there. I want his address, phone number, work schedule, and anything else you can find."

"Okay sir, I'll get on it. Do you mind me asking what you're going to do with that information?"

"Yes, I do. You have your role here and it does not require you to know anything about this. Plausible deniability, right?"

Vincent glanced at Marybeth and they shared a quick moment of eye contact while Charlie walked around the couch.

"Sorry," she mouthed to Vincent, who returned a faint smile and gave a dismissive shrug.

Charlie joined the women on the couch and put his arm around his daughter. "Honey, we're going to get through this. Don't make any more videos and just lie low for a while, okay?"

"I already deleted my social media accounts. I want nothing to do with publicity anymore. It's not worth it."

"That's my smart girl. Do you want to head out of town for a bit? Maybe you and Mom can head to the condo in Naples for a bit?"

"Oh, that's a wonderful idea, Charlie. What do you say Mac? Does that sound like fun?"

Mackenzie lifted her head up and wiped away the tears that had yet to soak into her mother's hair. "Actually, it does. Some beach time with big sunglasses and a huge straw hat would be amazing. Mr. Leoni, do you think your daughter would want to go with us?"

"Possibly. She's home for a while and I'm not sure if she has plans. Send her a text and see what she says. I'll let the caretaker know you'll be coming down later this week," said Vincent.

"No, tell him we'll be there tomorrow," said Mackenzie with a smile. "Come on, Mom, let's go pack." She pulled out her phone and sent a quick text to Vincent's daughter.

The two women stood quickly and walked out of the room toward the grand spiral front staircase.

Charlie waited a minute for them to get upstairs before addressing his attorney. "I'm going to make that doc wish he hadn't been born. I want him so nervous about testifying against my daughter that he can't even piss."

"And I'm sure you can make that happen, sir. I will focus on the legal and public relations aspects of this situation. Remember, money can't always buy the outcome that you wish to see."

"Like hell it can't. I've done it before, and I'll do it again."

"Charlie, I wish the best for Mackenzie and your family. You know I do." Vincent stood as he finished his statement. "But what becomes of your business and family legacy if you lose in the court of public opinion? I will be consulting with some colleagues over the next few days, but will be available via phone or email. Let me know if anything changes."

Charlie waited for his attorney to exit the front door before pulling out his cell phone and making a call.

A gruff voice answered. "Yes, sir, how can I help you?"

"Shaun, I have another job for you. Off the record. Stop by my office tomorrow morning and I'll explain what I need."

"Absolutely, Mr. Hearst, I'll be there right when we open."

"Actually, do you mind getting there thirty minutes early? Fewer people around."

"Yes, sir, see you then."

Chapter Twenty-Four

"Hello, I'm here to see Clay Turner. Can you tell me how to find his room?"

"Sure, head down that hallway, fourth door on your right," said the nurse's aide without looking up from his computer.

Bryce saw the door was open and knocked on the wall before looking into the room. He smiled at what he saw. Clay was in a wheelchair next to his roommate's bed, helping him with his lunch.

"Is this a good time for a visit?" said Bryce.

Clay spun the chair around and grinned when he saw Bryce standing in the doorway. He looked down at the bag that Bryce was holding and rubbed his hands together. "It's always a good time if you're bringing me decent food."

"Chuck, you good for a bit?" asked Clay, looking at his roommate.

"Yeah, I'm good. Go spend time with your friend."

Clay pushed his chair back to his bed and then stood up.

"Woah, you're walking? That's great!" said Bryce.

"Not well, but I am. My back gets tired quickly from trying to stay upright. I use the chair a bit, but I hate the thing. Reminds me I'm not back to my normal yet."

"You'll get there in time. And protein will help you get there even quicker." Bryce held up the bag. "I brought us a sampler from Johnson's BBQ Shack. It's got pulled pork, ribs, brisket, and some corn bread casserole. Oh, and a side of mac and cheese."

"Awesomeness. Let's eat that in the dining hall," said Clay as he walked out of the room and down the hall.

Bryce kept pace and tried to be close enough to catch him should his back give out.

"Relax man, I do this trip thirty times a day. I'll be fine."

"Thirty? That seems like a lot."

"The physical therapist said I can do as much as I feel comfortable with. I should be out of here in a day or two. There's nothing they're doing for me I can't do at home." He paused and then continued. "Well, the dressing change in the middle of my back is difficult, but they can have a home-health nurse do that."

"I can help with whatever you need as well. This place doesn't seem like your style."

"Not hardly. But it is nice being the most eligible bachelor here. Chuck told me the number of people walking past our room tripled the day I moved in."

"Well, look at it this way. You're helping everyone else get some exercise."

His roommate laughed and gave a thumbs up before coughing loudly.

"Easy there, Chuck. Don't laugh when you are chewing. The speech therapist will yell at you if you get aspiration pneumonia," said Clay.

They walked to the dining room and took a table in the corner. Both men took chairs next to each other so they were facing out toward the others in the room.

Bryce opened the bag and laid out the spread of food and utensils. "This place does slow-cooked BBQ right."

"I've been doing some thinking since I've been laid up," said Clay. "I am going to start exploring some hobbies. Have you seen the grills that burn pellets and function like a smoker?"

"I can't believe I didn't brag about mine when you were over. I have a Recteq smoker. Those things are amazing. I turn it on with my phone on the way home from work. Then toss on the burgers to get close to temp and finally sear them on my gasser. Phenomenal."

"That's what I want to do. Make my entire neighborhood smell my dinner, starting at lunch."

"Be careful. They'll want to come over and eat it with you." Bryce took a bit bite of brisket and swallowed before switching topics. "Have you heard anything from your legal team?"

"I did. They came out here and met with me to get the full story, and then they were going to talk to your insurance company. Have you heard anything?"

"No, not yet. I don't know what they'll want other than a statement."

"Is this like a car insurance claim? I don't really understand how it works," said Clay.

"I don't really either. But I think you need to sue me and get a judgment awarded, then my homeowner's policy will cover the first part until it is maxed out. Then, the umbrella policy we own will kick in to cover the rest up to its maximum."

"And your umbrella policy is five million dollars, right? How much will your homeowner's cover?"

"Yes, and we have half a million coverage on that one," said Bryce before taking another bite of brisket. He shook his head as he chewed. "That is so juicy."

"So I should sue you for $4.5 million?"

"That might be a little too coincidental. I'm not planning to fight the lawsuit at all. The best thing would be if we could settle without a formal trial, but I don't know if the insurance policy forces me to defend it fully. I'll find out. I was thinking you sue me for seven million and then we settle for $3.5 million. That gives my insurance company some breathing room and they may settle rather than risk a full judgment with five million on the line."

"That's a good point. Another bonus is I don't owe attorneys' fees, since the fire department has a policy in place to handle things like this for us."

"It all sounds good out loud. The trick will be getting the insurance companies and the lawyers to go along with it." Bryce looked at his watch and excused himself. "I need to get home and get a nap before my shift tonight. It was good seeing you, Clay."

Bryce left the food and headed back to his car for the trip back home.

He wasn't home fifteen seconds before the kids had him surrounded, talking quickly.

"Do Dad next!" said Noah.

"What? What are you doing to me?"

"Your head! Mom did ours, and now it's your turn."

Bryce looked up at Val, who was sitting on a bar stool and smiling at him. "What are they talking about?"

"Just get over here and let me do your head."

Bryce let the kids drag him into the kitchen and sit him down on a stool next to Val. She unlocked her phone and opened an app before looking back at him.

"Okay, sit up straight. Give me a smile where I can see some of your teeth and then do what the phone tells you to do."

Bryce gave a half smile and stared at the camera on the phone.

"Turn your head left," instructed a digital voice. "Turn your head to the right. Look up. Look down." After it finished, Val looked at the screen and frowned.

"That was terrible. You need to go all the way in each direction and in a smooth rotation. Try again."

It took three takes before the result satisfied her. She spun phone around to show him a 3D rendering of himself that he could manipulate and spin in any direction.

"That is freaky, but kinda cool. What are you going to do with it?" he asked.

"It's a surprise."

"Are you going to make a," Bryce mouthed the word 'sex', "doll of me?"

Val busted out laughing. "Yeah. It would totally be your face on there if I made one."

Bryce put a hand on each child's back. "Kids, tell your mom to be nice."

"What? Why? She just got us cookies," said Noah.

Val raised her eyebrows and smiled at him. "You work in two hours, mister. You'd better get a nap if you're going to."

Chapter Twenty-Five

B ryce woke when his alarm sounded, but was still feeling tired. *Why are naps like vacations? Never long enough, and usually followed by a shift in the ER.*

He was an hour into the shift when he looked over at Peter and saw him still typing away at charts.

"Peter, why are you still here? You're usually out almost on time."

"Just doing charts. I barely have time to see patients, let alone chart on them. Emily quit this week and now I have to do all my own charting. It's been years, man."

"She quit? I didn't know that. What happened?"

"Said she doesn't need the job now because her boyfriend is rich. I don't think she's pursuing a career in medicine anymore, either."

"Huh, just seems odd," said Bryce.

"What does?"

"I saw her here the day of the QCC visit. I thought you must have been working, but she said he had forgotten something and came to pick it up."

"What did she forget? All she brings is that giant lunch box."

"I didn't ask. I was seeing patients and passed her in the hallway." Bryce paused and thought for a moment. "Come to think of it, I saw her in the back hallway near room twenty-five. Why would she have been back there?"

"Who knows man, she's nuts," said Peter.

"I believe you, but maybe it's more than that? I heard they found some expired IV catheters in some rooms, including down that hallway."

"Expired catheters? All I heard about was the dead rat."

"You mean 'rats'. There was a second rat found that day," said Bryce, chuckling.

"I heard about the one in the tube system. Where was the other found?"

"I'm not allowed to say. But, the person who found it said it was cold. Why would a dead rat on the floor be cold?"

"Are you saying someone put it there on purpose?" asked Peter.

"Maybe. As weird as it sounds, it's about the only thing that makes sense. I have heard about three rats in our ER. The first one was at the first QCC visit, and the next two were on the second visit. I'm not a fan of coincidences. Also, the catheters that were expired are not ones we use in his hospital. It seems someone brought them in to be found."

"Do you think it was Emily?"

"I have no idea, but you said yourself that she is nuts. Could she do something like that?"

"She thinks she's the most capable person on planet earth. I'd put nothing past her. What did the catheters look like?"

"I don't know. Let's find out." Bryce contacted Diane Hopkins on their communication device and asked her to bring one of the expired catheters to the physician's work area.

A few minutes later, she handed one to Peter to examine.

"Yep, I recognize them. We used these at my last hospital and I hated them. They didn't design the device that hides the tip of the needle very well, and it kept getting in the way. I nearly poked myself a few times trying to use them."

"Well, how did they get into our supply room and IV carts?" asked Diane.

Peter looked at Bryce, who was subtly shaking his head. He then looked back to Diane before answering. "I have no idea. I'm sure they use these catheters in many other hospital systems. We have a lot of traveling nurses here. Could be any of a dozen people."

Diane squinted at him. "So you're saying one of my nurses did it?"

"No, not at all. Just saying it could be anyone, really. Heck, you can buy them on eBay too."

"Great. That doesn't help us figure out what happened at all." Diane took the catheter back and headed back to her office.

"Sorry, I figured it was best if we didn't say anything yet."

"No problem," said Peter. "Do you think this review thing will cause problems?"

"Who knows," said Bryce. "I can't imagine them shutting down an ER over a few dead rats and expired catheters. We need to look into Emily, though. She always had that giant lunch bag with her. She could have had rats in there, right?"

Peter laughed. "I sure hope not. She used to keep my lunch in there. Do you want me to ask if she was tossing dead rats around our department?"

"That's a little too obvious, don't you think? We need to get a look at her apartment and see for ourselves. What do you think about a little reconnaissance mission?"

"She hates me right now and is dating someone else. I can't just go over and knock on her door. She'll immediately suspect something. And I'm not breaking into anywhere, that's your thing."

"Maybe we try a double date? You can try to lead her on a bit and see if she invites you over. Then poke around and see what you can find."

"I could do that. But you know me Bryce, I don't have good self-control around women. It could end up taking days to sort through the place," said Peter with a smile.

"No, you can't. Just get a look around and then find an excuse to leave. Maybe fake food poisoning. She's nuts, Peter. Keep telling yourself that."

"Yeah, but there's nuts, and then there's nuts, but hot."

"Ah, yes. The crazy-hot matrix."

"Exactly. She started in the wife zone, then quickly moved into the date zone. I only noticed recently she belongs in the danger zone."

"I'll have Val look at our schedule and get back to you. Maybe try to text back and forth and see if she'd be interested. Then we can work out a time."

"Okay, I will," said Peter, standing up from his workstation. "I'm going to finish these charts at home."

"Welcome to life without a scribe in the era of modern medicine," said Bryce as Peter walked away.

Chapter Twenty-Six

"Val, I need to leave for work in fifteen minutes. Do you mind if I wake the kids up so I can see them before I leave?"

"Well, it's almost nine. I suppose it's time to get them up. But I just love this peaceful time in the morning when they're asleep. I love them with me, but I love them sleeping as well."

Bryce laughed. "It's the age-old parenting paradox. I'll be right back."

He went slowly went upstairs, avoiding the creaky stair and keeping as quiet as possible. He entered Noah's room first and rubbed his belly gently. Noah responded by opening his eyes and letting loose a massive load of gas. His laughter picked up where the noise ended, and Bryce joined in for good measure.

"Why doesn't Mom think that's as funny as you do?" asked Noah.

"Are you asking me to explain women? We don't have enough time and I don't have enough knowledge." Bryce rubbed Noah's head. "Maybe your generation will figure them out. I'm headed to work; I just wanted to see you before I left. It's supposed to be a nice day, so we should play some basketball when I get off."

"Yep. Have a good day, Dad." Noah rolled over and snuggled into his pillow as Bryce stood and walked out of the room.

He quietly entered Hannah's room, finding her still asleep in her bed, modeled after Cinderella's carriage. He climbed in next to her and went to reach for her when she rolled over and grabbed his arm, snuggling in close.

How can I wake her up when she's so stinking' adorable? He reached with his spare hand and grabbed a stuffed animal from next to her pillow. He lifted her arm up gently, slid his out and replaced it with a stuffed animal. She snuggled into the plush creature and stayed asleep.

Bryce slipped out of her room and back downstairs, where Val was waiting with a tumbler of coffee for him. "Thanks babe. I am trying to cut back on Diet Coke, so coffee will be perfect."

"Cut back on Diet Coke? You're an ER doctor Bryce. Is that even allowed?"

"Hey, I cut out alcohol. Diet Coke should be a breeze. Oh, and I left Hannah asleep. She was too adorable to wake up."

Valerie smiled at him. "I struggled with that every day. They are perfect little angels while they're asleep. No whining, no backtalk, no messes..." Her voice trailed off, as she took a sip of her coffee.

Bryce's phone rang with a familiar number on the caller ID. "It's Detective Stephenson. I'll take this while I drive." He leaned in and kissed her quickly before walking toward the garage.

"Hi Detective, this is Bryce," he said into the phone after connecting the call.

"Dr. Chapman, I got some interesting results I think you'd like to hear."

"Oh yeah? What's that?" Bryce's voice changed pitch as he focused on backing out of the garage and down his driveway.

"It turns out Officer Jenkins was holding something else back besides his alcohol abuse."

Bryce felt his heart sink at those words. *Why do we have to tarnish his memory even more?*

"Yeah? What did you find?"

"He was pregnant."

Bryce laughed out loud at the absurdity of the statement. "Let me guess, that test result was from the same sample of blood that showed an alcohol level of 0.32?"

"Indeed, it was. My chief is on his way over to the coroner's office as we speak. I'm betting that coroner is going to wish he were one of the stiffs in his freezer by the time 'ol Booker is done with him."

"Don't forget Ashley Saxon. She's the one who collected the sample," said Bryce. *And screwed me over by saying my patient had cystic fibrosis. Now I'm neck-deep in a malpractice case that I can't defend because doing so would expose my theft of the semen sample.*

"Oh, I haven't forgotten about her. I'll be interviewing her soon about her visit to the ER. I want to know every step she took to get samples and how she confirmed the blood sample was from Jenkins. It'll be fun to make her squirm."

"Well, thank you for updating me, and I hope you give them hell. Is there anything else I can do for you?"

"Actually, there is. My chief and the rest of the department want this coroner gone, and as luck would have it, there's a primary election coming up."

"Right, but he's running unopposed. I mean, who else would even want the job?"

"That's a question I hope you can answer yourself. What would make Bryce Chapman run for coroner?"

"Oh no, I hate politics. Both sides publicly call the other evil, while behind the scenes they share a table in the back of the restaurant. I want nothing to do with it."

"I understand that. There are a lot of politics in police work as well. It's a necessary evil that I accept as part of the job. But sometimes it's possible to use politics to accomplish something worthwhile. Like getting a new coroner who gets the job done correctly. Who doesn't assume a person died of natural causes just because they can't figure out what happened? Someone who works on people, not animals."

"A veterinarian could make a fine coroner," said Bryce. "But this one certainly doesn't."

"Exactly. Which is why we need to find someone to challenge him in the election, and soon. The deadline for candidate certification is in one week," said Stephenson.

"I am telling you, I don't want it," said Bryce. The irritation in his voice becoming clear.

"Let me see if I can change your mind. Remember that case I mentioned about the stolen semen sample? Well, it turns out the story gets even stranger. Apparently, you thought that Kent Carpenter was murdered, and were all hot and heavy to find the real killer and clear your name. Then suddenly Clay Turner, a local EMS hero, was nearly cut in half by a pressure washer at your house. Pretty gruesome, from what I hear. But ever since that happened, it doesn't seem like you are putting much effort into finding out who killed your patient."

Bryce swallowed hard and tried to get his hands to stop shaking. He glanced in his mirror to make sure the lane was clear before turning off the road and into a random parking lot.

The detective continued. "I looked into Kent Carpenter a bit and even talked to his ex-wife. Turns out the guy was a sick freak. Probably best that he's not around anymore, wouldn't you say?"

Bryce cleared his throat with a cough, trying to ensure his voice was prepared to speak without cracking. "I'm not sure where you're going with this, detective. Kent's case has been closed and now I am defending the malpractice lawsuit. Clay's injury was an accident."

"Yes, an accident. That gave him a really nasty bacterial infection, the same one that killed Kent Carpenter. What are the odds of that?"

What? How did he figure this all out? Bryce wiped his forehead with his left hand, then wiped the sweat onto his scrubs. He turned the fan up and pointed the vents directly at his face.

"It's not what it looks like," he said.

"Oh come on doc, I've been around the block a few times now. It's exactly what it looks like. But honestly, I don't care. A sick freak is no longer walking the earth. Good riddance, I say."

Bryce did not respond, and the detective let nearly a minute go by before speaking again.

"Here's what I propose. You run for coroner and win, and I keep all those crazy thoughts in my head. If you don't run, or you don't win, then eventually I'll have time to investigate the circumstances around Kent's death."

"But the election is in nine weeks. That's not enough time to build a proper campaign and have a fighting chance. Even if I wanted to, I don't think I could win."

"Doc, I hate to tell you this, but I have you by the short hairs. Getting the current moron out of office will do more to help our city than determining what happened to Kent Carpenter. I'm thinking of the greater good for our citizens. So, are you up for it? I can promise you the support of the entire police department."

Bryce shook his head and leaned his forehead on the steering wheel. He responded with the only answer that made any sense. "Okay, I'll do it."

"Excellent!" came the shouted reply through the phone. "I will let the chief know. He'll be pleased."

Bryce sat up in his seat and ran his hands through his hair before sighing loud enough to be heard through the phone.

"What is it?" asked the detective.

"Mackenzie Hearst. As long as I'm being blackmailed, I might as well tell you what she told me the first time."

"Yes, please do. What did she say initially?"

"She said she was recording a video and looking down at her phone when she struck Officer Jenkins. At first, she thought she'd struck a deer and kept driving. She pulled over into the store parking lot and watched her video, at which point she realized she had hit a person. Soon after, she had a bout of psychogenic blindness which resolved while she was in the ER. When I came back to check on her, that's when everything changed. Her parents and their attorney were in the room and then the story was she had a violent sneeze, which caused her to jerk the wheel."

"Will you be willing to testify in court regarding what she told you?"

"If I do, I can lose my medical license and face a huge civil suit from the Hearst family. We need to find a way to get you that information without me violating doctor-patient confidentiality."

"Well, I'll work on that with the prosecutor. In the meantime, you need to fill out some paperwork at the county clerk's office. Looks like the race for coroner is about to get interesting."

Bryce hung up the phone and slammed his palm into the steering wheel. "Damn it!" he screamed for no one's ears but his own. "What am I supposed to do now?"

His phone beeped as a calendar notification popped up. He was due in the hospital in ten minutes. He checked for traffic and then pulled onto the road. *And now I'm supposed to work a shift while worrying about all this?*

Chapter Twenty-Seven

C lay Turner exited the law offices of his attorney, supplied by the fire station, with a spring in his step. It was a sunny day, and he had just received encouraging news. The attorney had reviewed the footage from Bryce's security camera and skimmed through his medical records, including images of the wound on Clay's back. Clay was told he had as slam dunk of a personal injury case as the attorney had ever seen. The pieces were coming together to ease Clay's conscience regarding his killing of Kent Carpenter and starting the malpractice case against Bryce.

He caught a whiff of French fries and his stomach reminded him he hadn't eaten lunch yet. He was standing right across the street from Taxman Brewing Company, a local brewery with a refined menu, and changed direction to stop in for a bite.

He took a table outside and sat down in a chair bathed in sunlight, feeling the warmth on his legs and back. *Can this day get any better?*

He ordered a bacon cheeseburger with a fried egg on top and a Belgian-inspired beer. The server brought the dark craft beer in a cold pint glass, promising the food would be out soon.

Clay sat back in the chair and closed his eyes, soaking up the positive energy of the day. He only had a moment to enjoy the feeling before the noise of a chair scraping across the brick patio snapped his eyes open. He watched as an attractive redhead sat down across from him and lifted her sunglasses off her face, tucking them into the front of her shirt and drawing Clay's eyes along for the ride.

"Can I help you?" he asked.

"I hope so. Are you Clay Turner?" The words would had have little effect if written on a piece of paper, but delivered with an Irish accent and a crooked smile, they drew him in quickly.

"Yeah, that's me. I don't believe met, Mrs..."

"Miss, actually. Lorena McCarthy. I'm an attorney who works in the building you just walked out of. I recognized you from the news reports about your injury and how the EMS community rallied around your recovery. How are you doing?"

"Much better. This is the first restaurant I've been to in the last few months. I'm feeling more normal every day."

"Wonderful. You look so strong and vigorous." She accented the statement by reaching out and quickly touching his right forearm. Her fingers slid down his skin briefly before she pulled her arm back.

"I've got a long way to go, but it's a good start. What can do I for you?" *Other than offer you a ride back to my place.*

"So, full disclosure, I'm suing the person who caused your injuries. I'm a medical malpractice attorney and am representing the family of Kent Carpenter. I believe you transported him to the hospital after his accident."

Clay nodded and took a drink of his beer. "Yes, that's right. But I transport many people. I will not discuss this case without an attorney present and a subpoena."

"Well, I'm an attorney and I'm here," she said with a smile.

"Thanks, but I meant one representing me."

"I know, just joking with you. Don't worry, I'm actually not here to discuss the case; I'm here because I need help."

"With what?"

"My practice. I need someone trustworthy and tough as nails. You started out as a fireman and then became a paramedic. You've been there and done that. Then you took a power washer to your back, and yet here you are. Sipping beer and looking like you don't have a care in the world."

"You left out the part where I did two tours in the Army. Turned eighteen just in time for Afghanistan."

"You're exactly the type of person I'm looking for. Besides medical malpractice, I also handle personal injury cases." She made a face of disgust and shook her head quickly. "Not the slip and fall nonsense. I only take the big cases with large potential paydays."

Clay took another drink of his beer. *Do you know about the settlement Bryce and I are working on?* "And how can I help you with that?"

"I need someone who knows accident scenes, medical care, is immune to intimidation, and a few other things I can't discuss yet." She scanned him from head to toe before continuing. "You're perfect."

"What salary range are we talking about?"

"A hell of a lot more than you make riding in the back of a truck."

"Do you have a card? I need to think about this for a while."

"No need for a card." Lorena flipped open her wallet and exposed her cellphone tucked inside. "What's your number? I'll drop you a text now and you can call me when you have a decision."

Clay gave her his number and quickly received a text containing a winking emoji.

Lorena stood and waved goodbye before heading back toward her office. Clay watched her until she passed behind a brick building and was out of sight.

"Sir, your bacon cheeseburger with fried egg. Can I get you anything else?"

Clay turned to the waitress standing by the table, waiting for a response.

"What? Sorry, I'm a bit stunned at the moment. I'll let you know."

This could be a dream job, but is it a trap?

Chapter Twenty-Eight

"Are you ready for this?" asked Bryce, standing outside the law office where they were about to be deposed for the malpractice case involving Kent Carpenter.

"No, not at all. I hate everything about it. This stuff makes me want to quit medicine," said Tom.

"I'm right there with you. There's got to be a better way than grinding everyone's lives to a halt so lawyers can make a ton of money and drag us through emotional hell for two years."

"Sometimes bad things just happen. The expectation should not be that we can save everyone from dying. Patients walk around living as unhealthy of a lifestyle as they can tolerate and then when it hits the fan, they race in, and we're supposed to save them from the consequences of their actions." Tom shook his head and stared at the ground. "I know you understand; I'm just venting."

"They're waiting for us in there. We should go," said Bryce.

"Why? Let them wait. They're probably making twice what we do per hour, anyway. Seven years of training to help put people back together medically, but it only takes three years of training to rip us apart legally."

Bryce held the door open for Tom and then followed behind him.

"I hate malpractice attorneys so much," said Tom as he and Bryce left the deposition hours later.

"What about the ones working for us?" asked Bryce.

"I guess they're okay. But they're still part of the Leviathan."

"Lorena puts on a good show, but I swear I could tell she was looking defeated. She knows we did nothing wrong. How were we supposed to know our patient was actually a murder victim?"

Tom looked sideways at his friend. "Are you still thinking this was murder?"

Bryce kicked himself internally, but kept his face neutral. "It's the only thing that makes sense. No healthy person gets that sick with that bug that quickly. I just hope whoever did it has moved on or died themselves."

Tom let the comment go and focused on the present. "So, what now?"

"Now we hope our testimony makes Lorena reconsider taking this to trial. She has a widow and kids without a father, but we have science on our side. We did nothing wrong."

"I wish I could feel that." Tom sighed loudly. "I know we did nothing wrong, but it's hard to feel it with this lawsuit hanging over our heads."

"Maybe we'll get lucky, and they will drop the suit. I know that's what I'm hoping for," said Bryce. *Which reminds me, I need to check on how Clay's discussions with my insurance company are going.*

Bryce walked into his house and greeted his family quickly before grabbing a Diet Coke and sitting down on a lounge chair by the pool. The same chair he sat in while talking with Clay and trying to determine if he was the one responsible for Kent's murder. He pondered how things had changed in the last few months. He had caused serious bodily injury to a person in retribution for two murders and now he was being forced to run for coroner to keep his sperm bank theft quiet. *I hate lawsuits, but am now using one to clear another.* Bryce sighed at the irony and then dialed the number for Clay.

"Hey Doc, how's it going?"

"Fine. Just got done with the deposition for my malpractice suit. Have I told you how much I hate malpractice attorneys?"

"Yes, you have. A few times, actually. But I'm glad you called. I just talked to my attorney and he is optimistic they will settle my case against you out of court. I mean, your security camera footage shows exactly what happened. Combine that with the photos from the operating room and he said any judge will probably award a maximum settlement."

Bryce sat up quickly in his chair and paced around the pool deck. "Fantastic! Did he give any indication of how quickly it might happen?"

"Within a few weeks. He's pressing them for a quick settlement to avoid filing a lawsuit. Have you heard anything from your insurance company yet?"

"No, not yet. I want to call them, but I'm concerned they may get suspicious if I know about the potential lawsuit."

"Gotcha. Well, I'm about done with rehab. Should be out of here in a few days. Maybe, by then, we can have something in writing," said Clay.

"I hope so. Once we do, we'll find a lawyer to approach Lorena and make an offer directly to Kent's ex-wife. She'll be obligated to run it by them. Immediate closure, limited lawyer fees, and an essentially equal payout. That would sound very appealing to me."

"Me too. Let's get past this and onto better things. I'm looking at doing some volunteer work and have some ideas for employment outside of the EMS community."

"Good for you, Clay. Let's meet for lunch when you get out of there."

Bryce ended the call and laid back on the chaise lounge chair. He took a drink and then closed his eyes, letting the sun cover him like a warm blanket.

A few minutes later, a splash of cold water across his legs woke him up.

"Dad, how was that splash?" asked Noah, who was now swimming in the pool.

Bryce dried his phone off on his shirt and sat up to see both kids in the pool, and Valerie sitting on the edge with her legs in the water. "It was pretty good, but I'll show you what a real splash looks like." He stripped off his clothes until he was in his boxer jocks, then entered the pool with a running leap with his body folded into a jack-knife position.

After the swim, the family was sitting around the table on their back porch as they waited for the suits to dry. Sitting in the middle was a bowl of queso dip, and each person took turns dipping a chip in and eating it like a gang of workers pounding in a railroad spike.

"Kids, should we show your father what we made him?" asked Val between bites.

"Yes!" they said in unison.

"Can I go get it?" asked Noah.

Val smiled and nodded at his enthusiasm. He scooted back from the table and raced inside the house.

"He sure has your enthusiasm for life, Bryce." She looked at her husband, who was wiping cheese off his chest. "And eating ability," she added.

"Hey, be nice. And I just cleaned myself in the pool." He smeared the cheese onto a chip and ate it.

"So attractive..." said Val, shaking her head.

"Here it is, Dad!"

Bryce turned around to see a miniature version of himself in his son's hand. It was an oversized head sitting atop a smaller body. The figurine was wearing a white jacket and had a stethoscope around its neck.

"Hey, that's me!" said Bryce. "Did you guys make that?"

"Yep!" said Noah. "Mom helped us use the 3D printer, and then we all painted it to look like you. Do you like it?" Noah sat it down in front of Bryce. A spring supported the head and attached it to a small base.

"I'm a bobble-head? I absolutely love it. Thank you, guys." He reached out to hug his kids before leaning in to kiss Val. "If you drop any cheese on your chest, I'll take care of it for you."

"Thanks, Bryce."

"It's the least I can do. Kids, I'm going to take myself to work with me. I have the perfect place in my car to mount him between shifts, too. And I think we need bobble-heads of the whole family now."

"They're on the printer right now, actually. Should have them finished before bed," said Val.

Bryce laughed and dipped another chip into the queso. "I love your quirkiness, babe. It's so easy to relax, after a hard day, when you do things like this."

Chapter Twenty-Nine

C hief Sammy Booker drove his Tesla Model S police cruiser toward the city building where the coroner's office is located. He skipped the usual satellite radio music and instead drove in silence. Each minute that passed brought him closer to the confrontation he'd been wanting to have for several days. He knew Jenkins had not been drunk, but had no evidence to fight back with. Now that they knew the blood sample came from a pregnant patient, it was obviously not Jenkins' blood.

Unfortunately, the damage had already been done. The public believes the first narrative that they hear of any event. Even if that later turns out to be completely wrong, the majority will still believe what they heard first. The accusation is always more impactful than the retraction and apology.

He parked the Tesla and hurried through the security checkpoint. He walked around the screening station and down the long ornate hallway. Several people tried to engage him in conversation, but quickly lost interest when they saw the look on his face.

Chief Booker knocked on the office door and then pushed it open without waiting for a reply. He entered the office and saw Zachary

Pullard sitting at his computer. His eyes opened wide at the sudden entrance of the Chief of Police.

"Chief, I did not expect to see you today. What can I do for you?" He stood and extended a hand toward the chief who shook his head and sat down instead.

"I wanted to talk about the autopsy of Michael Jenkins."

"Is this about him being pregnant?"

"You're damn right it is," said the chief. "We told you he was not a drinker, but your office published the result, anyway. I want to know how that happened."

"Chief, we triple checked the results. We recalibrated the machine. We did everything we could to verify the result before making our conclusion."

"The hell you did. You kept checking the evidence that you had, but never questioned whether the evidence actually belonged to my officer, did you?"

Zachary Pullard leaned back in his hair and held his arms up, palms outward. "Chief, how were we supposed to know that the blood from the hospital wasn't from him?"

"Sounds like your chain of custody sucks. Can you imagine what the prosecutor would do to me if I gave him a bag of evidence from the wrong person? It might jeopardize many cases in one fell swoop." The chief leaned in closer and continued. "But you know what else it would mean?"

The coroner briefly shook his head and shrugged his shoulders. "What?"

"It would call into question all the work my department has done in the past. Defense attorneys would look to re-examine evidence and request new trials. If an officer screwed up that bad, what else have they screwed up before? It would cause people to question the officer, the training they received, and the Chief of Police who is in charge of that officer."

The coroner stared back without responding, but his breathing had sped up.

The chief continued. "There would be calls for investigations and even my resignation. But you can imagine how much worse it would be if it turned out that I was related to that officer?"

The coroner stood up quickly and exhaled in a huff. "Thank you for coming by today, chief. I don't need your innuendo and veiled threats. I run my department the best way I know how, just like you do."

The chief stood and met his stare. "I have no problem believing that, Zac. That's why we're going to support a candidate to challenge you in the upcoming election. Our city needs solid leadership in the coroner's office. The blood alcohol report on Michael Jenkins is the final straw."

The coroner sneered at the chief. "Good luck. The deadline for registering a candidate is just around the corner." He walked around the desk and opened his office door. "Thank you for coming by. It's got to feel weird to intimidate the only man who can arrest the Chief of Police."

Chief Booker laughed deeply, filling the room with the sound of his chuckles. "Yeah? Come at me, if you will. Just remember, if you're going to take a shot at the king, you better not miss."

He turned and walked out of the office, pulling the door nearly closed but stopping short of actually engaging the latch. He walked away, but could still hear the comment through the open door. "That son of a bitch."

Chapter Thirty

C hief Booker returned to the department and began making waves immediately.

"Set up the conference room and alert the media; I want to go live in an hour."

A flurry of activity followed his order and soon the conference room had transformed into a TV set ready for a live broadcast. Several news channels were present with their cameras prepared to broadcast the feed live to their viewers.

"One minute!" The warning came from an administrative aid, putting the finishing touches on the podium's appearance.

The chief walked to the podium and adjusted his uniform one last time before starting at the reporters. "Let's get started."

The hushed conversations in the room stopped when the chief began to speak.

"Hello, this is Captain Sammy Booker. I am the Chief of the Indianapolis Metropolitan Police Department. I wanted to provide an update in the investigation into the death of our brother, Michael Jenkins. Zachary Pullard's office initially reported that Officer Jenkins was significantly intoxicated at the time of his death. I can now say with confidence that this is completely untrue. The sample used by their office also tested positive for pregnancy, something we can all agree Officer Jenkins is unlikely to have been dealing with when he died."

"The coroner will hopefully conduct his own conference to answer your questions about how this could have happened. I am here to correct the record and clear the name of our fallen officer. We have requested the collection of additional samples to determine the true blood alcohol level, which I guarantee will be zero."

The chief looked around the room and met the gaze of the other officers in the room. Men and women he'd celebrated with, cried with, and stood shoulder to shoulder with to protect the city. "As a final order of business, I wish to endorse Dr. Bryce Chapman in his campaign for coroner. Dr. Chapman is a local Emergency Medicine Physician who works at Washington Memorial Hospital. He treated Officer Jenkins the day of the accident. He was as upset as the rest of us when the false information came out and has promised to improve the quality of work performed at the coroner's office."

"The citizens of Indianapolis deserve to have confidence in their government, to know that reported information is correct, and to have each death meticulously reviewed to ensure we leave no crimes undetected. I truly believe that can best happen under the direction of Dr. Bryce Chapman."

He scanned the room again before zeroing in on a news camera. He stared directly into the lens and finished the conference with a promise. "IMPD will stop at nothing to prevent and solve crimes, to keep our city safe. Even if it means assisting in the removal of an elected official from office. Thank you for your time."

Chief Booker turned and walked away from the podium to a chorus of cheers from his fellow officers.

Bryce's phone rang and showed an incoming call from Val.

"Hey babe, what's up?"

"When were you going to tell me you decided to run for coroner?"

Bryce paused before replying. "Uh, I didn't know that I had decided to. What are you talking about?"

"The IMPD chief just told the world that you are."

"What? Where?"

"He just had another press conference and announced that IMPD is endorsing you for coroner."

"Detective Stephenson talked to me the other day and strongly suggested that I put my name in the hat. He basically told me he figured out I stole Kent's semen and likely assaulted Clay. He essentially said he'd investigate me for both unless I beat Zac Pullard in the election."

"Well, I guess you need to win, then. How can I help?" asked Val.

Bryce closed his eyes and sighed before responding. "Thank you for rolling along with these punches. Honestly, I don't know. The detective said they'd have someone reach out to help me get started. Some political consultant. I didn't expect it to move this quickly or I would have said something to you."

"I'm with you for the long haul, Bryce, so we need to find a way through this."

"We will. I promise." *I'm not sure how, but I don't plan on going to prison for theft and assault.*

Bryce parked his car in the physician parking lot and ended the call with Val. *It's getting a lot harder to be excited about coming to work lately. Something has got to give.*

Chapter Thirty-One

"Mom, can you toss us the sunblock?"

"Sure Mac, here you go," said Marybeth as she lobbed the sunblock to her daughter.

"You were right. This trip is exactly what I needed. I haven't had that dream since we've been down here and I feel so relaxed."

"Yeah, thanks for letting me come also, Mrs. Hearst. It's been totally awesome spending time with Mackenzie again," said Isabella Leoni. "I can see why my dad likes it so much here. The view from this pool is top-notch."

"No, thank you for coming down. A mother can only comfort her daughter so much. Sometimes a girl needs a friend to stroll the beach with and lose herself in the moment."

Marybeth glanced at the time on her phone and smiled. She typed a quick text.

> Was your flight on time? What's your ETA to the condo?

She sat up in the chair and pulled the cover-up over her head, revealing her toned abdomen and arms. Her chest stood proudly underneath an American flag printed bikini.

"Wow, Mrs. Hearst, you're going to turn more heads in that suit than we will."

Marybeth smiled at the words. "I will take your compliments all day long. But, I'm just here as an advertisement for what Mackenzie will look like in thirty years."

"I hope so, Mom; you're beautiful. Dad sure is lucky."

"Yes, he is, but do you think he knows that? He's too busy with his businesses most days to notice. Down here, everyone notices. Let me give you some advice, girls." She pulled her sunglasses down to let the women see her eyes directly. "When you get to be my age, you maintain your physique for yourself. Don't worry about trying to please anyone else. Just live the most active life you can. Sometimes that means leaving your husband at home and jetting off to Florida with your daughter and a close family friend."

"Tell me about it. There's something special about this place. Every time I come down to Florida, I ask myself why we live in Indiana. People buy cars in Florida, right? Why doesn't Dad open a dealership down here? I'll run it for him."

"It's the eternal question, dear. Is the vacation spot your happy place because of what it is? Or is it because you leave all your stress and worry back at home and let your hair down? If you move here, all the stress of daily life comes with you and it may not be the same."

"Who cares? All that is with us no matter where we live. Why not trade the nasty gray Indiana winters for warm Florida winters? I can just find a new vacation spot to escape to."

Marybeth's phone vibrated on her leg. She flipped it over and saw a new text.

I'm in the car, be there in ten minutes.

She replied quickly.

Girls at the pool. Just come on in.

"Girls, why don't you take a walk on the beach? I'm going to head to the room and start on lunch. Meet up there in an hour and a half?"

"I don't know, this feels pretty good right here in the chair," said Mackenzie with her eyes closed.

Come on girls, give me a moment to myself. Well, at least away from you.

"Here's fifty dollars. Why don't you see if a beach vendor will sell you a margarita or two?"

Both girls shot upright in their chairs. "Deal!" they said in unison.

"We may be underage, but we're over developed. That has its benefits," said Mackenzie. "See you in an hour and a half!" She snatched the fifty from her mom and they waked walked across the pool deck toward the beach.

"If it's two hours, that would be fine!" shouted Marybeth before gathering her things and hurrying toward the elevator bank.

Marybeth entered the condo and left the door unlocked. She stripped off her top as she walked back toward the master suite, dropping it on the floor outside the door. She pulled off her bottoms and left them outside the bathroom door.

I hope you can follow the breadcrumbs. She smiled as she pictured him entering the condo and seeing the swimsuit on the floor. Imagined him hearing the shower running and the mental image he'd have of her under the dual rain shower heads. Her hands drifted over her body, pretending they were his.

The visitor arrived right on schedule and found the front door unlocked. He entered quietly and looked around for the object of his attraction but found only a swimsuit top laying on the carpet. He set down his monogrammed leather briefcase and luggage and picked up the suit, running his fingers across the fabric.

Now where's my girl who can't keep her suit on? He walked into the bedroom and heard the soft sound of running water and saw the swimsuit bottom near the bathroom. He stepped sideways to change his angle, looking into the bathroom to see a hazy outline of a naked woman in the shower. *Bingo.* Sitting just outside the shower door were two folded bath towels. *You little minx, you planned this.* His hands moved to his neck and quickly removed his tie, then unbuttoned his shirt. The pants fell a few seconds later, smothered by a pair of socks, shoes, and underwear.

"Mackenzie, come on. Those clouds look terrible and it just got ten degrees colder. Everyone is heading inside."

"My mom said we had two hours and I want another marg!" said Mackenzie, holding up a nearly empty plastic cup.

"I don't think we even have two minutes. We need to get inside. I'll get you one after the rain comes through."

"Fine," said Mackenzie, rolling her eyes and shaking her head. "We can help my mom make lunch. I'm starving anyway."

The girls made it onto the pool deck just before the skies opened up and the downpour began. They hurried into the building and paused inside the door, laughing at each other's soaked appearance. The girls dried themselves off and then the chill of the air conditioning took over, leading to goosebumps on their skin.

"We need to get out of these suits," said Isabella.

"And then eat."

They hit the button for the elevator and were soon on their way toward the Hearst penthouse condo.

Marybeth heard the shower door open and spun around to see who it was.

"You made it! And wore the proper attire." She held her arms out and pulled her lover into the shower with her.

"Ow!" he yelled, backing away. "You still take scalding showers?"

"Relax, I'll turn it down. I thought you liked it hot?"

"You Marybeth. I like you hot, not the water." He leaned forward and turned the mixing valve to a cooler setting and then pulled her into his arms. "That's better."

After several minutes of mutual showering, she turned off the water and reached out to retrieve the towels.

"I need my towel for my head. Will you use your towel to dry me?"

He smiled and quickly complied as she wrapped the towel around her hair. Thirty seconds later, they fell into bed; the towel laying on the ground only feet from the bathroom.

"I can't believe it's been a year," he said. "Want to try that position we left off in?"

"We've got just over an hour. I think we can start there and see where we end up," said Marybeth as she raised up on her knees.

Chapter Thirty-Two

Shaun Kimball arrived at work forty-five minutes early, or fifteen minutes before he was to meet Mr. Hearst. The last time he received a call like this from his boss it led to a payoff equal to ten times his annual salary.

He stared at the building, curious as to what this next assignment was going to be.

A loud rap on his driver side window caused him to jump and lean away from the noise. He turned to see Charlie Hearst laughing while staring inside his vehicle. Shaun unclipped his seatbelt and exited the vehicle.

"Don't do that to me, I about crapped myself," he replied in his gruff voice.

"You should have seen yourself," said Charlie between laughs. "You looked scared as a cat at the dog pound. Come on, let's get inside."

The two walked behind the main sales building to a metal entry door. Charlie entered a five-digit code and the door clicked open. He pulled it open and held it for Shaun and then followed him inside.

The door opened into Charlie's private office and the two took seats on opposite sides of the large desk. Shaun sat quietly and waited for Charlie to speak.

"Shaun, you've been with me for quite some time now and I appreciate that loyalty. Your connections have helped our profits significantly by maximizing efficiency of our parts deliveries."

Shaun nodded and replied. "Happy to do it sir. Your support has helped my finances significantly."

"Glad to hear it. I've got another task for you that is very important to me and my family. As you probably heard, my daughter Mackenzie was involved in an unfortunate situation where her car struck a police officer standing next to the road."

"I did hear that. Very unfortunate for everyone. How is she doing?"

"She's a good girl with a great heart. But she's young and naïve. She thinks that honesty is the best policy and can't see a different way through this. She told a doctor in the Emergency Room that she was looking at her phone when she left the lane and hit the cop."

"I thought that happened when she sneezed?"

"That's what we decided to blame it on. If she admitted what happened, she would probably spend years in prison. The only ones who heard her initial statement is this doctor named Bryce Chapman and the nurse. No way she'll say anything."

Charlie reached into the top drawer of his desk and removed a piece of paper which he slid across to Shaun.

"There's a picture of him along with his address, phone number, and work schedule for the next two weeks."

"What do you want me to do with this information?"

"I want you to scare him into not testifying. He is the only one who heard her confession. If he won't testify, then they can't nail her for negligent homicide."

"Can't he be subpoenaed and forced to testify?" asked Shaun.

"Sure, they can subpoena him. But if testifying would lead to something bad happening to his family, maybe he would refuse the court order. What's a contempt charge compared to protecting your family from harm? Plus, he can lean on the doctor-patient privilege. He can claim to be a pure as snow doctor fighting for his patient's privacy."

"What are the rules here? Is it like Chicago?"

"No, not yet. I want him scared, not dead. Can you do that?"

"I can intimidate him and put him on edge; that's no problem. But how will he know the meaning behind it?"

"I'll handle that. A little man-to-man chat should clear that up right quick."

Chapter Thirty-Three

The girls exited the elevator and entered the condo. They immediately heard noise coming from the master bedroom and could hear Marybeth's voice.

"Hey, whose stuff is that?" asked Mackenzie, pointing at the luggage and briefcase sitting in the entryway.

Isabella looked at the briefcase, and the gold-colored lettering embossed on the leather. Her hand went to her mouth in disbelief.

She turned to show her friend but saw Mackenzie had walked toward the noise coming from the master bedroom. She ran after her and opened her mouth to warn her friend, but Mackenzie's scream filled the condo first.

"Mom! What are you doing?"

Isabella caught up to her friend and looked inside the bedroom, seeing Mrs. Hearst straddling a man. She could pick that hairline out from a crowd a hundred yards away. "Hi, Dad." She put her hand up to shield her eyes and turned to walk toward the other bedroom.

"Shut the door!" yelled Marybeth.

Mackenzie groaned and reached in to grab the door handle, then pulled the door shut with a slam. She stood outside the door and stared at the floor. Her feet felt as confused as her heart.

"Grab some beer and get in here," said Isabella from the doorway of the guest bedroom. "I think we need to talk."

Mackenzie looked up at her friend and then walked toward the kitchen, returning shortly with four cans of beer. She set them on the small table between the two twin beds. Isabella leaned in and grabbed one and then tossed another to her friend.

"What the hell was that?" asked Mackenzie as she popped the lid open on her beer. "My mom is cheating on my dad with your dad." She took a long pull on the can. "How messed up is that?"

She looked at Isabella sitting on the other bed, sipping her beer and staring straight ahead.

"Why do you look so calm? Are you just in shock, like I am?"

Isabella looked at her friend and tried to speak several times before finally closing her eyes and sighing. "Mackenzie, it's not what it looks like."

"What's not? My mom was naked on top of your dad. What else could it possibly look like?"

Isabella stared back at her friend; her face showing the beginning of speech but never starting a sentence.

"What? Just say it."

"It's just... I've caught them before. The same thing happened back home two years ago, but it was at my house. My dad was supposed to be at the office all day, so I ditched school and came home to have a few drinks by the pool. I walked outside and found them in the shallow end. Their suits were still on the lounge chairs."

"Are you freaking kidding me?" said Mackenzie, her voice rising in another surge of anger. "You knew about this the whole time? How long has it been going on?"

"I can answer that, if you'd like to hear it from me," said Marybeth from the doorway.

Mackenzie turned her head and closed her eyes. Her left arm shot out and raised its palm toward her mother. "Not now. Let me get this second beer down first. I'm going to need it."

"Two beers and a margarita in an hour? Don't you think that's a bit much for a nineteen-year-old?"

Mackenzie opened her eyes and stared at her mom through squinted eyes. "I don't know Mom, is it any worse than two men in two days for a fifty-year-old?"

The room stayed silent for a few moments before Marybeth spoke. "Very well. Finish your beer and then come out on the balcony. You need to know the back story." She walked out of the room and joined Vincent in the main room before walking toward the balcony. "I'm only forty-eight," she whispered to Vincent.

"Really? I was going to guess twenty-five the way you were moving a few minutes ago."

She smiled and grabbed his hand as they opened the sliding glass door and took a seat on the balcony.

"Do you want something to drink?" asked Vincent.

"Yes, thanks. A bottle of wine would be lovely."

Vincent slid the glass door open again and heard Marybeth call after him. "Oh, and get yourself something too!"

The bottle of pinot noir had rested for years in their wine cabinet after a long and arduous journey from the Willamette Valley in Oregon, and was halfway gone by the time Mackenzie and Isabella joined their parents on the balcony. The girls chose seats that faced the adults but also gave a view of the water.

"So, lay it on me. What's going on," said Mackenzie. Her voice was flat; the anger having coursed through her, replaced with a depressed curiosity.

"Thank you for coming out to talk. Let me start by saying that I love your father very much." Marybeth filled her wineglass and then continued. "But that has nothing to do with who I choose to sleep with anymore."

"Ugh, Mom. That is so bad. Is that the type of marriage you want to model for me?"

"Just wait. It wasn't always like this. When we were first married, your father idolized me. I was his queen. His trophy. We went on a date night at least once a week. We'd go dancing, hiking, and even bowling. It didn't matter what it was. We were together, and we were happy."

The girls sat quietly and listened, while Vincent poured himself the last portion of the wine.

"But then he opened his first dealership. The hours were awful. He was there at least eighty hours a week, more if it was a holiday or a special promotion. I rarely saw him. Our weekly date nights turned into monthly, then they just stopped altogether."

"So what, you got bored and started cheating on him?" said Mackenzie.

"No. Please let me talk. You need to stop interrupting me." She paused and smiled at Vincent before laughing. "Especially when I'm entertaining."

He grinned and winked at her before gesturing for her to continue.

"There was one particular time when the hours got even worse. Some nights he wouldn't even come home. I got worried, so I went to the dealership to check on him. That's when I caught him. Screwing his top salesperson in a convertible in the middle of the showroom floor."

"Bob? The white-haired guy?" asked Mackenzie with a fresh look of surprise on her face.

Vincent and Marybeth both lost control of themselves at that line and laughed so hard they could barely breathe. The laughter proved so infectious that even Isabella and Mackenzie joined in.

"No dear, this was a long time ago. You were barely walking. It was some bimbo named Patty."

"Aunt Patty? The one who wore so much makeup?"

"Yep, that's her. She wasn't really your aunt, but she was over at our house so much she started calling herself that."

"I don't understand. How could you just put up with it?"

"It took some time, honey; it really did. At first I tried to ice him out and told myself I would not sleep with him until he admitted the affair. But after a month, he hadn't even tried. It was then I realized that our relationship had changed, and he didn't need that from me anymore."

"But you stayed with him and allowed her to be at our house?"

"What was I supposed to do, Mac? Divorce him? Take you and half his money and drive off into the sunset to find Prince Charming? I got what I wanted from the relationship. A beautiful daughter. If I busted him, it would mean you would have barely seen him."

Mackenzie wiped a tear from her eye and adjusted herself in her chair, ending up closer to her mother. Isabella put a hand on her back and massaged gently.

"After a year, he showed no signs of slowing down, so I decided it was time to have a talk. I walked in on them and this time just started talking. You should have seen their reaction. I simply told him he was done being away from home so much and that the new rule was he got fifty hours a week to himself. The rest of the time, he was to be with his family. I told him I didn't care what he did when he wasn't home, but he was going to be present in your life and we were going to give the appearance of a happy family."

"But what about you? How did you deal with it emotionally?" asked Mackenzie.

"By then I had worked through the stages of grief and was firmly in the stage of acceptance. Having you grow up with two parents was my number one goal."

"I'm so sorry, Mom; I had no idea what you were dealing with. You did all of that just for me? It must have been humiliating to stand by his side knowing what he was doing."

"Nope. Not at all. I never felt more in control than knowing I was choosing how it was going to go. He knew if he broke the time commitment rule, I'd crush him legally and financially. We've gotten along well over the past decade. There is still love there, just not the way the poets would describe it."

"So how did you end up with Mr. Leoni?"

"That surprised us both, I think," said Marybeth, glancing sideways at Vincent. "Do you want to tell that story?"

"It brings back some tough memories, but it led me to you." He looked at the girls and spread his hands open like a dealer at a blackjack table. "I'm going to leave out a lot of details for privacy reasons, but I'll tell you the important parts. Mackenzie, your father had a few side businesses he was engaged in that were separate from the car dealerships. Those were done off the record and skirted the law in some regards."

Mackenzie bowed her head and sighed. "Just when I thought I couldn't lose any more respect for my dad."

"Hang on, there are some redeeming parts to the story. Anyway, he made the wrong people very upset when a transaction did not go smoothly. It ended up costing the other parties significant amounts of money and led to several of them going to prison. In retribution, they kidnapped Isabella and held her for ransom."

"What? You were kidnapped? When?" asked Mackenzie, spinning toward Isabella and putting a hand on her arm.

"When I was ten. They had me for two days and then released me."

"They didn't release you of their own good will. Charlie Hearst paid them two million dollars in cash," said Vincent. *That I borrowed from him first, but you'll never know that Isabella.*

"Dad spent two million to free you from a kidnapping?" Mackenzie's jaw hung open, incredulous at what she heard.

"Yes, and then another million to make sure it never happened again."

"What does that mean? He paid them another million to stay away?"

"Not exactly. He paid someone else a million dollars to make sure they never harmed anyone again."

"I don't even want to know," said Mackenzie, leaning forward and cradling her head in her hands.

"Good, because I will not say any more about it. It was during that time period that your mother and I connected the first time. I was staying at your house to be close to the situation. I was a complete wreck. Wasn't eating. Wasn't sleeping. All I could think about was if you were okay or not." His voice cracked on the last sentence. He attempted to conceal it with a cough, but the next sentence wouldn't form either. Marybeth leaned toward him and gave him a long hug, after which he could continue.

"After we paid the ransom, I drove out and picked Izzie up from where they had left her. It was like I received a second chance at being a dad. That night we celebrated and connected on such a deep level. Charlie, your mother, and I. Charlie stepped out for a bit and that's when your mother and I first..."

"It's okay; I get the gist of it. Sorry for getting mad at you two earlier. I did not know what you both had been through." She turned to her friend and continued. "And they kidnapped you? How did that never come up in conversation?"

Isabella laughed. "How would I have told you without explaining why? I don't even know the complete story myself. I learned a few things tonight, too."

"First your mom died and then you were kidnapped. My mom sacrificed herself for me since I was two, and I have taken it all for granted. I'm the epitome of a spoiled brat." She finished her statement and leaned back in her chair.

"I can't go through life this entitled. It's not fair to any of you. I want to come clean and admit what I did." She paused and let out a quick sigh. "I was looking at my phone when I hit that officer." She looked up at the others and saw three heads nodding back at her. "I need to take responsibility. But how can I do it at this point?"

"I have thought about that for some time," said Vincent. "First, I'm proud of you for coming to this conclusion, Mackenzie. I will work with the city to see what they will offer as a plea agreement.

The bigger challenge is figuring out how to tell Charlie. I don't know what he's going to do."

"I do," said Marybeth. "He'll yell and scream, maybe break something. He'll spew some nonsense phrases in a Texas drawl and then, when his tantrum is done, I'll tell him what he's going to do." She tipped her wine glass up and finished the contents before standing up.

"Now then, since this is all out in the open, what do you say we all go out for lunch?"

A chorus of agreement greeted her before twelve chair legs scraped on the concrete as their occupants rose to their feet.

Chapter Thirty-Four

"Dr. Chapman, you have a visitor," said the registration clerk who had poked her head around the corner. "He's back in trauma."

Bryce stood and walked toward the trauma rooms, curious about who was there to see him. Detective Stephenson? The coroner?

He opened the door and saw a crowd of people gathered. They were smiling and taking turns shaking hands with Clay Turner.

"There he is, my attacker and my savior," said Clay, pointing to Bryce.

The two walked toward each other and shared a firm handshake.

"Good to see you back in the hospital, Clay. How are you doing?"

"So much better now that I'm out of that rehab facility. I can't get the smell out of my nose though. It's like I'm at Goodwill."

"Is your wound healed?" asked Bryce.

"Yeah, completely. No more dressing changes, and they said I can get more aggressive with my therapy. At this point my only limitation on what I can do is pain, but that's getting better every day."

A nurse broke in with a question of his own. "When will you be starting back at the fire house? We miss you bringing patients in."

Clay grimaced and replied. "I'm not sure I'll be able to, at least not for a while. I can't lift much at all. I wouldn't be much help on a crew."

He looked across the crowd and spoke to them all at once. "Let me give you guys some advice. If Dr. Chapman invites you over to his house, make sure he knows you're already baptized, and if he has a pressure washer in his hand, run!"

Everyone laughed at the good-natured comment from Clay, including Bryce.

"But you've been born again, Clay. So maybe it was a good thing?" said Bryce.

"I'm not sure I'd go so far as to say it was good, but I'm certainly in a better place now in many ways. Since I can't work at the moment, I signed up to teach CPR classes at high schools in the area. I'll be helping these kids learn how to save lives, and maybe encourage some to consider a career in pre-hospital care."

"That's awesome! Good for you," said Bryce.

Clay finished greeting everyone and thanking them for taking care of him that day. The team slowly dispersed and headed back to their patient assignments until it was just Bryce and Clay standing together.

"Hey, big news," said Bryce. "I talked with my insurance company this morning about your case and they want to settle. They said they expected a maximum verdict and prefer to save lawyer fees and a million dollars by settling for four million. They needed my approval before writing up a settlement offer."

Clay brought both hands up to his head and pinched his fingers in his hair. "What? Are you serious?"

Bryce nodded. "Yeah. Never thought I'd be happy about losing a four-million-dollar claim, but this should clear up a lot of issues. We can move forward with an offer to settle the malpractice case with Kent Carpenter's family now."

Clay's smile eroded and was replaced by a stern look. "Actually, I was thinking about that. I'd rather just keep the money and let the courts sort out your case. You didn't do anything wrong and I'm sure the jury will agree."

The words stung Bryce like a slap to the face. "What? That's not what we agreed–"

Clay interrupted him with a burst of laughter. "Just kidding, man. I wanted to see the look on your face when I said it. Sorry, bad joke, but I just had to."

Bryce exhaled in a long sigh and turned around in a slow circle. "Oh man, you had me there. A million thoughts ran through my mind at the same time."

"I wouldn't do that to you. We're sort of in this together, right?"

"Blood brothers," said Bryce, extending a fist toward Clay, who matched with his own.

"Speaking of your lawsuit, guess who ran into me at lunch the other day?"

"Who?"

"Lorena McCarthy. Apparently, her office is in the same building as my attorney. I ate lunch at an outdoor cafe a block away and she just sat down like I invited her."

"That sounds like her. Never met a situation she didn't think she could control."

"As hot as she is, I bet she's usually successful. And that accent..."

"She's the enemy; don't forget that. What did she want with you?"

"She offered me a job. Said she recognized my tattoos from the news report about my injury and knew I wasn't working right now. Said she needs someone with medical knowledge to screen cases for her and maybe some investigating, too."

"That's a pretty big coincidence. She's suing me and suddenly she's buddying-up to the person I injured? Do you think she's really trying to figure out what we're up to?"

"I'll let you know. We're having dinner together this weekend," said Clay with a wide grin.

Bryce groaned and shook his head. "Why do all my friends keep sabotaging themselves with women?"

"Relax. I'll keep my guard up."

"Okay, please do. Don't let her get you liquored up. If your tongue gets loose, it may get you in trouble again."

"Touché."

Bryce scanned around the room quickly before continuing in a hushed voice. "I found a lawyer who has agreed to be the intermediary and make an offer to Kent's family to drop the lawsuit. I'll let him know to move forward and see if they are interested in formalizing something. We may be close to putting this whole thing to rest."

"I hope so. Once it's over, I'll feel better about offering to make breakfast for Lorena." Clay's smile had not faded a millimeter.

Chapter Thirty-Five

"Thanks for coming with me today," said Bryce. "I'm not a fan of politics and appreciate your support in this."

"No problem. Actually, I'm curious about what they're going to say," said Val.

The two walked into a modern office building full of glass and various pieces of art displayed throughout the lobby. A secretary sat at a desk just inside the door.

"Good morning. Do you have an appointment with someone?" she asked.

"Yes, we're meeting Steven Harris," said Bryce.

"Perfect." She looked at her monitor for a moment before responding. "He's in office 203, today. The elevator is to your right."

Bryce thanked her and walked toward the elevator with Val. "Today? Does he change offices?"

"I think this is a shared office space building. For people that don't need an office every day. They can have a secretary and access to an office whenever they need, but don't pay as much as having their own dedicated space," said Val.

"Interesting. And cost effective."

They exited the elevator to find a tall man in a suit standing there to greet them.

"Doctor Chapman? Valerie? I'm Steven Harris. Pleased to meet you."

They exchanged handshakes and then proceeded to his small office, which was little more than an empty conference room with a computer and phone.

"Let me explain a bit about what I do, and then we can talk about your current situation. I am a lawyer who specializes in political campaign consulting. Neither a Democrat nor a Republican, I simply vote my conscience in the privacy of a polling booth. I work with candidates from across the political spectrum to help them develop a cohesive strategy for fund-raising, platform development, and campaigning."

"What if the candidate doesn't want to do any of those things?" asked Bryce with a smile.

"So that brings us to you, then. Why are you running for coroner?"

"You're a lawyer, right? So anything I say here is confidential?" asked Bryce.

"Yes, that is correct," said Steve.

"I have no confidence in the current coroner's conclusions. There was one particular case he got wrong, and it led to me being sued for malpractice. There are other cases I have heard about, but this is the one that affected me directly. Now with the death of Michael Jenkins, there is a second case they screwed up that directly affects me. The coroner's report pissed off the police because of the false report on the officer's blood alcohol. A detective approached me to run for office to defeat him and bring competence to the position."

"Why did they choose you? Surely there are plenty of other people out there they could choose from. No offense, of course."

"Let's just say they had a way to motivate me to run that made it difficult to say no."

Steven nodded slowly. "Okay, so you need to run for office, but don't want to do it."

"Correct."

"Well, that doesn't really change anything other than we're going to need to motivate you to put energy into something that doesn't excite you."

"That's not entirely true; it's very important that I win. It is the reason I couldn't say no. I'm prepared to do whatever it takes to win."

Steven smiled at Bryce. "Very cryptic, but that's what makes politics fun. Well, the first thing we need to do is form an entity that you can use for fund-raising and spending. You're running for coroner; it's not like that's a massive campaign usually. I think you'll be able to do what you need to for under fifty-thousand dollars."

Val coughed and gasped at the same time. "Fifty-thousand dollars? The election is a few weeks away. How are we going to have time to spend that much?"

"Do you have any idea how many households there are in Marion County? Or how much a standard sign costs to stick in the ground to support a candidate?"

"You can spend fifty thousand in the blink of an eye. Ideally, you'll only pay for hard merchandise and services, and find enough people to volunteer time. You shouldn't need to pay anyone to show up."

"I have the support of IMPD. They have promised to do whatever they can to help."

"That should help immensely. Coroner is a non-political office so voters are going to have to select a name. They can't simply pull the lever or push the button to vote straight ticket. Name recognition is huge in this type of election. Unfortunately, the current coroner received over a quarter million votes in the last election. You're going to need to do better than that."

"I need to get more than a quarter of a million people to vote for me?" Bryce repeated the line slowly and with a slight shake of his head. "How is that possible?"

"Name recognition. You need to get your name out there."

"Bryce made the national news for the save we had in the Bahamas earlier in the year. Would that help?"

"Sure it will. Anything you can do to get on television or in the paper now would help as well. If they hear your name and then see a sign, that builds the connection they need for when they see your name on the ballot. I will get you on several news programs and in as many newspaper articles as I can before the primary."

"I read it's possible to win the election outright in the primary. Is that true?" asked Bryce.

"Yes, it is. Since this election has no party affiliation, if anyone reaches fifty percent of the vote in the primary, they win the election. Primary elections have much lower turnout, so if you have a motivated base you could win the whole thing. It's how AOC beat Joe Crowley. Low turnout elections can surprise you."

"When would I take office, if the election is over in the primary?"

"Worst case, it would be January, but usually the incumbent resigns and the mayor appoints the victor to the position to finish out the term."

Bryce looked at Val and spoke. "What do we owe you for your services? Is that part of the fifty thousand?"

Steven raised his hands and spread them apart dismissively. "Don't worry about that. My fee has been covered."

"By whom?" asked Val.

"They wish to remain anonymous if that's okay with you. From a reporting standpoint, it's not a big deal. Technically, I waived my fee to do this pro bono, and that covered a favor I owed someone else. So my in-kind donation to your campaign will be disclosed, but not who I owed a favor to."

"Politics and favors," said Bryce.

"Yep, and welcome to it," said Steven through a grin.

Chapter Thirty-Six

"So, what did you think of that meeting?" asked Bryce.

"It's all so overwhelming. You know I hate politics, Bryce. Everyone claims to be representing the people, but the truth is most of them are simply representing themselves or their family."

"Right? The term 'public servant' is absurd. They are usually serving their own interests. But I like to think local politics may be different. It's like minor league baseball. These people often have other jobs as well, and work to better their community."

"I guess you'll find out soon enough," said Val.

"Why is that?"

"Because you're Bryce Chapman. Things just sort of work out for you. You get what you want."

Bryce smiled at his wife. "What are you saying? That I'm just lucky?"

She grabbed his right hand and looked at him for a moment without speaking. "No, it's not luck. It's some strange combination of charisma and personality. People just like you."

"I see you mentioned nothing about my good looks or physique," said Bryce with a frown.

"Awe, honey, that goes without saying. But I don't think it's your dad bod that draws people to you."

"Dad bod? Ouch."

Val laughed and squeezed his hand tighter. "I need to keep your ego in check."

Before Bryce could reply, his phone rang. The caller ID on the car's LCD screen showed a local number he didn't have in his address book. He thumbed a button on his steering wheel to answer and it broadcast the call through the car's audio system.

"Hi, this is Bryce."

"Doc, this is Charlie Hearst. Ya' got a minute?"

Bryce gave Val a look of uncertainty before replying. "Yeah, I'm just driving."

"Good. Listen, I wanted to talk to you man to man about the legal situation we found ourselves mixed up in. The case against my daughter Mackenzie is moving forward, and I need to know what you're going to tell the prosecutor at your deposition."

"I'm going to tell them exactly what she told me. And I'm not sure it's appropriate for us to be talking right now."

"Are you referring to the violent sneeze that caused her to jerk the wheel?"

Val saw Bryce's face tighten in sync with the sudden increased grip on her hand.

"No, I'm referring to her original story, where she said she was recording a video. You know, the one she told before you showed up and told her to lie about it?"

"Listen doc, we need to figure this out right quick. I will not let you ruin my daughter's life. If you want a battle, I'm ready and rarin' to go."

"I don't want a battle. I want the truth to be told. Why does there have to be a battle?"

"Because when it's your kin in trouble, you protect them, come hell or high water. Or some jerk ER doctor."

"Okay, we're done here. Have a great day."

"Doc, one quick piece of advice. I fight fire with fire. If you put my family in trouble, I'll be obliged to do the same."

Bryce smashed his finger into the steering wheel control and ended the call. "I miss the days where you could slam a phone back on its cradle." He looked over at Val, who was pushing a button on her phone. "What were you doing just now? Our family is getting threatened at you're playing on your phone?" The irritation was obvious in Bryce's voice.

Val dropped her head so she could roll her eyes to look up at her husband. She swiped her finger across the screen and then tapped it. Charlie's voice filled the car again, and his threat came through crystal clear.

"Oh, you recorded that? Brilliant move."

"Duh. I compliment you, and then two minutes later you're scolding me for something I didn't do?"

Bryce sighed, and she felt his body go limp. "I'm so sorry. That call scared me and pissed me off at the same time. I should have trusted that your instinct was to help."

"Yes, you should have. But, apology accepted. I'll send you a copy of the audio, so we each have one."

"Good idea. Last time we lost some recorded footage it caused some serious headaches," he said.

"We?"

"Fine, I lost it. But to be fair, it was my first time stepping into a seaplane and I was caring for a guy we just saved. I was a little distracted."

"Other than Noah and Hannah, I think that's the best thing we've done together. That was pretty fantastic."

"Yet. Best thing we've done together, yet."

"You think we'll be able to top that some day? We rescued a guy who drowned and got him back with CPR and no equipment in a tropical paradise. How do you top that?"

"I don't know, but I'm sure we can. Who knows what the future holds?"

"With you, I have no idea, but I'm sure it will be exciting." She let go of Bryce's hand and sat up in her seat. "I think you need to send this to that detective you're working with. Hearst just openly threatened us."

"I will. Not sure what he can do with it, but I'll send it to him."

They finished the drive and then shared a quick meal before Bryce headed in to work.

Chapter Thirty-Seven

"Whew, I need some air," said Paula, reaching for the fan perched in the far corner of her desk. She turned the knob all the way to the right to get the maximum air flow.

"You OK, Paula?" asked Bryce, who was just walking past her, headed to a patient room.

"I think so, just felt like I couldn't catch my breath. I'll be okay in a minute."

Bryce nodded and continued down to the second room down the hallway. *Knee pain in a fifty-year-old. This should be easy.* He opened the door and saw a pleasant-looking man lying in the bed, a hospital gown in place and exposing his legs below mid-thigh. *Someone actually put a patient in a gown. Amazing.* The patient's right knee was swollen and a little red.

Bryce introduced himself and started asking questions about the patient's knee. "How long has it been red like that? Does it hurt?"

The patient rubbed his knee and tried to bend it before wincing and laying it flat again. "It's been getting worse for three days. I had it replaced a year ago and have been doing great. It didn't bother me until we went to the seafood buffet a few days ago. The next day it started hurting."

The patient's wife had done her best to not interrupt, and she used her husband's pause as a time to interject. "I told him not to eat that many oysters. I don't care if it was an all-you-can-eat, it was just stupid. He must have had fifty of those slimy things."

Bryce smiled. "I love oysters. My favorite ones are at Boshamps, down in Destin, Florida. Add some hot sauce and you're ready to rock. Did you really eat fifty?"

The patient nodded sheepishly. "Was that a bad idea, doc?"

No, eating something to extreme excess is rarely a bad idea. "Well, they are high in purines, and that can trigger a gout or pseudogout flare. The problem is you have an artificial knee and we need to make sure that it's not infected. I'm going to use a needle to aspirate your joint and send a fluid sample to the lab to see if it's infected or just an arthritis flare like gout. I'll go get the supplies and we'll get that fluid drained. You should feel better once the fluid is out."

Bryce exited the room and walked toward the supply room on the opposite side of the department. He glanced over to the physician's workstation as he passed and saw Paula with her head down on the desk.

That's odd. She never naps at work. He touched her shoulder. "Paula, you okay?"

No response. This time, he aggressively shook her shoulder and yelled her name. She took a deep inhalation, her neck arching back as she did so, then was motionless again.

"I need help here!" shouted Bryce. "Get a crash cart!" He reached down and pulled Paula to an upright position, her head falling backward over her chair. He placed his fingers over her radial artery at the wrist. *No pulse!*

Nurses and techs assembled quickly. One pushed the resuscitation cart that had the monitor and defibrillator on it and another pulled a stretcher as close as possible.

"What happened?" asked a nurse. "She was fine a few minutes ago."

Bryce reached down and picked up Paula the way a father would lift a sleeping child from a car. He placed her on the cot and checked again for a pulse while nurses placed her on the monitor. *Still no pulse!*

"Let's move her to trauma, get an IV and an EKG. Get RT down here now!" he ordered. He leaned forward and began chest compressions on Paula, wincing as he felt her ribs give way. He made eye contact with a nurse and asked him to reach under the bed to retrieve the bag-valve-mask system and began delivering breaths to Paula as they wheeled down toward trauma.

"Bryce, what happened?" asked Tom Sharpe, who had stepped out of a patient room.

"I don't know. I found her down at her desk. Grab the ultrasound machine and meet us in trauma."

The team hurried down the hallway as fast as they could safely go. Each person performing their tasks efficiently, but quietly. They had each provided medical care to pulseless patients hundreds of times. But this was different. This was their coworker. Their friend.

Bryce looked down at her body as they entered the trauma room. Come on Paula, what happened?

"She has a rhythm!" shouted the nurse, who placed Paula on the monitor. "Tachy at 180."

"Is it wide or narrow?" asked Bryce.

"Narrow."

She's in Pulseless Electrical Activity. Remember the mnemonic. The H's and T's. Bryce scanned his memory and ran through the usual causes of PEA. "Hey Tom, look with the ultrasound and see if she has any clot in her leg. She was complaining about leg pain the other day."

Thromboembolism. If she has a clot, then we need to get it broken up now. He watched Tom place the ultrasound probe on Paula's right thigh just past her groin. He saw the femoral vein sitting next to the artery and noted some debris inside the normally hollow appearing vessel. "Can you compress that?" he asked.

"No, not at all." Tom followed the vein further down her leg to the knee. "This clot is huge, Bryce. It's her entire femoral vein. She must have had a massive pulmonary embolism."

"Someone get TNKase to bedside now. Push it as soon as we have an IV and the drug mixed. Someone take over on compressions. I need to intubate her," said Bryce.

Respiratory therapy had the equipment laid out for Bryce, who quickly placed a breathing tube in her trachea, despite the added difficulty of chest compressions moving the airway back and forth.

"Put a call out to cardiothoracic surgery and tell them I need them down here for possible ECMO on a patient with a massive PE," shouted Bryce.

"I have the clot busters ready," said a nurse.

"Push it, fast. She probably weighs about sixty kilograms, give her thirty milligrams." The nurse nodded and attached the syringe to an IV in Paula's right wrist. She depressed the plunger until six milliliters were delivered and then disconnected the syringe. She attached a saline flush syringe and smashed the plunger to the hub with her thumb, flushing the medication through the IV tubing and into Paula's vein.

Bryce looked up at the clock on the wall. Less than five minutes had passed since he found Paula face down. But how long was she down? The ER is busy. Surely someone would have seen her within a few minutes.

"Let's check her blood sugar. Does anyone know her family? We need to call them," said Bryce.

"I know her husband. I'll call him right away," said the registration clerk from the entrance to the room before walking away quickly.

"What's next?" asked Tom, standing next to Bryce.

"We continue to do compressions and give her fluids until hopefully the TNKase allows her heart to pump blood again. If that doesn't happen, I'm going to push for her to get on ECMO."

"Do you think cardiothoracic surgery will place her on the bypass machine after receiving lytics? Those are huge arterial catheters that need to go in."

"I know, but what other options do we have? Maybe a thoracotomy and direct massage of the pulmonary arteries to break up the clot, but that's pretty drastic and may cause more harm than good."

"Hey, are you guys doing interrupting my day with talks of ED ECMO?" The words were innocent enough and came from a usually friendly cardiothoracic surgeon who had just entered the room.

Bryce shook his hand and brought him up to date on who the patient was and what he believes happened. "Do you think she's an ECMO candidate?"

"Well, we don't even know if she has a PE," he said.

"What else could it be? Several days of leg pain, has a clot in it on ultrasound, and sustained a PEA arrest with a heart rate of one hundred eighty. What else does that?"

"You're right, it's just hard to do something this invasive without knowing for sure. Is there anyone around to sign consent?"

"Well, she's currently dead. Are you worried about making things worse and then getting sued? If we don't get her back in the next few minutes, we need to consider taking this resuscitation to the next level. Paula is the kindest person who works here. She'd do anything for any of us, and we're going to do whatever we can for her." *You may own the scalpel, but I own the resuscitation.*

"Let's stop and do a pulse check. Tom, have the ultrasound ready to look at her right ventricle." The team stopped compressions and several people checked Paula for a pulse. Tom placed the ultrasound probe on her chest and a grainy image of the heart displayed on the screen. The monitor showed rapid electrical activity, but the heart was barely twitching on the screen. Not enough motion to pump blood and generate a discernible pulse.

"That RV is blown. It's got to be a PE," said the cardiothoracic surgeon. "Okay, you convinced me. I'll get a perfusionist here and we'll proceed with ECMO as soon as we can, if she doesn't get a pulse back."

A nurse resumed chest compressions, and the surgeon walked out of the room to gather supplies. The team continued to help their friend, a somber mood keeping conversations to a minimum.

Come on Paula, keep fighting.

Bryce searched his brain for medical tips and tricks to help his secretary and friend. What he found was something in his heart. His favorite verse of his favorite Christmas song, played by Paula not one hour ago.

"Hark! The herald angels sing, Glory to the newborn King." He sang the lyrics as loud as he felt he could manage without his voice cracking in emotion. Paula loved Christmas music and streamed the classics from her workstation every hour of every shift.

"Peace on earth, and mercy mild. God and sinners, reconciled," added the nurse doing chest compressions with a much better voice than Bryce had managed. The entire team joined in for the third line. The spontaneous a capella performance continued while each person continued their task at hand. Someone hung a second liter of fluid on a new IV and squeezed in with a pressure bag.

"Christ by highest Heaven adored, Christ the everlasting Lord!" Bryce's voice restarted the song at the second verse as several had gone silent after the well-known first verse ended. He watched the monitor and noted the electrical activity on the monitor, a task made difficult by the movement of her chest wall from compressions.

The surgeon returned with several pre-packaged supply kits and laid them out on a table. He paused and looked at the team as they continued to sing the second verse. A perfusionist arrived a few seconds later, pushing a large heart-lung bypass machine. The surgeon opened the packages and organized them in the order in which he'll need them. He then put on his sterile gown and gloves, a nurse helping secure the gown in the back. "She's the one always playing Christmas music, isn't she?"

Bryce nodded and continued to sing. "Hail the Heaven-born Prince of Peace! Hail the Son, of Righteousness!". *Okay Paula, if you were going to come back, now would be a great time. I chose this song for this verse. If you don't get a pulse in a minute, this surgeon is going to put you on a heart-lung bypass machine.* "Light and life to all He brings, Risen with healing in his wings."

The surgeon stepped to Paula's side and took over the lead vocal as he splashed her groin with iodine. "Mild He lays His glory by, Born that men no more may die, Born to raise the sons of earth, Born to give them second birth." He rubbed the area dry with gauze and laid out a plastic drape over the planned incision area.

"Hark! The herald angels sing, Glory to the newborn King...". The surgeon held the last note as he leaned over and picked up the scalpel. He placed his fingers over Paula's left femoral artery and ended the song. "Okay, hold compressions. I'm going to make my incision."

The nurse doing chest compressions stopped and leaned back. Everyone was looking at the surgeon's hand as he moved the scalpel toward her leg. Then he paused and looked up at the monitor.

Bryce followed his eyes and saw the heart rate was now registering 140 instead of 180.

"I believe we have a pulse," said the surgeon. "Will someone look at her heart with the ultrasound? Try to cycle a blood pressure," he said.

Bryce beat Tom to the ultrasound probe and placed it on her left chest. The screen showed that her heart was beating significantly better. "It's not normal, but it's way better than it was. I think the clot busters are doing their thing."

"I agree. I think we should hold off on ECMO for now. How do you feel about using a pulmonary artery catheter to break up and suction out the clot instead? Now that she has a pulse, that seems like the best option."

"Absolutely. How can we help you get ready for it?" said Bryce.

"I'll make the calls. We'll take her to the lab and get it started in about ten minutes. Just continue fluids for now. I'll drop an arterial line in when she gets to the lab. Nice work." The surgeon peeled his gown off and stuffed it into the garbage can before leaving the trauma room.

"When Paula has recovered, she is going to love this story," said Bryce.

"Are you kidding me? That was the most powerful thing I've ever seen!" said Jackie Sirico. "We're all going to be in the room and sing it with her when she's feeling up to it."

Tom caught Bryce's gaze and hold it for a few seconds. "That was bad ass Bryce. Even for you. I'm going to nominate you for an award over this one."

Bryce wiped a tear from each eye and nodded back to his friend and mentor and tried to shake off the emotion. "Thanks for the kind words and your help. I've always wanted a Daytime Emmy."

The team finished the usual procedures for a patient on a ventilator as Bryce entered orders for sedation, labs, and a chest X-ray.

He took one last look at Paula and headed out of the room

"Wait!" called a nurse from behind him.

Oh no, what happened? Bryce spun around and rushed back to the beside, glancing at the monitor and vital signs. "What's wrong?" he asked.

"Nothing. She just moved her left hand. I thought you'd like to know," said the nurse.

Bryce smiled and thanked her. He reached down and held Paula's hand for a few seconds before asking the nurse to start an infusion of a sedative. *Glad you're waking up Paula, but it's time to go back to sleep. You have a long road ahead of you.*

Chapter Thirty-Eight

"Kids, I need you to calm down," said Val. "The TV crew will be here in a few minutes, and I don't want you all hot and sweaty."

The two stopped chasing each other and plopped down onto the couch, looks of boredom spreading quickly across their faces.

"How do I look?" asked Bryce. He stood in the family room wearing a black suit with a red tie.

"Do you want my honest opinion?"

"Of course, unless it's mean..."

"You look like you're running for Congress. This is a county coroner position and you're an ER doctor. Maybe wear something that helps people understand that?"

"Ah, okay. The tired and burned-out look will be easy, but how do I let the viewer know how much my soul has been destroyed by the administrative burden?"

Val laughed at her husband and replied, "you'll figure it out."

Bryce ran upstairs to change and returned a few minutes later wearing a pair of khaki pants with an embroidered scrub top.

Val nodded. "Much better. Professional, yet ready to rock out medically."

The TV crew arrived a few minutes later. The crew set up equipment in the family room, while a reporter introduced herself.

"Hi, I'm Martha Martin. I'll be interviewing you on camera. We won't be broadcasting live so don't be nervous; we can always go back and do another take on a question. I thought we could start with an introduction of your family and then have your wife take the kids out of frame and we'll continue on. Does that sound okay?"

"That's fine, I guess." Bryce looked at Val, who nodded her agreement.

"Great. Let's setup on your couch here. Do either of you need anything? Or can we begin?"

"Nope, let's go," said Bryce. He led Val and the kids around power cords for the large portable lights and took a seat on the couch.

Martha sat on a cushion opposite the Chapmans and adjusted her hair one final time. She looked at the cameraman who gave her the thumbs up sign and began recording.

The reporter's demeanor changed instantly as she switched into her television persona.

"Good evening, we continue our election coverage series with another candidate interview. This time, we are in the home of Dr. Bryce Chapman, running for coroner against Dr. Zachary Pullard, whom we interviewed last week. Dr. Chapman, would you mind introducing your family?"

"Sure Martha, I'd be happy to," said Bryce with a smile to the camera. "This is my wife Valerie, and our two children, Noah and Hannah." The Chapmans smiled together for a moment before Hannah looked at her mother and pulled on her sleeve. Val shook her head and tried to dismiss the request.

"You have a beautiful family. The children are adorable."

"Thank you very much. They're the reason I work so hard."

"Mommy, I need to pee," said Hannah in a loud whisper, picked up clearly by the camera.

Bryce's faced flashed momentary annoyance, but the reporter laughed it off. "Don't worry, take her to the bathroom and we'll redo the opening." She spoke to the cameraman while Hannah ran to the bathroom. "Working with kids and animals, eh?"

A few minutes later, the camera was rolling again as Martha continued her interview.

"Doctor Chapman, can you tell us why you decided to run for coroner? You just made it in before the ballot deadline. Why the late entry?"

"Honestly, it was the coroner's report on Officer Jenkins' blood alcohol level. I took care of him that day in the Emergency Department and felt a strong connection to him and his family. When I heard that report, I was livid. It did not fit the clinical picture I saw that day and it didn't mesh with what his friends and family knew about him either. So I decided I could just yell from the sidelines, or I could suit up and step onto the field myself. And here I am." He smiled at the camera and waited for a follow-up question.

"What makes you qualified to be coroner?"

"The role of coroner is mainly an administrative one. The person must coordinate with pathologists, police, crime scene investigators, family, and so many more people to determine the true cause of death of a person. Ensuring we get it right is so important. Not just for the person who died, but for those who cared about them also. Like Officer Jenkins, for example. His family went through an emotional roller coaster of public reaction. It must have been so hurtful to be told your loved one was a closet alcoholic, who was drunk on the job, when you know he wasn't."

"I see. And can the voters expect your office to get it right every time?"

"Can they expect it? Yes. Can I deliver on that? I'm not sure. But I'll do my level best to make sure that we do. We cannot miss a murder and assume it was a natural death. Our citizens deserve to be protected both while they're alive, as well as once they have died."

"Thank you, Doctor Chapman. Can you tell us a bit about your background? I think most of our viewers probably watched a video of you and your wife in the Bahamas from earlier in the year."

"Guys, come here! Doctor Chapman's interview is about to start."

Several nurses and techs gathered in an empty patient room to watch the interview on the evening news. They shared good-natured laughter at the cheesy lines and smiles Bryce offered the camera.

"He is pretty slick; I'll give him that," said Tom.

"He's got my vote," said a tech.

"If he raises my taxes, I'm going to stop cleaning up after his procedures," said a nurse.

Another nurse slapped him on the arm. "He's running for coroner. The worst he could do is put some embarrassing cause of death on your death certificate."

Chapter Thirty-Nine

"Bryce, I need you to stick around today after your shift for a meeting," said Ashford Tate.

"Why? Who are we meeting with?"

"Our favorite person. Lorena McCarthy."

"Oh man, what does she want?"

"There's been a twist in the Kent Carpenter lawsuit that she wants to discuss, but without the hospital attorneys."

Sounds like she got a call from my other attorney. Sweet!

"Okay, I'll come to your office when I'm done."

"Take your time; I don't mind entertaining her a while," said Ash with a wink.

"You dog; I'll be there soon."

Bryce's shift ended well, and he only turned over one patient to the on-coming doctor. He grabbed his backpack and headed toward Ash's office. The smell of perfume in the hallway became stronger the closer he came to Ash's office. *I bet he keeps the door shut as long as he can to keep that in there.*

"Hi, Doctor Chapman, come on in," said Lorena. *You're inviting me into someone else's office? Is there a place where you don't think you're in charge? You'd probably even ask St. Peter if he needs any advice.*

"Thanks," said Bryce, pulling the door to the office closed behind him. "Sorry, there are people who come down this hallway, and I thought we'd like to keep our discussions confidential."

"Of course. This makes it much more intimate. Now, I'd like to talk about a settlement offer I received on this case."

"Settlement offer?" said Ash with raised eyebrows. "I didn't know the hospital approached you with a settlement offer."

"That's the thing," she said. "They didn't. This came from another lawyer. I got a phone call yesterday offering Kent's family two million dollars as a settlement for his death, with the condition that it end the malpractice suit."

Bryce tried his best to act surprised. "Really? Wow! Any idea where the offer came from?"

"I have no idea. Do you?" asked Lorena, staring into Bryce's eyes.

He maintained her gaze and shook his head. "The only person I know who has that kind of money is Niles Proffit, the CEO of the company who owns this hospital, among others. I saved his son down in the Bahamas earlier this year. Maybe he's trying to repay me."

"Perhaps," said Lorena, spinning a pen in her hand. "Or perhaps there's another angle at play."

"What do you mean?" asked Ash.

"There are other sources of money." She shifted her gaze from Ash back to Bryce. "Insurance settlements, for one. I have yet to meet a doctor that didn't have a large personal umbrella policy."

"That's because we're all terrified of people like you," said Bryce.

"Oh, come on. I'm not scary. I just help the people that you didn't."

The insult hung in the air uncomfortably long before she continued speaking.

"Anyway, it doesn't really matter where the money is coming from. What matters is what my client does with the offer."

"How are you going to advise them?" asked Ash.

She sighed before answering. "I'm going to recommend they accept it. Truth be told, off record of course, I'm not entirely convinced this was malpractice. I agree with you that the coroner's report is shaky regarding the cystic fibrosis claim. Seeing as how that is the linchpin in my case, I think it's reasonable to take the settlement and put this matter behind us."

Bryce exhaled deeply. "Wow, that's a relief. Do you think she'll accept it?"

"I do. This isn't a game show. No one is going to risk two million dollars for the chance to get a little more. And, other than a malpractice attorney, who wants to go through a long, drawn-out trial? Certainly not some ex-wife busy with two kids."

"Well, I'd like to buy our mysterious benefactor a beer. When do you think you'll have a final word on this?" asked Ash.

"I'd say a day or two." She stood up and straightened her skirt. "It's been a pleasure meeting with you, gentlemen. I'll let you know." She opened the door and walked through it before pausing and turning her head toward Bryce. "You know, there's an old Irish saying. Do you know why the Irish are always fighting each other?"

"No, I don't. Why?"

"Because we have no other worthy opponents. Nicely played, doc. I'm impressed."

When she pulled the door closed, Ash looked at Bryce with squinted eyes. "What did she mean by that?"

Bryce smiled and held his hands up while shaking his head. "I have absolutely no idea."

"I don't believe that for a second."

"Well, let's just say you owe me a two-million-dollar beer and leave it at that."

"I thought you don't drink anymore?"

"I don't. I'm going to put it on my trophy rack. You don't drink a two-million-dollar beer."

Ash put his right hand on his forehead and shook his head. "You never stop surprising me, Bryce."

Chapter Forty

B ryce left Ash's office and sent a text to Val.

> Bryce: Let's eat at our favorite Mexican restaurant tonight. Time to celebrate.
> Val: What are we celebrating?
> Bryce: The end of a headache.
> Val: Great, I'm in. Margs, for me. You get the kids.

Bryce smiled and walked through the department. His brain blocked the cacophony of typical sounds from the ER out as it focused instead on the joy of knowing the malpractice case had just vaporized. He continued through the hallways without slowing down or hearing the several people who had tried to strike up a conversation with him.

It's finally over. Sucks for Kent and his family, but we did nothing wrong and that damn lawyer knows it. Definitely worth losing my umbrella policy and never being insurable again to get the case off my back. I hope they enjoy their millions.

Bryce pointed his key fob at the Yukon and pushed the remote start button like Mickey Mouse in Fantasia. With a swipe of his hand, the SUV came to life with the roar of the engine accompanied by music. *Sorry Mickey, no orchestra today. Just a little Zac Brown Band to help me celebrate.* He reached out and knocked his bobble-head to get it rocking along with his mood.

Twenty minutes later, he pulled into the parking lot of the Mexican restaurant and saw Val's vehicle with an open spot next to it, which he quickly filled.

He found his family sitting at a table, both kids facing the door with Val's back to him. He snuck up behind Val and reached his hands out to surprise her.

"Daddy!" yelled Hannah, causing Val to spin around and see Bryce standing behind her like a zombie on the hunt for brains.

"Glad you could join us; I saved you a seat," she said, tapping the chair next to her.

Bryce sighed and dropped his arms before walking over to hug his kids and then sitting down.

"You guys are supposed to let me scare Mom when I'm sneaking up like that. Anyway, how was your day?"

"We went to the water park and I went down the biggest slide they had!" said Noah, reaching his hand way above his head. "There was a huge pool at the bottom and I made a giant splash at the end of the ride. Mom, show him the video!"

Val smiled at her son's enthusiasm and swiped through her phone until she had the video pulled up.

"Woah, that's impressive Noah," said Bryce. "Did you have a good time too, Hannah?"

His daughter nodded and spoke a soft reply. "I didn't do the slide, it was too big. But I did the river a bunch with Mom." She extended her finger and swirled it around in circles to show the lazy river path.

"Well, that sounds like a great day. Daddy had a good day today, too. Remember those things that Mommy and I were dealing with that were making us sad?"

The children nodded back at their dad.

"A big one just went away today, and now we're here to celebrate."

Val picked up her strawberry margarita and held her glass over the middle of the table. The kids raised their lemonades, and Bryce raised his water to finish the toast.

"Bolus," said Val, taking a large drink.

"And titrate," said Bryce, rubbing her back. "Hopefully you tired the kids out today and they'll go to sleep easily."

"Oh, I'm sure they will. Why do you think I'm drinking tequila?" She winked at him and placed her hand on his thigh, squeezing gently.

"I got some good news today. Lorena McCarthy showed up for a meeting with Ash and me. She received the settlement offer from my lawyer, and expects Kent's ex-wife to accept it. That will clear the malpractice case and provide for his kids' future."

"That is definitely worth celebrating. So will Lorena be out of your life once and for all?"

Bryce chuckled. "A few weeks ago, I would have said yes, but she approached Clay with a job offer. Some sort of private investigator. I'm not sure if it's legitimate, or a way to figure out what's going on with these insurance payoffs to clear malpractice cases. I told him to be careful."

Val dipped a chip in queso and chewed it while pondering Bryce's answer. "Maybe this is a good thing. He can make sure she doesn't start looking into things."

"I think she may have a suspicion already. Before she left the meeting, she told me 'well played'. The good news is, I'm not sure she cares about things she's not getting paid to worry about."

"Lawyers," said Val after blowing a puff of air through pursed lips.

Chapter Forty-One

M ackenzie Hearst walked slowly down the softly carpeted
hallway of their home and knocked quietly on her mother's
door.

"Come in!" said her mother, prompting her to push the door
open and walk in.

"Oh, hi Mackenzie. Are you okay? I didn't know you were home."

"I've been home for a while. Can we talk for a bit?"

Marybeth sat up in bed and pulled the comforter down before
patting the mattress next to her. "Climb in bed with me and we'll
talk like we used to do when you were little. I miss those days."

Mackenzie settled in close to her mother and leaned against her
shoulder. "Mom, these last few weeks have been awful. I know what
I did, and Dad won't let me tell the truth about it. Even if I can beat
the charges, I don't think I want to. Does that make sense, or am I
just being stupid?"

Marybeth stroked her daughter's hair. "You're not being stupid,
honey; you're being responsible. You're a good person who had a
very unfortunate thing happen, with devastating consequences to
someone else. Your father won't let you control it, and you probably
feel you're just drifting in the wind."

"That's exactly how I feel. I can't hang out with any of my friends. When I do, it's just weird. I feel guilty for having a good time while I'm lying about what happens. It makes me feel like a bad person and I can't keep living like this. Can I just tell them the truth and accept whatever punishment I deserve?"

"Of course you can. The angst and guilt you feel is because you're a good person who's being forced by your father to do something out of character. What would you do if there was no one else involved?"

"I would call the prosecutor and tell them exactly what happened. I'd tell them Dad told me to lie and how awful I feel about it." She sighed and snuggled in toward her mother. "Maybe if I'm honest and remorseful, they'll go easy on me."

"We can have Vincent speak with the prosecutor again if you'd like and see what sort of plea bargain they could agree to. It would probably involve some prison time, but you're young and can probably put this behind you. I'll support you in whatever you decide. But, I'm curious. What spurred this conversation?"

"I just feel so bad for his family. They can't get closure because this is dragging out and they probably know I didn't hit him because of a sneeze. I saw Mrs. Jenkins interviewed on the news yesterday and she looked so broken. I could see it in her eyes. And I know it was me that–," Mackenzie started sobbing and took a moment before she could continue. "It was me that did that to her. I killed her husband and ruined her life." The sobbing progressed to wailing and Marybeth did her best to hold her daughter as she expelled the feelings that she'd been holding in for weeks.

After a few minutes, Mackenzie had recovered enough to speak again. "I know that ultimately it's my fault, but I blame Dad for a lot of what has happened since. I was still in shock and he told me to lie. What kind of father does that to his daughter?"

"One who thinks he can solve any problem through bribery, extortion, or intimidation. Your father cares deeply about you. He's just not a good person. I have some news of my own about a conversation I'd like to have soon."

Mackenzie rolled over and looked at her mom. "Yeah? About what?"

"I think it's time I divorced your father. He served his purpose in helping to raise you, but now you're grown up and making wise decisions despite his poor counsel. I think we'll both be better off if we're out from under his roof."

"Oh Mom, I'm sorry."

Marybeth laughed. "Oh honey, don't be. This marriage has been dead for years. It's beyond time I dust off this classic and get it back on the road."

"Dust off? You look great, Mom."

"Thanks dear. And guess what? You'll look even better when you're my age. As long as you don't get any prison tattoos."

Mackenzie laughed at her mother's attempt to lighten the mood. "I hope I won't be there long enough to be tempted."

Chapter Forty-Two

"Twelve cars? That's all we sold today?" yelled Charlie Hearst into his speakerphone.

"Yes sir, that's correct. Across every dealership. We haven't had a day that slow since the snowstorm two years ago."

"Damn it!" said Charlie, kicking his desk.

"Sir, I know I'm just your accountant, but this situation with the police officer is killing us. We get as many phone calls from people yelling at us as we do potential buyers. Our secretaries don't even want to answer the phones. The sales force is removing their employer's information from social media. We're on a bad trajectory here."

Charlie stood up and leaned forward on his desk. "You think I don't know that, you stupid sum'bitch? I'm going to head down to police headquarters and jerk a knot in their tail." He punched the phone unit to end the call and stormed out the back door of his office and into his Cadillac Escalade. Once he was on the road, he yelled to the wireless calling feature. "Call Chief Booker."

After a few rings, the chief answered the phone.

"You have a lot of nerve calling me right now, Charlie," said the chief.

"Look Sammy, we need to put this behind us. It's killing my business," said Charlie.

"My name is Chief Booker, and honestly, I don't give a damn about your business right now. Your family is killing my officers!" yelled the chief.

Charlie paused before replying in a softer tone. "I am truly sorry for that. You know I am. But we go back a long way. How much have I donated to your campaigns over the years? How many cars have I supplied your department at a minimal markup? Discounted repairs for your department's personal vehicles? Jobs for–"

"Yeah, you've done all of that. And then you accuse my officer of being drunk on the job and blame him for getting struck by your daughter. Are you trying to make a moral equivalency here?"

"No, Sammy, I'm not. Look–"

"I told you, it's Chief Booker. We're done here. I have no use for politics and will find a new supplier for our vehicles. You can keep your money and your favors. I'll see you in the courtroom at the preliminary hearing for your daughter. Should be any day now."

The call ended abruptly, leaving Charlie alone in the silence of his SUV. He yelled an expletive and began looking for a place to turn around.

Marybeth Hearst spread her towel on the chaise lounge and stretched out in the sun. Her wide brimmed straw hat negated the need for the oversized sunglasses, but her sense of fashion dictated they remain in place for appearance's sake.

She looked over at her friend and smiled. "Thank you for coming, Susan. I appreciate your friendship and support, especially right now."

"Are you kidding? I wouldn't miss this for the world!" Susan laughed and began removing the foil wrapper from the top of a bottle of champagne. "Go ahead; make the call."

"Okay, here I go."

Marybeth called Charlie and put pressed the button for speaker-phone when he answered.

"Not a good time right now honey, I just got off the phone with Sammy Booker. I think our friendship is over."

"Sorry to hear that, Charlie. Listen, I have a few things I need to say. Are you alone?"

"Just me and the road."

"Okay. Look, I talked to Mackenzie and Vincent, and they are going to negotiate a plea deal. She's going to admit to distracted driving in exchange for leniency at sentencing."

"What? We can beat this. She doesn't deserve a conviction on her record. She's nineteen!"

"Yes, she does, and she knows it. If she doesn't accept the consequences of her actions, it will start her down the wrong path in life."

"You can't do this. I won't agree to it."

Marybeth sighed. "Charlie, it's not up to you. Mackenzie is an adult, and it's what she wants to do. But that's just one thing I wanted to talk to you about."

"Great, what else ya' got for me?"

Marybeth looked at her friend and flashed a nervous grin. "I want a divorce, Charlie."

"No, Marybeth, don't do this. Not right now."

"It's been a long time coming, Charlie. I tolerated your behavior for all these years because Mackenzie needed her dad in the home. Now she's an adult and your behavior is negatively affecting her. So we're done. We can have Vincent draw up an agreement if you'd like, or I'll hire my own attorney."

"Where are you? Let's talk about this in person."

"I'm eating lunch at Iaria's downtown. I just ordered. Want me to add something for you?"

"Yes, get me whatever. I'll be there in half an hour."

"Fine, but I'm not changing my mind, Charlie."

She ended the call and turned to look at Susan, who was laughing uncontrollably.

"That restaurant is an hour away from here. Nicely done!" she said as she handed Marybeth a glass of champagne. "What should we toast to?"

"New beginnings."

The ladies clinked their glasses together before Marybeth drained hers in a single gulp.

Chapter Forty-Three

Vincent Leoni walked into the Marion County Prosecutor's office and signed the guest registry. A secretary asked who he was meeting with and then led him into a small conference room with a solitary window above a four-person table.

He sat down and opened his briefcase, setting a legal pad on the table in front of him, then leaned back in the chair and tried to prepare himself for what was to come. His legal abilities needed to be perfect to fight for the daughter of his friend and lover, while admitting wrongdoing. It would be a delicate balancing act of legal tight-rope walking.

The door opened quickly, and the Marion County prosecutor entered, interrupting Vincent's moment of reflection.

"Sorry to keep you waiting; it's been one of those days." He extended his hand toward Vincent, who had just stood up. "Derek Chappelle, Marion County Prosecutor. Good to meet you."

The two shook hands and then took seats opposite each other at the table.

"Thank you for meeting with me," began Vincent. "As you know, I am representing Mackenzie Hearst in the matter involving Officer Michael Jenkins."

Derek nodded and gestured for him to continue.

"You need to understand that her father is Charlie Hearst, the largest car dealer in central Indiana."

"That fact has nothing to do with anything, counselor. Justice is blind, remember?"

"You and I both know that, but he doesn't. But despite that, the fact remains and it has presented some challenges in representing Mackenzie."

"Such as?"

"Let's just say her father had a significant influence on her recollection of the facts from that morning."

The prosecutor leaned back in his chair and picked a silver pen out of his pocket. "Are you saying that Charlie Hearst lied to the detectives?"

"I'm not saying anything in particular. I'm simply giving you some back story into how we got to where we're at today. Mackenzie is a good person who feels terrible about having struck and killed the officer. She would like to discuss what you could offer in terms of a plea deal."

"A plea? We know she did it. She lied to us about it. And the victim is an upstanding member of the Indianapolis Metro Police Department. He left a widow and two children. Why should I offer her a plea? The city wants her convicted of anything I can make stick."

"Because she is sincerely sorry. She has stopped making videos on social media and is planning to become an advocate to educate youth about the dangers of distracted driving. She would have given the detectives a different story had her father not shown up that day in the Emergency Department. You can talk to the ER doc, Bryce Chapman. He'll tell you."

"No, I can't. He won't talk to us because their conversation is privileged."

"Mackenzie will waive her right to doctor-patient confidentiality. She wants this behind her. She wants closure for the Jenkins family."

"Vincent, why the sudden change?" The prosecutor dropped his pen onto the table and held his palm up in the air. "I have been trying to get a confession out of her for weeks to avoid this trial, and now you walk in and lay it out all out. What changed?"

"I have been asked to handle the divorce of Charlie and Marybeth Hearst."

"Woah, the king of car sales is losing his queen?"

"You could say that. They haven't exactly been sharing the same throne for quite some time."

"Fine, so what do you propose as a plea deal? She is facing one to six years in prison for reckless homicide. She needs to spend some time in prison. I can't present a deal to his family that doesn't include a period of incarceration."

"We understand that. I propose a one-year sentence, half of it suspended. She is eligible for early release after three months. Then she'll have one year of probation during which she must not use a phone while driving, or she finishes out the entire year in prison."

"Three months? She killed a police officer," said the prosecutor, shaking his head.

"By accident. She glanced at her phone while driving. No different from looking for something that fell on the floor while you drive. She's a good kid with a good heart."

The two lawyers stared at each other, letting the deal hang in the air.

Derek broke the silence with a sigh. "Fine. I'll talk to the officer's wife and see what she thinks about it. You realize this does not prevent a civil suit, right? I fully expect her to sue Mackenzie for wrongful death."

"She could do that, but I can assure you Mackenzie has no significant assets, and she owned the car outright. Marybeth Hearst has asked me to make contact regarding an out of court settlement that would save everyone the strain of a prolonged trial. Not to mention the legal fees."

The prosecutor stood up and replaced the pen in his pocket before extending a hand in farewell. "I'll let you know as soon as I hear. Good to meet you, Vincent."

Vincent Leoni stood up and returned the handshake. "You as well. Take care."

He made it to his car before calling Marybeth to update her on the situation.

"Vincent! How are you? We were just talking about you!". The words carried more excitement and energy than their normal phone calls, causing him to smile, close his eyes, and imagine the look on her face.

"I'm fine. Sounds like you are having a good time, too."

"Yes! Susan came over and we're just finishing a bottle of champagne."

"Oh yeah? What are you celebrating?"

"Just told Charlie that I'm going to divorce him. He thinks he's coming to meet me now, but I sent him to Iaria's. He doesn't know I'm sitting by the pool with Susan." She broke out into a fit of laughter.

"Iaria's? I'm five minutes from there. When did you talk to him?"

"Maybe ten minutes ago. You can probably beat him there if you wanted. How funny would that be? He thinks he's meeting me but walks in to find his lawyer sitting there?"

Vincent checked his mirrors and then swerved across two lanes of traffic to make a right turn. "I'm turning around now. Is there anything you want me to say?"

"Don't tell him we talked. I'm sure he'll have you write up the divorce papers. No need to tell him we're lovers."

"Well, it's quite a conflict of interest. I could get disbarred if he filed a complaint."

Marybeth pursed her lips and exhaled in a huff. "Oh please. You think he wants to invite the legal profession to look into his dealings? I'll be fair in what I am asking for. And I will get everything I want, too."

"Very well. I'll go have a glass of chianti and see what happens. Enjoy the day with your friend."

Chapter Forty-Four

"Can I have a bottle of your chianti, please? Two glasses," said Vincent.

"Yes, good choice. Will you be ordering food as well today?"

"Maybe just a basket of garlic bread. Wait, garlic cheese bread actually."

The waitress nodded and left to enter the order.

Vincent adjusted himself in the seat and hoped for a glass of wine in his system before Charlie showed up. He has been the Hearst family attorney for over twenty years and knew nearly every detail of Charlie's business dealings. While it's true that Charlie moved mountains to get Isabella back from those who kidnapped her, it's also true they only kidnapped her because of the business he was engaged in.

He had suffered for years watching Marybeth exist inside a fake marriage, bound by social appearances rather than love. Himself not pursing a relationship of his own, as the object of his desire was within arm's reach, but unable to be touched as he wished.

The waitress brought the bottle of chianti and filled two glasses, setting one in front of Vincent. "Who's the lucky person who gets to drink the other glass of wine?"

"My boss. I think you'll recognize him, but I'm not entirely sure he'll drink it. There's a decent chance it will end up on my suit."

She gave him a concerned frown. "Well, don't you worry. If there's any trouble, I'll get Angelo from the kitchen to help you out. He'll turn your boss into ground beef in seconds."

Vincent laughed and raised his glass in salute. "That's kind of you to offer, but I don't think it will come to that."

Charlie arrived a few minutes later and scanned the room, his gaze pausing when he recognized Vincent Leoni sitting in the corner with two glasses of wine. He strode quickly to the table and wasted no time in getting to the point.

"What are you doing here? Where's Marybeth? She told me to meet her here."

"She's not here. She told me you wanted to meet for lunch, so I am. I ordered a bottle of wine. Why don't you take a seat?"

Charlie pulled a chair out and then sat down. "She told you I wanted to meet for lunch? Why?"

"I figured you would be the one answering that question, not me. But I have news regarding Mackenzie."

"Yeah? What?"

"She wants me to broker a plea deal. She wants to admit fault and put this behind her."

"Absolutely not! My daughter will not be going to jail!" Charlie's shouted response drew glances from several patrons sitting at tables around them.

"Relax, this is not the place for you to lose control," said Vincent. "She's an adult, Charlie. She gets to make her own decisions. I just finished a meeting with Derek Chappelle and he is considering a plea deal. One-year prison term, six months of it suspended. She would likely be out after three months if she behaves herself."

"Three months in prison?" Charlie swore quietly and turned his head away from Vincent. "I just can't believe what's happened these last few weeks. A month ago, everything was fine. Now my business is falling apart, my daughter may go to jail, and my wife wants a divorce."

Vincent made a choking sound while swallowing his wine. "What did you say? Marybeth wants a divorce? When did that happen?"

"Just got off the phone with her. She told me I'm a bad influence on Mackenzie."

Vincent tried hard to not let his face reveal what he was thinking. *Well, let's see. You told her to lie to the police and not take responsibility for killing someone. You have cheated on her mom for the last fifteen years and are involved in many illegal activities. Can't say I disagree with her on this one.*

"Did she say how she wants to handle the divorce? Is there any hope for a reconciliation?"

"Right away. This ain't some hissy fit; I think she's finally done with me."

"I'm sorry to hear that, Charlie." *Would it be too awkward if I moved in right away, or should I wait until the divorce is finalized?*

"So if they accept the plea deal, there won't be a trial?" asked Charlie.

"That's correct. And we won't have to worry about the ER doctor testifying to what she said initially."

"Will they come after her for giving a false statement?"

"No, that would be part of the deal."

Charlie quickly finished his glass of wine and then refilled both of their glasses.

"Hey, that's my job," said the waitress, who had just walked up to the table holding a basket of garlic cheese bread. "Don't you know it's bad luck to change the person who pours wine from a bottle?"

"Lady, my luck can't get any worse than it is right now," said Charlie.

Vincent smiled to himself. *Luck? Or consequences of your actions?*

Charlie took a large drink of his second glass of wine and slumped into his chair. "Vincent, I'm tired. I've been runnin' like a fish lookin' for water."

"Yes sir, you have."

Charlie sat silently and stared forward for over a minute. His body was in the room, but his mind was a hundred miles away.

Vincent stared at Charlie and saw the defeat in his posture. A man who nearly single-handedly created the largest car empire in the state, yet in the process lost his friends, his daughter, and now his wife. Vincent considered he now viewed the man he once considered a friend. Empathy was too much to ask for. Pity required too much effort. Scorn seemed about right.

"Do you want me to draw up a divorce agreement?" he offered.

"Yeah. Make it an even split, if she'll go for it." Charlie stood up and pushed his chair back from the table. "And try to find a buyer for my business. It's time to liquidate before they become worthless."

Vincent sat in disbelief as Charlie turned and walked out of the restaurant.

"Your shirt still looks pretty good. Did things go okay?" asked the waitress after Charlie had left.

Vincent turned and smiled at her. "You know, it did. Much better than I expected."

"I'm happy for you. But Angelo will be disappointed. He was looking forward to stepping out of the kitchen."

"Sorry to disappoint him. Oh, can you add on a crème brûlée and a limoncello?"

"Now you're celebrating?"

Vincent finished his drink and sat it down close to the waitress. "Yes, I am. Been waiting ten years for this day."

Charlie rushed out to his car, his pace quickened by anger and fear. He dialed a phone number and listened until it went to voicemail. "Damn it! Answer your phone!"

He tried two more times, but it went unanswered. He then fired off a quick text.

> Plans have changed. No overtime tonight, just show up to work as usual tomorrow morning.

Shaun Kimball sat on his back porch, finishing his second beer of the afternoon. Normally, he didn't start drinking this early, but Mr. Hearst had given him the afternoon off to prepare for tonight's action.

He looked at the white Toyota FJ Cruiser parked behind his shed and laughed. "So many wasted cars. Damn government. They just about bankrupted us over that one."

He crushed the empty can and then threw it at the car, striking it on the hood. Reaching into the cooler next to him, he pulled out a third beer and popped the top open. His enjoyment of the fair weather and fresh air caused him to not notice the buzzing of a cell-phone ringing in his backpack on the kitchen counter.

He sipped his third beer and mentally planned how he was going to spend his earnings for the upcoming job.

"Sorry doc. It's just business," he said out loud to ease his conscience.

Chapter Forty-Five

Bryce arrived at the hospital early to check on his friend and patient. He entered the ICU and scanned the wall signs, looking for Paula's room number. The only time he went upstairs was to respond to a code, and usually he just followed a nurse to get there.

After a few wrong turns, he found himself in front of her room. She was sitting up in bed and talking to a man seated in a chair next to her. Bryce knocked on the frame of the door and entered when Paula saw him and waved her hand.

"Hey Paula, how are you doing?"

"So much better, Dr. Chapman. They told me what you did to diagnose and treat me so quickly." Her voice quivered, but she made it through the next line. "You saved my life."

The man sitting next to her stood up and leaned across for a handshake. "I'm Paula's husband. Thank you so much Dr. Chapman. She tells me stories about you all the time. It's so good to meet you."

Bryce shook his hand firmly and found a seat on the other side of the bed. "I just wish I had suggested you get the leg looked at more formally. You are so dedicated to your job that you're in that chair for almost twelve hours straight. You need to get up more and get the blood circulating."

"You're telling me. I'm just glad you were working that night. I don't know if anyone else would have picked up on what was happening so quickly."

"Oh, I bet they would. Maybe a minute or two slower, but they would have gotten there." Bryce added a wink to let Paula know he appreciated the compliment. "Are you breathing okay?"

"Yes, other than some soreness in my chest."

"Sorry about that. You had about ten minutes of CPR before you got a pulse back. I'm sure you have several broken ribs."

"It's much better than the alternative." She reached over and grabbed her husband's hand. "Doc, they told me about how you started everyone signing 'Hark the Herald Angels Sing'. Did you know that's my favorite song?"

"I did not. It's one of mine, too. I love when there's a trumpet or a whole brass accompaniment. The goose bumps hit instantly."

"Well, I feel like it has given me a second birth. That song it going to mean so much more to me from now on. Thank you, again."

"It was my pleasure. You are an integral part of the patient care team in the ER, Paula. I want you to take time to recover, but I would love to have you back in the trenches with us some day."

Her husband beamed at the compliment.

Paula nodded her head with resolve. "Oh, I'm coming back alright. I just need to get some healing in these wings first."

The three continued with small talk until a nurse interrupted for the one-hour vital sign assessment. Bryce leaned in and hugged Paula and shook her husband's hand again before heading back down to the ER.

Chapter Forty-Six

B ryce walked out of the hospital thirty minutes after his shift
ended and hopped into his Yukon for the trip home. He waited to call Valerie until he was past the commercial area and traffic had
thinned out.

"Hey, it's me. I should be home in about fifteen minutes. Are the
kids still up?"

"Hi, Dad!" came the reply of two children simultaneously.

"Hey guys, I see I'm on speakerphone. Are you getting ready for
bed?"

"Mom is reading us a story first."

"Oh, nice. I'll be home soon and will sneak in to give you guys a
hug. Did you have a good day today?"

Bryce smiled as he heard the children recount their activities of the
day. His focus on their words and the road ahead of him caused him
to not see the car run the red light behind him.

Shaun Kimball had been sitting in the white Toyota FJ Cruiser for
thirty minutes, waiting for the right vehicle to drive by. He waited in

the parking lot of an empty storefront holding a book visible above the dash. But his eyes were focused on the road rather than the words on the page.

Charlie Hearst had given him clear instructions to intimidate Bryce. To send a message, loud and clear, that cooperating with the prosecutor would be a bad idea for him and his family.

So Shaun sat in the car, waiting for the black GMC Yukon to pass by. After forty minutes and almost a dozen black Yukons, he saw Bryce drive past, his left hand held up against his head.

Gotcha.

Shaun pulled out of the parking lot and accelerated to catch up to Bryce. The traffic light ahead of him turned yellow, and he floored the accelerator, running the light by a full second. He checked his mirrors and saw no red or blue lights, or any other cars, for that matter. He scanned ahead and saw no traffic either, which brought a smile to his face.

Love me some quiet country roads. Get ready doc, you're about to have a bad day.

He pulled up into Bryce's blind spot and slipped a Halloween mask over his face. He double checked his seat belt was fastened and then accelerated until he was just even with Bryce's front bumper.

You may want to put that call on hold, doc.

He floored the gas pedal and served right as hard as he could. The front right panel of the FJ Cruiser smashed into the front left panel of the Yukon and both cars briefly dipped toward each other as they made contact. The lighter FJ Cruiser had momentum on its side and its wheels turned right, causing the Yukon to veer to the right. Bryce also reflexively steered away from the other vehicle, exaggerating the impact force of the FJ Cruiser.

Shaun kept the pedal to the floor and sped down the empty road as a cloud of smoke and screeching tires filled the space behind him.

"Kids, I'm off tomorrow. Do you want to invite some friends over and have a pool party? We can use the snow cone machine if Mom can find some syrup."

"Yes!" came two more excited replies.

"Bryce, don't get the kids wound up at bedtime, please."

"Sorry Val, I wanted them awake when I got home. I figured some excitement may help that. I'm ten minutes out. Need me to stop and–" Bryce cut his sentence off and switched to a yell as his car jerked to the right and his driver's window filled with a large white vehicle. He dropped the phone from his hand and jerked the steering wheel away from the impact, quickly rotating his car beyond a safe turning radius at highway speed.

His tires resisted the lateral force and skidded for a few feet before they caught traction and flipped the Yukon over like it hit a tripwire. The SUV flipped violently, smashing his phone and every free item in the car onto the ceiling. His Yukon made three complete rotations on its axis, finally coming to rest upside down and on the shoulder, facing the wrong way.

Chapter Forty-Seven

"Bryce!" screamed Valerie, jumping up off the bed. "Bryce, what happened? Are you okay?" She waited a few seconds before yelling his name again, but got no response.

"Mommy, what's wrong?" asked Noah, a look of terror on his face. "What happened to Daddy?"

"I don't know, I don't know!" she said as she dialed 911. The phone connected, and a recording informed her of extended wait times to speak with a dispatcher.

"Kids, get in the car, now." Noah was close behind her as she ran down the stairs with Hannah. She tucked the phone into her shoulder and grabbed her keys from the hanger by the garage door. She quickly strapped Hannah in as Noah secured himself in the booster seat before backing out of the garage and sped out of the driveway. A loud screech came from the undercarriage as her car slammed down off the curb.

"911, what's your emergency?" said a calm voice through the car's audio system.

"It's my husband, Bryce Chapman. He was just in a car accident, but I'm not sure exactly where. I think it's on US 31 South, just past the Worthsville Road intersection. He's driving a black GMC Yukon."

"Yes ma'am, we just received a report of that accident via an OnStar representative. We have police and EMS on the way as we speak."

"Oh thank God, where is he? Is he okay?"

"He is a mile south of where you guessed. The OnStar agent stated all airbags deployed, and he was wearing his seat belt. The car sustained significant damage, and they could not make contact with him."

"I will be right there. Let him know I'm coming if you're able to contact him." She ended the call and focused on the road ahead as well as the cross streets.

"Mom, you just missed a stop sign," said Noah from the back seat.

"I don't care!" screamed Valerie, failing to hold back her emotions.

Hannah began crying at the tone of her mom's voice and soon Noah joined in.

Val looked at the sky and said a quick, silent prayer. *God, please protect Bryce from injury and my children from my behavior.*

"I'm sorry kids, I didn't mean to yell. I'm just worried about your father. Please forgive me." She reached behind her and rubbed a leg of each child.

In a few minutes, she could see flashing blue and red lights on the road ahead. As she approached the scene, she could see the Bryce's Yukon was upside down and surrounded by police and EMS personnel. A firetruck was approaching from the north, its lights adding to the strobe effect and making it difficult to see.

Shaun Kimball continued down the road after smashing into Bryce and causing the Yukon to roll several times. Within a minute, the car was shaking violently and veering to the right. He pulled the car onto the shoulder and jumped out quickly. Instantly he saw that both right tires were flat, and the car was sitting on the rims. Looking back north, he could see fresh scratches on the road surface from the metal rims. Hansel and Gretel would have been proud of the trail he had left.

"Damn it," he said. "I need to get the hell out of here."

He jumped back in the car and drove half a mile on the shoulder until he came upon a county road heading into the woods. He made the turn and limped the car a hundred yards off the main road before parking it in the underbrush next to the road.

He pulled out his phone and to call Charlie and noticed numerous missed calls and texts, all from Charlie. Shaun shrugged and called him back. The call connected after the first ring.

"Thank you for finally calling. Did you get my messages? Abort mission. Mackenzie is going to take a plea deal. We don't need to intimidate the doc."

"Well, too late now. I just flipped his car over a few times."

"Son of a bitch! Why didn't you answer the phone?"

"You told me to call you when it's done, not to watch the line in case plans changed. That's a burner phone. I didn't expect anyone to call me on it."

Steven held the phone away from his head while Charlie screamed a rant of profanities. When the volume subsided, he put it back to his ear. "What's done is done. What we need to focus on is the current problem."

"Awe hell, what kind of problem? Did he die?"

"I sure hope not. The car flipped a few times, but those things are built like tanks. He's probably fine. The problem is my car. I lost two tires and I'm driving on the rims. I only made it about two miles away from the scene of the accident."

"Where is the car now?"

"It's stashed off some country road. We need to get a flat-bed tow truck out here or have someone bring me two tires. There wasn't even a spare on this one."

"Well, that car doesn't exist, remember? I'm an hour away. Do you know anyone close who can help you out?"

"Do I know someone with two extra tires that are the correct size and who is available at this time of night? No, I don't. We're going to have to get something from the dealership."

"I can't have anyone else involved in this. Stay where you are. I'll be there as soon as I can."

"Hurry, there are police coming from every direction."

Shaun heard the line go quiet and shoved the phone into his pocket. He walked into the woods far enough to where he could see the road and vehicle, but they could not see him. He hoped.

Chapter Forty-Eight

V alerie drove her Land Rover through the median and parked on the far shoulder, just beyond the emergency vehicles.

"Kids, stay here. I'm going to check on your dad."

She exited the vehicle and ran toward his car. She saw an EMT laying on the ground and stretched halfway inside the vehicle.

"Bryce!" she yelled as she reached the vehicle. "Is he awake?"

A police officer turned to face her. "Ma'am, we need you to stay back. Let the paramedics work on getting him out. Do you know the driver of this car?"

"Yes, he's my husband, Dr. Bryce Chapman. He's an ER doctor at Washington Memorial. I have our children in the car."

"He's breathing!" shouted the EMT from inside the vehicle. "He has a strong pulse, but it's fast. Probably about 130. He's suspended from the seat belt and his head is hanging free, not smashed against the roof. Hand me a C-collar." He quickly secured the collar around Bryce's neck and ensured that his airway was still open.

"Those are good things, ma'am," said the officer standing next to Val. "Is your husband the one running for coroner?"

Val nodded but couldn't speak. Her hands here clenched in front of her mouth, tears streaming down her cheeks.

The firefighters arrived and took control of the scene. At this point it was a rescue operation of an entrapped occupant, something firefighters are better trained for than paramedics and EMTs.

"How many victims? Is the ignition turned off?" asked the first one to arrive at the car.

"Solo occupant. He was belted in and airbags deployed. Looks like he rolled a few times. He is unconscious but has a pulse and is breathing. I don't see any obvious injuries," said the EMT who had crawled out from inside the vehicle.

A fireman laid down on the road surface and looked inside the vehicle. "I don't see or smell any fuel leaks and the ignition is off. I think the scene is safe to begin the extrication and get this poor guy to the hospital."

Val turned away at that last sentence. She pulled out her phone and called the number for the Washington Memorial Emergency Department, pressed nine for the secret menu bypass and soon was speaking to the secretary.

"Emergency Department, how can we help you?"

"This is Valerie Chapman, Dr. Bryce Chapman's wife. He's been in an accident. Can I talk to the doctor who's working now?"

"Yes ma'am, right away. I hope he's okay." The secretary placed the call on hold and, several moments later, the call was reconnected.

"Val, this is Tom. What happened? Is Bryce okay?"

"Oh Tom, I'm glad it's you working. I don't know. He was headed home and flipped his car several times on US 31. The car is upside down and he's still inside it. They are trying to figure out how to get him out. They can't see any injuries, but he's not awake."

"Oh no, that's terrible. Is he breathing? Does he have a pulse?"

"Yes, they said it looks like he's just asleep."

"Well, that's a good start. If he doesn't have outward injuries, hopefully he'll be okay. Significant internal injuries usually happen on deceleration injuries, like running into a concrete wall. My shift is over soon. Peter Thrasher is taking over, but I'll stay and help when he arrives. Who is watching the kids?"

"I have them with me. I'm going to have to bring them to the hospital with me."

"Okay. I'll call my wife and see if she'll take them back to your house if that's fine with you."

Val sighed audibly. "Oh, that would be wonderful, thank you."

"No problem. Just assume it will happen. If Rebecca doesn't answer, I'll call you back. Bryce is a tough man Val, he'll pull through this. We'll be praying for you guys."

Val ended the call and jogged back to the car. She found a female police officer standing next to it, trying to distract her kids with conversation.

Val interrupted to add, "Hannah, Noah, your dad is doing okay right now. They are trying to figure out how to get him out of the vehicle."

She nodded at the officer. "Thank you for thinking of my children through all of this."

"No problem, ma'am. I have a few of my own. I know this can be scary and confusing for them. We've been talking about my car and how loud the sirens are, and if I'm allowed to turn the lights on and drive as fast as I want."

Val heard a loud metallic pop and looked back at Bryce's car. Another pop followed quickly, and then the driver's door fell to the ground next to the vehicle. She thanked the officer again and walked back toward Bryce's upside-down SUV.

"Okay, let's get the rear hatch open and prepare for extrication. I need two backboards and a few extra hands. Someone get those rear seats out."

She watched as several firefighters set about the tasks at once. They opened the rear hatch, but it wouldn't quite lay flat. Two firemen jumped on it and the metal bent, allowing it to lie on the ground. On the sides of the vehicle, a firefighter removed the rear seat from both the passenger and driver side, creating more room to work inside.

Once the rear hatch was open, they went to the front of the vehicle and inserted a backboard sideways through the driver's and passenger's door. They lifted it up, so it was holding Bryce's thighs in place against the seat. A paramedic reached in to activate the seat adjustment system to lay the driver's seat as flat as possible. This allowed Bryce's weight to be held by the seat belt across his chest rather than his neck and positioned his body more flatly.

They slid a second backboard in through the rear hatch until it struck the steering wheel. Two people crawled in the passenger doors and got as close to Bryce as they could. One held his head and neck while the other cradled his chest.

"Ready for seatbelt release!" shouted one firefighter.

Another reached in with a seatbelt cutter and cut the lap belt, after which Bryce's legs rested on the sideways backboard. He then reached further in and cut the portion over Bryce's chest, which allowed his upper body to gently lower onto the second backboard, thanks to the strength of a firefighter crouched next to him.

Once he was flat on the board, they carefully dragged it out the rear hatch.

"Hey, careful," came a quiet voice from the rear of the vehicle.

"He just said something!" shouted a firefighter.

Val ran to his side and knelt next to the board. "Bryce, can you hear me? It's Val."

He opened his eyes and looked at her before giving a faint smile. "Yeah, I hear you. What happened?"

"You were in an accident, sir. Your car rolled over several times. We're going to take you to the hospital, but first we need to roll you over."

The paramedics took over and log rolled Bryce into a proper position on the board. They secured straps across his chest, hips, and legs to ensure he wouldn't move. Next, they added padded supports around his head and secured them to the board.

"Lift on three," said a paramedic before counting up, and then the group lifted the board off the ground. They set it down on a stretcher and secured it in place before pushing it toward a waiting ambulance.

"The kids," said Bryce. "Are the kids okay?"

"Sir, you were the only one in the car."

"Thank God. What happened?"

"We're not sure, but you flipped your car several times."

"I did? Are my kids okay?"

The paramedics glanced at each other when Bryce repeated the same question. "Let's get him out of here."

Val followed Bryce to the ambulance and kissed his forehead before they loaded him up, careful to avoid the pieces of glass on his skin and hair. "I'll be right behind you, Bryce."

Val watched the ambulance drive away and then turned back toward the SUV.

What happened, Bryce? Why did you flip your car?

She stared at the vehicle, trying to make sense of the situation. Both sides of the vehicle were destroyed, but the front and back of the vehicle were mostly intact. The crash busted out every window, and personal items were strewn about the road.

She bent down and looked inside the vehicle, scanning everywhere she could see.

There!

She knelt down and reached through the passenger compartment and grabbed the loop of a black cable. She pulled it toward her until she came to the micro-USB adapter on the end.

Damn it, where did you go?

She pulled out the flashlight on her phone and scanned deeper through the vehicle, not finding what she was looking for. She then stood up and walked around the vehicle before tracing its path back north along the road surface.

Her eyes locked on something shiny just inside the grass. She went over and picked it up, smiling at her good fortune.

Maybe we'll get some answers as to what happened.

"Ma'am, I'm going to have to ask you to hand that over. It's part of the evidence of this crash investigation," said an officer, holding out his hand. "If your husband had a dash cam, that video will help us figure out what happened."

"You're right, it will. And you can have it right after I make a copy. Our family has a history of losing important video evidence, and I will not let it happen this time." She jogged toward her car and jumped in the driver's seat, quickly pulling a U-turn through the median and heading toward the hospital.

Chapter Forty-Nine

"Washington Memorial, this is Medic 32. How do you copy?" The EMS radio blared its static-laden traffic through the doctor's workstation in the ER.

Tom had been waiting for the call and picked up the phone to respond. "This is Dr. Tom Sharpe. Copy clear, go ahead with your traffic."

"Hey doc, we're on our way with one of your partners. I believe you're aware of this patient?"

"Yes, I am. How is he doing?"

"He's awake now and doesn't have any obvious injuries. He's amnestic to the event but otherwise is following commands fine. Vitals are stable except for a heart rate of one hundred and twenty. We'll be there in five minutes. Do you request anything further?"

"No. We'll see you in Trauma Room One. Drive safe. Washington Memorial out."

Tom put down the phone and noticed a few nurses standing around him. "Well, I guess you guys know who's coming in. Send out a Trauma One alert."

"Doc, he doesn't meet Trauma One criteria. Are you sure you don't want to page it as a level two?" asked a nurse.

"He's one of ours. I want everyone here and ready to go if we find something." He looked at the team standing around him. "I'd do the same for any of you. Let's get the room ready."

He looked at the secretary and asked her to page Peter Thrasher to the trauma room.

The team quickly assembled in the trauma room and had everything in place when the medics rolled in with Bryce strapped to the backboard.

Tom noted the glass pieces covering his friend's body and clothing. He had a few small abrasions but overall there were no obvious injuries. The team picked up the backboard and moved him over onto the ER bed in one well-choreographed and practiced move.

"Hey Tom, how's your shift going?" said Bryce, staring up at his friend.

"It was over five minutes ago. You're keeping me here late. Extremely inconsiderate to my family, Bryce," said Tom before beginning his assessment. He quickly moved through Bryce's body and found no concerning signs of injury.

Peter arrived and grabbed the ultrasound, performing a quick focused exam to assess for potential internal bleeding. "Bryce, the ultrasound looks good. No fluid where it's not supposed to be, but it looks like you need to pee."

"Tell me about it. I was trying to wait until I got home. Glad I didn't piss myself in the accident." His face formed a confused expression and looked up at Tom. "I didn't piss myself, did I?"

"No, you didn't. Thank God."

"What's going on here?" said a feminine voice from the foot of the bed. "I was about to start a case when I got the trauma notification."

"Elisa, Bryce decided to come back rather dramatically after his shift ended. He rolled his car a few times, but I can't find any outward sign of trauma. Ultrasound was negative for fluid. We're about to pan-scan him."

She walked to the side of the bed and did a quick exam herself. "No sign of injury, yet you're going to CT most of his body? I thought you guys hated the trauma pan-scan?"

"He's one of ours. I don't want to miss anything," said Tom.

"Ah, but if he wasn't one of yours, it would be fine if you missed something?" Elisa let the words hang in the air before smiling and continuing. "Just messing with you. But see? The American College of Surgeons recommends these scans in trauma patients because it's poor form to miss things. Even if it's an insignificant finding, it's important to document all the injuries."

Peter turned around before his eyes rolled back in his head. Half the nursing team saw the move and tried to conceal their smiles.

"Did anyone do the rectal exam yet?" asked Elisa. "We need to make sure his spinal cord is intact."

"Hang on, I promise you it's fine," said Bryce. "Let's skip that and get me off the backboard."

"Are you refusing care?" asked Elisa. "Someone please document that the patient is refusing our recommended care. I don't want to get sued later."

"Elisa, come on. This is our colleague on the table. Knock it off," said Tom.

"Oh, relax. You told me you don't see any injuries. He's going to be fine. You know as well as I do the CT scans will show nothing. I'm trying to lighten the mood. Your faces look like Bryce only has minutes left to live."

Tom sighed and nodded in agreement. "Okay, fine. Will you help us roll him off the backboard?"

The team logrolled Bryce off the board and removed some glass that was underneath him. They raised the head of the bed up a bit, allowing him to sit upright, though he still had the cervical collar on.

"We're ready in CT if you want to bring him over," said the radiology tech from the doorway.

A nurse unlocked Bryce's bed and prepared to move him.

"Wait, where's Val?" he said.

"She's not here yet," said Tom. "Rebecca is on her way in and is going to take your kids back home. She can spend the night and however long it takes until you guys can go home."

Bryce smiled before his lips trembled and the emotion of the events overcame him. Tears filled eyes and then ran down his face to fill his ears. He brought his right hand up to wipe them away, but Elisa grabbed his wrist.

"Wait. Don't do that. Your hand is covered in glass." She pulled a 2x2 gauze from her pocket and ripped it out of the package. She then used it to dab the tears and dry his ears before he went to the CT scanner. "Bryce, you're going to be fine. Your family is fine and will be here any moment."

"Thanks, Elisa. I truly mean that." He tried to turn to face her as he completed his statement, but the collar restricted his movement. A minute later, he was on the CT table staring at the spinning unit inside the chassis.

Chapter Fifty

Valerie entered the ER waiting room, carrying Hannah and holding Noah's hand. The triage nurse stepped around the desk and met her.

"Are you Mrs. Chapman?"

"Yes, I am. Where's my husband?"

"He's in the back. Can I take you to the quiet room first? The chaplain is there and can watch your children if you'd like while you see him."

"That would be great, thank you."

They walked through the short hallway and entered the quiet room, where the chaplain introduced himself to Valerie and the kids. He had a coloring book and some crayons, and did his best to distract the kids while Val exited the other door to the department.

"Right this way, Mrs. Chapman," said a nurse as she led Val through the hallways toward the trauma rooms. "If he's not in the room, he's probably in the CT scanner and should be back soon. I heard Dr. Sharpe say he could not find any injuries on your husband other than some scratches. We're all hoping he does well."

Val nodded her thanks but followed quietly behind the nurse. Soon they arrived in a trauma room and found it missing its bed and patient. Bryce's clothing sat on a table along with his phone, watch, keys, and wallet.

"Looks like they're still in CT. I'll stay with you until—"

The doors popped open, and the trauma team returned with Bryce. He was sitting up in bed, but still had the cervical collar in place. He saw Val standing in the room and raised his hand to wave.

"Hi, honey."

Val waited for his bed to be locked in place before leaning down to give him a hug.

"How are you doing?" she asked.

"I have a headache and am sore, but overall, not too bad. Do they have any idea what happened yet?"

"No." She reached into her pocket and removed the dash cam. "But I found your dash cam on the side of the road. The police wanted to take it, but after what we went through the last time we lost a memory card, I wasn't about to let this get away without making a copy."

Bryce smiled at his wife. "That's my girl. Always thinking."

During their trip to the Bahamas earlier in the year, Bryce had lost the GoPro camera that was mounted on his head after they successfully resuscitated Tony. It contained personal videos and the footage showing that Bryce was not the instigator of the event, but Tony Proffit. A college student from Duke found the camera on a trip the next day and tried to extort Bryce for half a million dollars to not release the private videos to an adult website.

Val helped identify who the student was and, once they found where he lived, Bryce had driven down with Tom Sharpe and recovered the memory card through a physical confrontation.

"Is there somewhere we can make a copy of this before I turn it over to the police?" asked Val.

"Let me see if the CT techs have any spare thumb drives. They put images on them now for patients who are being transferred out of our system," said Tom before exiting the room.

"Where are the kids?" asked Bryce.

"They're in the quiet room with the chaplain. Rebecca Sharpe is going to take them back to our place until you are ready to be released. How many days do you think you'll be in the hospital?"

"Days? I think you mean hours. Once my scans are back, I want to get out of here and find out what happened. I honestly feel okay other than a headache and some nausea. Probably just a concussion."

Tom returned and informed them the CT techs can create a copy of the dash cam footage if they would like.

Val handed him the memory card and thanked him.

"Bryce, I got a call from the radiologist. So far, your head and neck CTs are negative. Do you want to get that collar off?"

"Absolutely," he said, reaching up and unstrapping the Velcro.

"Hang on a minute. You know that's not how this works." Tom held his friend's head steady and helped him through a gentle range of motion test, asking if the motion caused any increase in pain.

"Tom, I'm telling you, I'm fine. That Yukon is built like a tank. I'm going to have to get another one."

"I'll be right back with the copy of your card."

Tom excused himself, and then it was just Bryce and Val alone in the room.

"Bryce, do you think someone caused this? Charlie Hearst was pretty clear in his threat to you about testifying," she said.

"I suppose it's possible. I drive home that way all the time and there's nothing that would make me swerve. It's a flat highway straight through cornfields."

"You should talk to your detective friend. Have him look into it and see if he can find anything."

"Let's look at the video first. After I get out of here."

Tom returned a few minutes later along with one of the police officers who was at the scene of the accident. Val received a stern lecture about taking evidence from the scene as she handed over the memory card. The officer interviewed Bryce but learned little, as he couldn't remember anything about the accident.

The officer concluded the interview with a personal comment. "Dr. Chapman, we need you to bounce back quickly. You have an election you need to win next week."

"I should be good to go in a few days. I appreciate the support of you and the rest of your department."

"Don't mention it." The officer reached into his jacket and removed something, holding it out toward Bryce. "If you're going to win, you need your good luck charm."

Bryce reached out and took the item from the officer and held it up. "My bobble head! Where did you find it?"

"It was lying on the floor of your car. Well, the roof, I guess. He's a bit dinged up but not too bad, considering what he went through."

"That makes two of us. Thanks again, officer."

The officer nodded and walked out of the room, holding the door for Peter, who was just about to pull it open himself.

"Hey Bryce, I got the good news from the radiologist. The rest of your CT scans are essentially normal. How do you feel?"

"Not my best day, but I think I'll be fine. I'd like to get up and walk."

Tom and Peter each lowered a rail a side of the bed and helped Bryce sit on the edge. He looked at Val and smiled. "Want to take a walk?"

"I think Peter should spot you instead. If that goes well, I'll help walk you out."

Bryce slid off of the bed and onto his feet. He wavered for a moment, but then steadied and could walk around the room with Peter close by to assist if needed.

"I think I'm good. Can we get out of here? I don't need any discharge instructions."

"Please take it easy, Bryce. We'll get your shifts covered for a few days. You're probably not going to be able to do much for the next forty-eight hours. Go home and rinse all that glass off of you," said Tom.

The chaplain poked his head around the curtain and waited for an opening in the conversation before speaking. "Doctor Chapman, Mrs. Sharpe is here to take your children, but I heard you might go home soon. What do you want me to tell her?"

"Can you bring the kids in here? I'd love to see them."

The chaplain agreed and returned shortly with the children. They looked tired but perked up when they saw their father. The kids waved at Bryce but stayed close by Valerie, nervous to approach their father in an unfamiliar situation.

"It's okay kids, I'm fine. Can I get a hug?" said Bryce as he held his arms out wide.

Val placed her hands on their backs and encouraged them to walk over to the bed.

Bryce embraced his children as Val looked on with a nervous smile. "I'll go pull the car around. Meet you out front?

"Yeah, we'll be there, thank you." He asked the nurse who had just removed his IV if she could bring in a wheelchair, which was quickly brought to the bedside.

He lifted each child and placed them next to each other on the chair, and pushed them out of the room.

The nurse whispered to Bryce as he passed. "Nice move. You get a rolling walker for support and they think you're just giving them a ride."

Bryce hushed her quietly. "Don't give away all my secrets."

Chapter Fifty-One

Both kids fell asleep shortly after leaving the hospital. Val drove carefully and tried to take turns gently to ensure they stayed asleep.

"Do you want to drive by the scene, or take a different way home?" she asked.

"I want to see it. You guys keep telling me what happened, but I have absolutely no memory of it."

Soon they pulled up to the scene of the accident where a fire truck and crew remained to assist in the cleanup. A flat bed tow truck had rolled the Yukon back onto its tires and was dragging it onto its bed.

Bryce gave a low whistle. "Wow, that car is absolutely destroyed. How did I survive that? And what happened?"

"I don't know, Bryce. I'm just glad you did."

"All of my work gear was in that car. I'm going to need a new stethoscope before my next shift."

Val shook her head and slapped him on the leg. "Would you stop worrying about work for a minute? You almost died."

"'Almost' is the key word in that sentence. Since I didn't, I get to keep working. Just the facts of life. Let's get home and watch the dash cam video. Maybe it caught something."

They passed the accident and then continued on toward home. A few minutes later, they saw flashing lights down a side road in a thickly wooded area.

"Lots of action for the police tonight," said Valerie. "I wonder if it's another accident."

"Strange place for an accident. Maybe a drunk driver or a kid speeding?"

When they arrived home, Bryce got out of the car and opened one of the rear doors. He undid the seat belt for Hannah and tried to lift her up before wincing and drawing back.

"It's okay, I can carry them in. You should shower and clean up," said Val.

Bryce agreed and went straight to their guest shower in the basement. He took much longer than usual as he rinsed the dried blood and glass off the best he could.

Once finished, he looked at himself in the mirror while he dried off. *You have got to pay more attention, idiot. What if the family was in the car?* He wrapped himself in a towel and headed upstairs, finding Val in their bed with her face illuminated by the laptop screen.

"Hey, do you feel better?" she asked.

"Yes, much. Are you pulling up the video?"

"I actually watched it once already. You sure you're up for watching this?"

"Why? Do I look stupid on it or something?"

"No, just wondered if it was too much to handle right now."

"I'm an ER doc. We just keep rolling with the punches."

"Yeah, but usually you're not inside a car while rolling."

Bryce grimaced at that comment. "Well played." He eased himself into the bed and leaned toward the laptop. "Show me what you got."

She advanced the video to just before the accident and hit play. Bryce heard his voice as they talked on the phone and then saw a white vehicle smash into the front left side of his SUV. The camera angle dipped down as the car slowed quickly from the impact, and then veered right as Bryce reacted to pull his vehicle away from the other.

What happened next left him speechless. As the car began to roll, all the windows shattered and broken glass floated in the air. The camera lost its mount when the windshield vaporized and then it twisted around, recording what its lens saw, in 4K quality video. Bryce saw his head and upper body pulled far to the right as the car continued to roll left. Then the video ended abruptly.

They both stared at the screen for a few seconds before Val spoke first.

"That must have been when it unplugged itself. I found it on the side of the road behind your car."

"Who was driving the other car? It looks like they swerved into me on purpose."

"That's what I thought too. Hopefully, the police can piece something together. Let's worry about that tomorrow. For now, we should say some extra prayers and get to sleep. We have a dinner date coming up soon."

Val set the laptop on the floor and rolled over to face Bryce. She cuddled up to his side and put her hand on his chest. "You're not allowed to leave this family yet, Bryce."

Chapter Fifty-Two

"Thanks for letting me know. I appreciate it." Detective Stephenson hung up the phone and leaned back in his chair.

"Hey Brett, you'll never guess what that call was about."

Greg's partner spun around in his chair and held his arms out. "You're right, so why don't you just tell me?"

"It was the report on the car we found in the woods near the Chapman rollover. We already knew it was probably the car that slammed into him and caused the accident, but they found something unexpected."

"Greg, quit pretending to be a suspense writer and just tell me what they found."

"Hey, I'm not pretending anything. I finally finished the outline of my novel."

"Yeah? What's it about?"

"It's about this badass cop who solves cases despite working next to a complete moron who continually distracts him from what he's trying to do."

Brett laughed and threw a paper clip at his friend. "Any similarities to actual persons or events are purely coincidental, though, right?"

"Obviously. Anyway, it turns out the car doesn't exist. They recorded it as destroyed in the Cash for Clunkers program a few years ago."

"So how does it end up running a doctor off the road in the middle of the night?"

"That's where it really gets interesting. Guess which car dealer accepted it in trade for the program?"

"Hearst?"

"Exactly. The same guy whose daughter was treated by this doc the day she killed Jenkins."

"So why would someone cause a significant accident and then dump the car right down the road?"

"I don't think they planned to. When we found the car, it had both passenger tires shredded and sitting on its rims. There is a nice trail of scraped asphalt leading right to the car."

"So, who was driving it?"

"That's what we need to figure out. Looks like I'll be taking a trip to see Charlie Hearst soon."

"Maybe run that by Chief Booker. I heard they had a falling out the other day. He may want to be involved in the interview."

"Thanks, I will."

"Chief?" Greg Stephenson knocked on the door and peered around the open door.

Chief Booker looked up from his computer and waved the detective in. "What is it?"

"Update on the accident involving Dr. Chapman from last night, sir. We recovered the vehicle that was involved in the collision. It has damage matching what we would expect based on the impact seen in the video."

"Very good. Nice work, detective." The chief looked back at his computer and continued typing.

"Sir, there's more. The BMV database listed the vehicle as destroyed a few years ago in the Cash for Clunkers program. It shouldn't have even existed. Hearst Automotive is the company who accepted the car in trade and certified the destruction."

The chief leaned back in his chair and folded his hands behind his head. "You don't say."

"I got a warrant for Charlie Hearst's phone records and found he received a call five minutes after the doc's wife called 9-1-1. It came in from a number registered to a burner phone."

"I think I am going to like where this is going."

Detective Stephenson smiled and continued. "Hearst's phone began pinging different towers within minutes. He drove toward one of his dealerships, where he stayed for about fifteen minutes, and then headed toward the scene of the accident."

"But he never made it, did he?"

"No. He received another phone call from that number a few minutes after our deputies spotted the car stashed in the woods. He turned around and headed straight home."

"So whoever tried to run Dr. Chapman off the road was by the vehicle when we found it and warned Hearst."

"That's what we think happened, yes. I was planning to drive out there and interview him. Brett thought I should loop you in on this one."

"He's right," said the chief, standing up from his desk and tossing his keys to Greg. "My car; you drive."

Detective Stephenson pulled the chief's Tesla into the long asphalt driveway of the Hearst estate and stopped at the gated entrance. He pushed the visitor button and announced Chief Booker was here to see Charlie Hearst. A few seconds later, the gate began sliding sideways and soon was open far enough to drive through.

As they neared the house, Charlie Hearst jogged out the front door and lifted a finger up, signaling the officers should wait a moment. He continued toward his Escalade, parked at the base of the front steps, and climbed into the driver's side.

"Pull around the other way and stop in front of him. I want to see what's inside his car," said the chief.

Stephenson pulled the wheel left and went around the circle drive the other way, stopping across the driveway and blocking the Escalade's path.

Charlie smacked his steering wheel and rolled his window down before leaning out. "Hey, what are you doing? I need to put my car away and then we can chat."

"Just leave it in park. Try to get a look inside the vehicle," said the chief as he opened his door and exited the vehicle. "We'll be quick, Charlie. I wanted to chat with you about something that happened yesterday."

Stephenson walked up to the passenger side of the and tapped the glass window. Charlie looked over and pushed the button to open it. "What can I do ya for?"

"There was a terrible accident last night. Someone sideswiped a car, and it ended up rolling several times, sending the driver to the Emergency Department."

Charlie leaned back from the window and whistled. "That's terrible to hear. I hope he was okay."

"He?" said Stephenson. "How did you know who we're referring to?"

"The driver whose car flipped. Just picked a pronoun. It's how people talk. Hopefully, the car was one of mine; I only sell high-quality vehicles."

"Actually, both vehicles involved were yours," said Chief Booker. "The driver who flipped his car is Dr. Bryce Chapman, the doc who took care of Mackenzie that day in the ER. Strange coincidence, wouldn't you say?"

Charlie adjusted himself in the seat and shifted his gaze between the two officers.

"The craziest part about it though," said Stephenson, "was the car that caused the accident was listed as destroyed several years ago. Hearst Automotive received it as a trade-in and certified it as destroyed to get the Cash for Clunkers credit. So how does a car that you supposedly flattened, rise from the scrap heap and nearly kill an ER doctor who is about to be subpoenaed to testify in the prosecution of your daughter?"

Charlie's breathing had become quicker and audible over the engine noise, but he didn't answer.

Chief Booker leaned on the car door and looked Charlie in the eye before nodding his head in the direction of the rear of the car. "Last question. Do you always drive around with two spare tires in the back of your car? What are the odds they would fit a Toyota FJ Cruiser?"

"I'd like you two off my property until you have a warrant."

"That's fine; we're finished anyway," said Stephenson, leaning away from the Escalade. "Oh, one more thing. When you use a burner phone to communicate with your hired goons, you need to buy two of them, you cheap bastard. You made it really easy to figure this all out. Have a great day."

The officers turned and walked back to their car and then reversed away from the Escalade before heading down the driveway.

The chief looked at Stephenson and grinned. "Well, I'd say that went well." He pulled out his cell phone and scrolled through the contact list until he found the one for the prosecutor. "Time to loop Derek Chappelle in on this."

Chapter Fifty-Three

"Police just released video of an incredible car accident last night involving Dr. Bryce Chapman, the ER doctor running for coroner. Officers believe the white vehicle seen here struck Dr. Chapman's car intentionally, causing it to roll several times, and sending the doctor to the very hospital he works at. A hospital spokesperson confirmed Dr. Chapman was evaluated and released last night. Police are asking for any information you might have as to the motive of this intentional act, and if you saw the vehicle in question, a white Toyota FJ Cruiser. The question we have is why would someone intentionally sideswipe him on his way home? Could this be about the upcoming election? Tune to the news at six o'clock tonight for answers."

"Yes! Perfect!" Steven Harris yelled at his television while standing in the kitchen. He grabbed the remote control and clicked through several local news channels. They were all running video of the crash, along with reporters discussing what it might mean. "You cannot buy better coverage than that." He took his coffee mug with him to the screened-in porch and dialed Bryce's phone number.

"Bryce? It's Steve Harris. I just saw your video on the news. Did the police release that to help your campaign?"

"I have no idea; I just woke up. Val's here. Let me put you on speakerphone. Which channel did you see it on?"

"It was on literally every local news channel. Do you know how many voters just saw that video and were told someone probably doesn't want you to win bad enough to try to take you out? That's fantastic!"

"Excuse me, you're saying it was a good thing that someone almost killed my husband? How can you say that?"

Steve smiled and shook his head. *Amateurs.*

"Relax. I'm paid to consider the political side of everything. Of course I don't want any harm to come to Bryce. Since they released him last night and is at home now, I assumed he's free of any major injuries. Is that correct?"

"Yeah, I'm okay. Just stiff and sore. Do you think this will help my chances in the primary?"

"Absolutely. You were polling behind Zac Pullard by about fifteen points last week. It wouldn't surprise me if this puts you over the top. I'm talking about an outright win in the primary. The other candidates are not drawing much attention and shouldn't be much of a factor. You're running on a platform of improving accountability in government and someone tries to take you out. Who wouldn't support the person who others are afraid to allow to win?"

"I hope so. I need to win this election."

"Then what are you doing in bed? Election is in two days. Get out there and milk this for all it's worth. Hell, maybe even put on a cervical collar and get interviewed by a few TV stations."

"I'm not going to fake injuries to gain the sympathy vote. I'd rather give the appearance of being unbreakable."

"Hey, that works too. The point is, you need to be seen by as many people as you can after this accident."

"I'm going to be cycling through the largest polling locations on election day."

"Okay, I hope that's enough. You're the one with something on the line. Good luck, doc." Steve ended the call and took a drink from his coffee before spitting it back into the cup. "He'd better win this. Already cost me a cup of coffee."

Chapter Fifty-Four

"You about ready?" asked Bryce.

"I am, but are you sure we should do this? It's been less than forty-eight hours since you rolled your car a few times. Would you rather stay in tonight?"

"No, I'm good. Getting out will make me feel more normal again. But I'd like you to drive if that's okay."

"Sure, though I can't put my makeup on in the car, so you need to give me a few minutes," said Valerie. "I'm still nervous. This is going to be awkward, isn't it?"

"Yeah, probably. But we need to get Peter and Emily together in a way that didn't seem too obvious. Who doesn't like a nice dinner out with friends?"

"Is she your friend, though? I thought she is the one allegedly sabotaging the department with expired products and dead animals?"

"I don't comment on your friends, Val. It comes across as rude."

Valerie laughed as she walked toward the garage. "Please, if any of my friends are playing with dead animals, I'd like you to say something to me. What's her vibe, anyway? They have dated for a while and she's been his scribe, but does she have other career aspirations?"

Bryce called upstairs to the kids, who came running for a quick goodbye hug. The grandparents had a fun night of board games and movies planned for them.

He continued their conversation while Val started the car and headed toward the restaurant. "She was pre-med in college and has been trying to get admitted to medical school for several years now. Her scores were decent, on the low end of the usual range, but close enough to where she should have gotten in somewhere."

"If her grades aren't the problem, then what is?" asked Valerie.

"I think you'll see what you meet her. The interview seems to be where she loses points."

Peter parked his Maserati Levante Trofeo in the parking lot of Emily's new apartment and sent her a text. Two minutes later, she exited the building wearing a yellow sleeveless dress, hanging just shy of her knees. She wore her hair pulled back in a loose ponytail with her eyes obscured by oversized sunglasses. Peter whistled. *Why did I break up with her again?*

She pulled the door open and climbed in, filling the car with the light scent of perfume. "Thanks for picking me up. It's a shame you never took me out when we were actually dating. We had to break up in order for you to ask me out. How stupid is that?"

Peter chuckled. "Oh yeah, that's why."

Emily looked at him, confused. "What does that mean?"

Oh, nothing. "Sorry, just thinking back about something. Tonight's not really a date, just some friends getting together for dinner downtown and trying to blow off some steam. This QCC thing really has everyone on edge. Then Bryce gets run off the road, and it's high time for a normal evening out."

Emily opened her purse and pulled out a container of Chapstick. She looked at Peter as she applied it and then kissed her lips together. "Let's not rule things out just yet. Who knows, maybe we'll have a great time and it will turn into a date after all." She took off her platform shoes and rested her feet on the leather dash. "Gosh, I love this car. Remember all the fun times we had in it?"

Peter tried to remind himself tonight was only about trying to get invited back to Emily's apartment and searching for clues to whether or not she was behind the sabotage at the hospital. *Surely it can't be this easy, can it?*

They arrived at the restaurant and pulled up to the valet podium. Peter handed the keys to a fresh-eyed teenager, excitedly looking at his car. "Go easy buddy, it's still pretty new."

"Yes sir! I'll take great care of it," said the kid as he handed Peter a claim ticket and climbed into the driver's seat. Peter watched him take a quick selfie before driving around the corner to the valet lot.

He offered his arm to Emily, and they walked into the restaurant.

"Peter, you're just in time! The hostess told me our table is ready," said Bryce. "Emily, glad you could make it. This restaurant is fantastic. Have you ever been here?"

Emily smiled and shook her head. "No, I never have. But I've seen the cocktail sauce in the grocery stores. I hear it's pretty strong."

"It's the best decongestant I know," said Valerie.

The group followed the hostess past a century-old wooden bar that has hosted countless celebrities over the years. They navigated through narrow carpeted walkways between tables until the hostess stopped at one in the middle of the restaurant. She held the chair for Valerie, and Peter did the same for Emily.

"This should be a fantastic meal. I needed to get out of the hospital and it's been too long since Val and I have been on a date night."

"Tell me about it. Peter never really took me out, but this is a nice change. At least I get to meet you, Mrs. Chapman," said Emily.

"Please, call me Valerie. And Bryce hates being called doctor when he's not in the hospital. And just call him Bryce."

"Okay, thanks. Do you work outside the home, Valerie?"

"Not really. Since having the kids, I decided to stay home with them. I have a degree in mechanical engineering and have recently started dabbling with a 3D printer and selling some stuff online. I really enjoy having a creative outlet and the kids love watching items appear from a roll of plastic. It's like magic to them."

"She made a bobble-head with my face and even painted it. Looks amazing," said Bryce.

"Really? I would love a bobble head of myself," said Peter. "Can you make it so it only shakes its head no? I can leave that at my workstation for whenever nurses come up with a request."

The waiter arrived and interrupted the conversation. The four ordered drinks and their meals at the first interaction, a side effect of working in the ER where there often isn't time to even have a meal, let alone order each course at separate times.

"Emily, what are your career aspirations? Are you looking to go into the healthcare industry?" asked Valerie. She noticed Peter wince upon hearing the question.

"I used to think so. For a while I wanted to go to medical school but have recently given up on that idea. I spent three years applying and for whatever reason, I just didn't get accepted. It sucks, because I already know about as much as some doctors I've scribed for. I know I can do it. Anyway, now I think I'm going to go just find a guy and get married, then coast along on his coattails."

Valerie smiled back at Emily and chose her words carefully. "Well, that is certainly one way to do it. I made a conscious decision to be there for my children and gave up a promising career in order to do it. Excuse me, I'm going to hit the bathroom." She stood up, picked up her phone, and walked toward the rear of the restaurant.

"Emily, come on. That wasn't very nice. You just met her," said Peter. "Val's a good woman who works hard for her family."

"Yeah, let's talk about something else when she gets back, okay? The two of us have been known to defend our family rather aggressively."

Peter laughed out loud at that comment. "That dweeb in the Bahamas sure found that out."

"What dweeb in the Bahamas? I saw the video of you saving someone, Bryce. Is that who you meant?" asked Emily.

"Did you not hear that story? Yeah, that guy was drunk, being very aggressive with Valerie, and I had to step in to keep him and his friends away from her. He tried to punch me but missed. I pushed him away with my foot and then we both got out of there. When he tried to give chase, he got stuck under water and drowned. His drunken behavior nearly cost him his life."

Valerie returned to the table and sat down. She ran her hands through her hair and out a sigh. Sorry about that. What are we talking about?"

"Bryce was telling the story of the drunken douche that you both saved. Didn't you get a free week at an island paid for by his father for saving him?"

"Yes, we did. We really need to get that booked, Val. Who knew someone's stupid behavior could get us a free private island for a week?" said Bryce, lifting his drink up in a toast to his wife.

"What about your captain running into their boat first? Do you think that could have started everything off on the wrong foot?" said Emily.

Valerie turned to Emily with a quizzical expression. "That's not what happened. We were on the mooring ball when the other boat ran into the back of ours. Everyone on the other boat was drunk. But they sure sobered up quickly when we started CPR on Tony."

"Oh, okay. I didn't know," said Emily. She smiled and put a pleasant tone in her voice. "Are you planning to bring your kids with you on the trip or just adults?"

"Definitely the whole family. We decided to stick together for family trips for a while. When Val and I went to Exuma alone, bad things happened. Then she spent some time at her parents' house in Florida and I didn't like that very much. So for now, we're all in it together."

Dinner progressed amicably through the appetizer and main course, and then the waiter brought out the desserts. Four steaming hot chocolate lava cakes.

"You know what goes great with chocolate lava cake?" asked Emily. "A chocolate martini!" She flagged the waiter down and ordered another drink. The bottle of pinot noir she split with Peter had left her wanting a bit more.

"Do you guys think there's going to be an issue with the next QCC visit? Is it coming up soon?" asked Valerie. "I'm sick of how stressed out Bryce has been about it. Will they really shut down the whole ER?"

"I doubt it, but that has certainly happened before. It takes a pretty egregious problem for them to do that since it impacts so many patients. Finding a few dead rats doesn't help, and the expired products make them worry we are risking patient safety."

"If you ask me, there shouldn't be expiration dates on products. Does a plastic syringe really go bad?" said Peter.

"I bet it's the actual package it's in. Maybe it's only considered sterile for so long because the package breaks down?" said Emily.

"That's probably it," said Peter. "I'm gonna hit the bathroom, be back in a few."

"Actually, I'll join you. It's a half-hour ride home," said Bryce, standing up from the table.

"Now that the men are gone, how are things between you and Peter? You seem to get along well enough tonight. Is there a chance you'll get back together?"

"There's always a chance, I suppose, but I think I'm ready for a change. He's been a lot of fun, but I don't think he's marriage material, you know?" said Emily.

"I thought the same way about Bryce. Eventually, I realized having fun was a big part of marriage and I embraced it. Haven't looked back since."

Emily nodded and took a big drink from her martini.

"Well, how do you think things are going?" asked Bryce as they walked towards the bathroom.

"Fine, I think. She showed up dressed to impress and hasn't been shy about the alcohol consumption. It's like she's not worried about making any decisions. I supposed that could be bad or good, depending on what she's thinking. Or maybe she already decided how tonight is going to go."

They entered the bathroom and saw two classic floor-length urinals without a divider between them. "You go ahead," said Bryce, "I only came here to talk to you, anyway."

"You can tell this is an old restaurant. I mean, who puts two urinals close together like that anymore? Last thing I want is some guy asking me what model watch I'm wearing while I take a leak," said Peter.

Bryce laughed. "Nope. Eyes forward, no talking. Whatever you do, man, just don't screw her tonight, okay? Get in, look around, and get the hell out. If she's sabotaging our hospital, who knows what else she is capable of?"

"You're right. I'll be on mission. It's not that big of an apartment, and very few places to keep dead rats preserved. It's gotta be the freezer or a mini fridge somewhere, right? I'm not sure about the expired equipment. That could be anywhere."

"I wouldn't worry about that. If she has dead rats in a freezer, I think that's enough of a coincidence to assume she's the one doing it."

"But then what? Is what she's doing illegal? Where do we go with the information once we have it?" asked Peter.

"I'll run it by the detective and see what he thinks. Gotta be some law against bringing dead animals into a hospital and tossing them around."

Peter washed his hands, and then they headed back toward the table.

"All I'm saying is you two make a cute couple. I've enjoyed meeting you and wouldn't mind doing this again some day," said Val.

"Thank you for saying that. But he already broke up with me. Maybe you need to talk to him instead," said Emily.

"Welcome back, boys. Did you enjoy going to the potty together?" said Valerie, poking Bryce in the side.

"Bryce is very gentle, actually. He would make an excellent home nursing aide," said Peter.

"Whatever. Hey, we need to get rolling out of here. The kids like to see us before they go to bed. Thanks for joining us tonight, you two. Peter, I'll see you at shift change tomorrow night. The election is tomorrow, so I'll be out campaigning all day. Maybe we can celebrate my victory if the results come in early."

The two couples stood and exchanged goodbye hugs and handshakes. Peter handed his claim ticket to the same kid working the valet podium, and soon they were cruising back toward Emily's apartment. "Did you have a good time tonight?" he asked.

She reached over and grabbed his hand before closing her eyes and smiling. "Yes, I did. Peter, I miss this. I miss you. I miss us."

"Me too, Em," he said. They drove the rest of the way in silence, though it was easier for her since she fell asleep. Peter caught himself starting at her repeatedly during breaks in traffic.

Are you truly the one sabotaging the hospital? Or are you just a girl hopelessly in love with a guy who broke your heart?

Chapter Fifty-Five

Peter held onto Emily and led her through the short hallway toward her apartment door. She reached a hand behind him and grabbed onto his butt, giving it a firm squeeze. "I've missed that fine body of yours, Peter. You're not just going to run away once you drop me off, are you? It's been a long time since I've been on the Thrasher. It's still my favorite thrill ride, you know."

Peter squeezed her tighter and laughed. "I take over for Bryce tomorrow afternoon, so I guess I have some time to hang out. I think you may have had a bit too much to drink, though. Let's just get you inside first."

Emily fell backward onto her leather sofa and landed with a thud. She kicked her heels off and stretched out across all three cushions while Peter poured two glasses of water in the kitchen. He opened the freezer to grab ice and saw a brown cardboard box in the corner, marked with a bar code and an industrial label. He grabbed a handful of ice and leaned in closer to read the label, but Emily's voice from the other room startled him. "What are you doing? Get in here, babe." He shut the freezer door and sat down next to her on the couch. She put her legs on top of his and drank half the glass of water in one effort.

"What do you think of the hospital lately?" asked Peter. "It's gotten pretty intense with the accreditation review not going well. Everyone is on edge. I've never seen the administration of a hospital act so nervous. Bryce is pretty pissed and thinks someone is sabotaging us."

Emily took another drink of her water and sat the glass on the table in front of the sofa. "I don't know. I know that can be a serious problem if we fail the review. They could shut the ER down. If that happens, you'd have to go somewhere else for a job, right? We'd leave this city and just go somewhere else? Like maybe Florida? Or Hawaii?"

Could that be the reason she was sabotaging the accreditation reviews? Is she trying to force me to leave the city and take a job somewhere else? "I don't know. I haven't heard of an ER being shut down at a major hospital, but I guess it's always a possibility. If we can't pass the next inspection, I may have to go somewhere else."

Emily grabbed her dress and began to pull it up slowly up her legs. "That would be a shame. You were just getting to know some nurses, weren't you, Peter?"

What has she heard about my social life? "Yeah, I actually know a few of their names now. It's only taken me about a month."

"Oh stop it Peter, I know how they look at you. It's the same way I do. Do you remember how you used to look at me?" She pulled the dress up higher, revealing the lighter skin of her thighs usually hidden from the sun. He couldn't help but stare. "It's fun to look at each other, isn't it, Peter?"

Inside his head he saw Bryce's face and recalled what he was told a few hours earlier, *'Whatever you do, don't screw her, just scope out the*

apartment, and then we'll get the police involved if you find anything.'
But Bryce wasn't here right now. And neither was his willpower.

He adjusted himself on the couch, leaning forward to set down his glass on the table. He cursed his weakness for the opposite sex, but figured what could one more round hurt? *I'll scope the place out after she falls asleep and then leave before she's awake.* He placed a hand on her right calf and rubbed it slowly. "Yes, I do."

Emily closed her eyes and moaned softly. "I was hoping this was going to happen tonight. I even laid out our stuff in the bedroom. Let's go!" She sat up quickly and pulled her dress over her head, then threw it at his face. By the time he cleared it away, she was walking into the bedroom.

Sorry, Bryce. He pulled his arms behind his back and stretched before following her through the door.

He saw the room was empty, but heard the shower running. The bed had the comforter pulled back and looked very inviting. He leaned into the bathroom and saw Emily standing at the sink, taking her contacts out. "I'm going to shower and shave really fast," she said. "I wasn't sure I was going to have company tonight, so I didn't prepare completely. Why don't you make yourself at home and when you hear the water stop, come in and dry me off whatever way you want?" She playfully pushed on his chest to twist away from him and entered the shower enclosure. Peter watched her through the door for a minute before shaking his head and refocusing. He turned and walked out of the bathroom, the sound of the shower clearly heard throughout the apartment.

He scanned his eyes around the bedroom, looking for any evidence of her involvement in the sabotage. He quickly opened every drawer he could find, looking for expired equipment from their last hospital. Finding nothing, he listened again for the sound of the shower, which hadn't changed. He moved back into the main room and examined everything. Nothing jumped out at him until he went into the kitchen. He jogged to the freezer and went to re-examine the box. He leaned in and found the label that read "Domestic Rat, Preserved in Formalin".

Emily watched Peter exit the bathroom and counted to twenty. After the count, she slipped out of the shower and peaked into the bedroom, finding it empty. She then silently walked toward the bedroom door and peaked around it, finding Peter in the kitchen, face pressed into the freezer. Emily ducked back behind the door and quickly made her way back to the shower. She waited another ten seconds and turned off the water. "I'm all done. Are you ready to get started?" she yelled. "Hand me a towel, would you?"

Peter heard her voice and shut the freezer before hurrying back into the bathroom. He picked up a towel and held it out for her. Emily walked toward him and leaned in, wrapping herself in the offered towel. She took a second towel and wrapped it around her head like a turban. "Peter, go lay on the bed. And take off all those clothes. You're making me feel overdressed."

"Yes ma'am, you're the boss," he said before stripping off his clothes down to his boxers. He climbed into bed and rested with his hands behind his head, waiting for her to join him. *Wait a minute, why was the carpet wet?*

Emily walked out of the bathroom, typing on her phone. "Sorry, just finishing something up. What music do you want?"

"I don't care. I'm not here for the music, just the performer."

Emily smiled at him. "Well, I've taken a liking to Cake recently. The song 'The Distance' seems appropriate for now." She tapped her phone and a staccato guitar riff came from the speaker on her desk. She strutted toward him in sync with the beat and pulled on the towel tucked in to her chest, allowing it to fall to the floor. Peter laid still as Emily climbed onto the bed and straddled him, resting her hands on his chest. He reached up for her, but she caught his hands and threw herself forward, pinning his arms to the bed before leaning in to kiss him.

A metallic sound came from his left at the same time he felt something cold on his wrist. He looked over and saw she had him handcuffed to the bed frame. Emily sat up and pulled the towel off of her head. She leaned down and let her wet hair cover Peter's face while she reached toward his right arm.

Chapter Fifty-Six

"You still have those? We haven't used them in over a year," he said. "I hope you still have the key," he said with a nervous laugh. *Oh man, Bryce is going to kill me.*

"Relax, of course I have the key. But if I can't find it, then we'll just stay here and make love until we're old." She locked the second cuff into place on his right wrist, the other end connected to the metal bed frame, then grabbed her phone and turned the music up as high as it would go. She then typed another text and set her phone on the nightstand.

"Okay, now what? I can't do all my patented moves if I'm hand-cuffed to the bed. And who are you texting in the middle of this?"

The smile left Emily's face. She put her hands on his chest again and looked away. "Peter, we had everything. Life was perfect. We worked together, made good money, had a great social life. Then we moved here and you broke up with me. That crushed me, Peter. You destroyed my happiness. You destroyed us. I had given up on medical school and found my place in life, by your side. Why be a doctor when I can just marry one and still work in the hospital with you?"

Peter's skin flushed, and he adjusted himself on the bed. He tested the handcuffs but found them well secured. *Uh oh. Is she going to kill me before Bryce gets a chance to?*

"I wouldn't pull on those, could cause a pressure sore. I thought life was going well, but only because I didn't know any better. Once you dumped me, I was able to find better. I met a guy who has your good looks but comes from an enormous amount of money. We're going to travel the world together. Once we right a few wrongs here, of course."

Emily climbed down off the bed and exited the room. Peter looked around in a panic, searching for something he could reach with his feet. They found only clothing and bedsheets. He could not press his feet against anything to use for leverage, so he slumped back into bed, defeated.

"Emily, where does this end? What are you after?" he yelled.

She bent her head around the door frame. "I'm after happiness in my life, Peter. That can't happen with you in it. As to what my boyfriend wants, that's different. He wants revenge."

"Revenge? For what? Who are you dating?"

She walked back into the room holding a small round piece of plastic with a fabric strap connected to it. "Here, we're going to put this bite block in your mouth. I can't have you screaming and trying to call for help. I brought some things from our last hospital we worked at. They were all expired anyway, so I figured no one would miss them." She again straddled him and then smiled, the evil intent stretching her smile wider than natural. She wiggled back and forth a bit on top of him. "Poor guy, your body is obviously confused. Your head knows it's in trouble, but it seems your heart still has hope."

She let out a quick laugh and then continued. "How did the accreditation people like the expired goods? I see you found the rats as well. Honestly, I was proud of that one. The worst part was having to bring one to work every day since I never knew when the reviewers were going to show up. Have you ever packed your lunch in a container with a dead rat?" She made a face like she was going to vomit. "I wasn't even working the day of the last visit, but that idiot Diane posted on the department Facebook group about it, so I rushed right in."

She bent over his head and placed the strap behind his neck. This brought her breasts to eye level with Peter. He mentally kicked himself again and then stared at her face. The woman he had once loved was now his captor. *I don't like where this is going. If I don't try something now, I'm screwed.*

As the device neared his lips, he started coughing loudly and launching as much spit at her as he could. Emily made a face and sat back up, wiping her face with her hand. As she did this, Peter inhaled and suddenly bent his hips to lift his legs off the bed. He spread them wide and wrapped them around her chest. He slid his legs higher and locked his ankles around her neck, squeezing for all he was worth.

Emily grabbed his legs with her hands and struggled against his superior strength. She realized her hands were no match for his leg strength and quickly smashed her elbow into Peter's groin. He screamed and twisted his body away from the blow, throwing her off the bed and onto the floor. Her weight pulled his wrists against the handcuffs, but he did not let go. *You'll be unconscious in ten seconds.* She flailed her arms around, struggling to breathe as the strength slipped from her body.

"Peter," she gasped. "Don't. I'm pregnant."

Chapter Fifty-Seven

P eter heard the words and relaxed the grip on her neck a bit, but did not let go.

"You're what?"

"I'm pregnant!" she cried. "I didn't want to tell you, but you were about to kill me. Well, us."

Peter uncrossed his ankles and released Emily from his grip. She scurried backward, out of his reach and rubbed her neck.

"Thank you," she said.

"Sure, now let me out of these stupid handcuffs."

"Sorry, not gonna happen. At least not yet. You're the bait in the mousetrap." She laughed quietly and then continued. "Actually, the Bryce trap."

"What the hell does that mean? And when did you find out you're pregnant? How far along are you? Is it mine?"

"I'm not really pregnant, you idiot. I just said that so you'd let me go. Do you seriously think I'd let you impregnate me?"

"You're insane," said Peter, shaking his head slowly while maintaining eye contact with her.

"Am I Peter? Maybe we all are. You came back here expecting to, what, exactly? Search my apartment, find out I was the one sabotaging the ER, then go turn me in? To who? For what?"

Emily stood up and walked to the end of the bed. She made put her fingers in the air in a mock terror pose. "Help me! I found the girl who put a rat on the floor!" Her voice was getting stronger, and she proved it with a deep laugh.

Peter pulled his legs back onto the bed and pushed himself up higher, taking the tension off his wrists. "Why are you doing this?" he asked.

"Why not? What else am I supposed to do? The medical establishment has rejected me. I'll never be a doctor. You broke up with me. I have no family. I'm not about to just start over and pursue some different career. Screw that. I found my lottery ticket out of this mess. All I need to do is get Bryce here and then we're off to warmer weather."

She left the bedroom and returned holding a steak knife. "Now, let's get that bite block in you. Don't resist or I'll have to get pokey." She picked up the bite block and strapped it around Peter's neck and placing the device in his mouth.

Peter yelled through his open mouth, making loud but unintelligible sounds.

"Well, that won't do. You're making too much noise. We're going to have to quiet you down with something."

Emily scanned the room until she saw a pile of clothes on the floor from earlier in the day. She walked over and picked up two pieces of clothing and then stood next to Peter. She held a sock and a pair of underwear next to his head, pondering which to use.

"I think the sock will be too thick. Let's use these instead." She stuffed the panties into the hole in the middle of the bite block and then tucked the extra around the other openings.

Peter tried to talk again, but it came out quite muffled.

"Much better," she said. "Now, let's get some sleep. Tomorrow is a big day."

She turned off the light in the room, picked up a pillow, and then laid down on the couch in the main room. She opened a secure texting application and began a dialog with Tony.

> Emily: The cheese is in the trap. Are you still on schedule?
> Tony: Good. I will be there tomorrow around noon.
> Van is clean. Can't wait to see you.
> Emily: Me too. Drive safe. Love you.
> Tony: You too.

Emily exited the app and picked up another phone. She sent a quick message and then powered it off. She then switched back to her phone, scanning through Instagram photos of the Caribbean until she drifted off to sleep.

Chapter Fifty-Eight

E mily woke up to an apartment full of sun. She heard a tapping coming from her bedroom and remembered she was sleeping on the couch.

Oh yeah, Peter's handcuffed to my bed! She laughed quietly and jumped off the couch before walking into her bedroom.

"Good morning, Peter. Did you sleep well?"

He tried to reply, but the bite block and clothing made his words unintelligible. He closed his eyes and huffed before extending both middle fingers toward Emily.

"Nope, not anymore. I found someone to handle that for you. In fact, he should be here in a few hours." She looked around at her room and frowned. "I need to get this place cleaned up before he gets here."

Peter crossed his knees and grunted at Emily.

"What? Do you need to pee?"

He nodded, eliciting a groan from Emily. She looked around her room before walking into the kitchen. She rummaged through a few cabinets before returning with a two-liter pitcher. "We'll have to make this work. If you spill any, I'm going to make you lie in it."

She helped Peter aim into the pitcher and then dumped the contents into the toilet. She then rinsed the pitcher and filled it with water before bringing it back into the room.

"Thirsty?" she asked with a smile.

Peter shook his head.

"Suit yourself." She set the pitcher on the table next to the bed and started cleaning the room. He watched her shower and then air dry herself as she continued to clean her apartment for her guest. Eventually, she dressed and prepared to go out.

Emily's phone rang, and she answered it immediately. "Hey, are you close?"

Peter watched her as she listened to the reply and then ran to the window and pulled the blinds apart to look out. "Is that you in the white van? Okay, I'll be right down."

"My chariot awaits. I'll be back soon. Need to go vote against your buddy Chapman and pick up some things for our trip. Then we'll hang out and wait for him to show up."

Peter shook his head slowly and grunted.

"You don't think he'll come looking for you? Then I'll just send him a text from your phone to get him over here."

A loud knock on the apartment door made Emily spin around and walk out of the room. She opened the door and welcomed Tony inside.

"What are you doing? I was about to come down."

"I wanted to see what the apartment looked like and how Peter was doing." Tony walked into the bedroom and stopped in the doorway, staring at Peter.

"You have got to feel pretty embarrassed right about now, huh? Big powerful guy like you gets kidnapped by your former girlfriend?

And then you end up being the bait that leads to your friend getting killed. If I were you, I'd be pretty pissed at myself."

Peter stared back at him but didn't respond.

"Nothing to say? Fine. I wouldn't talk either. I'd have bent that bed in half and broken free within ten minutes of being locked up. But you're no man. You're some candy-ass meat head who is about to get his friend killed."

Peter mumbled something unintelligible because of the bite block.

"What's that?" said Tony, stepping closer.

Peter again mumbled something, but softer this time.

Tony took another step toward him and leaned in. "You're going to have to speak up if you want to be heard, little man."

Peter flexed his arms and then his lower body, raising his legs off the bed in a rocking motion. When he had enough height, he kicked his left leg out and struck Tony in the side of the head, knocking him backward a few steps.

"You bastard," said Tony, regaining his footing. "You're going to pay for that one." He quickly lunged toward Peter to get inside the reach of his legs and lashed out with his right hand, smashing into the left side of Peter's face. He pulled back and delivered another blow directly to Peter's head.

"Enough!" yelled Emily.

Tony turned to look at Emily, his arm cocked back to deliver a third blow. She took a step back when she saw the look on Tony's face. His eyes were wide with rage, mouth hanging open and breathing hard through it.

"He's not the one you're after. Let him be," she pleaded.

Tony huffed and lowered his hand to his side. He backed away from Peter and then checked his appearance in the mirror in her bathroom, his anger vanishing as quickly as it had appeared.

"Okay, let's get out of here. I want to be back and in position before Bryce shows up." He walked past Peter and shook his head at him. "Handcuffs or not, I could destroy you."

Chapter Fifty-Nine

B ryce woke at six o'clock and was out of bed in seconds. He stood at the side of the bed and stretched slowly as the pain and spasm of his car accident made themselves known again. After finishing his bathroom routine, he tried to sneak out of the bedroom but Val called his name he left.

"Bryce, you leaving already?"

"I have to. Polls opened ten minutes ago. I'll be out until they close. Would you mind bringing the kids and joining me at a few polling locations later?"

"Sure, but it will be after ten o'clock. Good luck honey, I hope you win this."

"Me too. There's a lot riding on the outcome. See you soon."

"Hey, wait. Did you hear anything from Peter?"

"Yeah, he struck out. Said he couldn't find anything yet, and it was going to take some more investigation. Then he added a bunch of kissy-face Emojis. I'm guessing they're back together, at least for now."

"I really like Peter, but he sure has a weak spot for women. It's going to get him in trouble one of these days."

"If it hasn't already. I think he's dated half the department already."

He closed the door and slipped quietly into the garage, where he grabbed a Diet Coke and then climbed into his car. He paused and then got out and found a six-pack cooler, filling it with more cans and ice, before finally backing out of the garage. *I'll cut down tomorrow.*

He glanced at the cardboard yard sign that displayed his name in large block lettering and encouraged his neighbors to vote for him for coroner. *Can't wait until I can throw that away.*

Bryce pulled out the list of the polling locations that had the largest voter turnout last election and plugged the address into the map on his phone. Ten minutes away. He sighed and began the trip to the first location.

When he arrived, there was a small line of voters standing outside waiting for their turn to enter and cast a ballot. Bryce parked his car, now adorned with large magnets displaying his name and candidacy, in a spot not quite the closest to the door. He put on a hat with his name on it and checked his appearance in the mirror. He looked down at his shirt, that also had his name on it, and sighed again. *Here goes.*

Bryce walked toward the entrance to the polling place and stopped near a parking island containing over a dozen political signs. He looked at another man standing there and saw they were holding a sign that read 'Chapman for Coroner'.

The man turned to see who was joining him and smiled when he saw it was Bryce. "Hey, are you Dr. Chapman?"

Bryce nodded and shook the man's hand, noticing a silver badge on his belt.

"We are happy to be out here supporting you, doc. That coroner's office should never have released the alcohol level on Jenkins until they had confirmed the sample was his. That's elementary level stuff right there."

"I agree. How long have you been out here?"

The officer beamed with pride. "I got here at 5:45 a.m. There's always a line outside waiting so they can vote and move on with their day before the lines get bad. There must have been twenty of them, and I'm pretty sure they're all going to vote for you."

Bryce's face widened into a smile. "Really? That's amazing. Thank you."

"No offense, but who really cares who the coroner is, right? I mean, who gives it a second thought unless there's a reason to care? Well, Zachary Pullard gave us a reason and now we're out here to make sure he is gone. Chief Booker said you're the man for the job and that's good enough for me."

The officer turned to the crowd and called out to get their attention. "Ladies and Gentlemen, this is Dr. Bryce Chapman, running for the office of coroner. I and the rest of IMPD would appreciate if you could vote for him. Let's bring integrity and competence back to the office. Michael Jenkins deserves nothing less."

Several people in the line clapped, and many more nodded their heads as he finished his speech.

"Thank for you saying that. It's very humbling to hear someone speak that way about you," said Bryce.

"Well, get used to it. There's one of me at nearly every polling location today. Someone organized a sign-up sheet and we are covering them in shifts. Crime isn't getting any better in the city and we need someone we can trust backing us up."

Bryce shook the officer's hand again and headed back to his car, more energized than he had been in days. Each polling location he stopped at had a similar interaction with at least one officer campaigning for him.

He pulled into a grocery store and purchased a cooler, a thirty-pack of Body Armor, and a bag of ice. He poured the ice over the drinks and brought one with him to give the officer at the next location he stopped at.

"Here, it's getting hot out. I figured you could use something to drink."

"Thanks, doc. I appreciate it. You are going to win in a landslide," said the officer as he opened the drink. "I usually hate politics, but voting out an incompetent idiot makes it tolerable."

Bryce began to reply, but was interrupted by his phone ringing. "Excuse me a second," he said as he answered the phone.

"Chapman."

"Hey Bryce, it's Tom. How's the campaigning going?"

"Better than I expected. There are police officers holding my signs at every location. I think I may pull this off."

"Good, you deserve it. Have you heard anything from Peter? He was supposed to be here at eleven but he's not, and when I call him it goes straight to voice-mail."

Bryce's excitement and happiness plummeted like Icarus; neither seemingly meant for such heights.

"No, I haven't. I sent him a few texts this morning and have heard nothing. He's never late for a shift."

"I know. That's why I'm calling you. Was hoping you knew something," said Tom.

"Do you need me to come in and cover for a while? Are you guys busy?"

"No, it's not bad. Ash is here for a meeting and he said let him know if it gets busy. Would be nice to have someone here when my shift ends, though."

"Okay, just keep trying to reach him. I'll take a detour from campaigning and swing by his place and Emily's to see if I can find him."

Bryce apologized to the officer and excused himself, heading back to his car at a jog.

While he drove toward Peter's house, he called Val.

"Hey, you weren't planning on leaving to meet me for lunch soon, were you?"

"Actually, yes, I'm just getting the kids ready to walk out the door. Why?"

"I just got a call from Tom; Peter didn't show up to his shift today. No one has talked to him since dinner last night."

"I thought you got a text from him later that night?"

"Well, I got a text from his phone. No way to know if it was actually from him or not."

"What are you saying? Do you think someone kidnapped Peter?"

"No. I mean, I don't think so. How would Emily even do that? I'm sure he just drank too much and overslept or something. Maybe he got in an accident; I don't know. I'll let you know what I find at his condo."

Bryce ended the call and tried to focus on the road ahead of him instead of the images of his friend in all sorts of perilous situations. Soon, he pulled into Peter's complex and parked in front of his building. Peter's Maserati was not in his assigned covered parking space.

Where are you, Peter?

Bryce looked around in case Peter had parked elsewhere, but quickly ran out of places to look. He pounded on the front door intermittently for two minutes before returning to his car, more apprehensive than before.

He found a text from Peter that contained Emily's new address and told his phone to navigate there. Fifteen minutes away.

Images of Peter in trouble became harder to shake from his mind. He turned on the radio and tried to distract himself as he followed the turns announced by the robotic female voice on his phone.

Bryce turned in to Emily's apartment complex and immediately saw Peter's Maserati parked in front of her building.

Thank God. Time to get up and go to work, you hedonistic fool.

Bryce jogged up the stairs to Emily's apartment and knocked on the door. No answer. He knocked louder and longer and still got no response.

He called Peter's phone, but it again went immediately to voice-mail. *Damn it!*

Bryce shoved his phone back in his pocket and then aggressively pounded on the door again, yelling Peter's name.

A door opened behind Bryce, who spun around quickly and took a defensive stance.

"Woah, easy there," said a neighbor, putting his hands up in front of him. "I'm just checking to see who is making all that noise."

"Sorry, I'm looking for my friend. His car is there, but he won't answer his phone, and I'm afraid he might be in trouble."

"Well, as loud as you pounded, I'm sure the problem isn't that he's just asleep. I heard someone leave here about half an hour ago. Are you sure he didn't leave with Emily?"

"Maybe, but I don't think so. He was supposed to be at work an hour ago."

"Oh, I didn't think he had a job. She said he just drifted around and did what he wanted. Independently wealthy guy, I guess."

"What? No. He's an ER doctor who works at Washington Memorial with me." Bryce pulled out his phone and showed the neighbor a picture of Peter.

"No, that's not him. Here, I took a pic a few days ago when they came over for drinks." The neighbor pulled up a pic and showed it to Bryce, whose mouth dropped open in surprise. He was staring at a picture of Tony Proffit.

"That's the guy who has been staying here?" asked Bryce, pointing to the picture.

"Yep. Nice guy."

"Okay, thank you. I need to get going. If you see my other friend, tell him to call me."

Chapter Sixty

"Stephenson," said Gregory, answering his phone on the first ring.

"Hey, it's Bryce Chapman. I need your help. I think a friend of mine is in trouble."

"What sort of trouble?"

"I think someone has kidnapped him. We have been looking into an issue at work and he was going to look around our suspect's apartment last night, and I haven't heard from him since."

"Your suspect? Was this breaking and entering? I can't be a part of this Bryce. If you think he's in trouble, call 9-1-1."

"No, it's not like that. They used to date. We all went out to dinner together and then they went back to her apartment. He was supposed to show up for work today at 11 a.m. but never showed up. He won't answer his phone, but I found his car at the suspect's apartment. I think he's in trouble."

"You think his former girlfriend kidnapped him? Is he a smaller guy?" asked the detective.

"No, quite the opposite. But he has a weakness for women and loses his mind in certain situations. Look, I'm going over there and if she won't open the door, I'm going to kick it down. I'd prefer if you were close by in case there is trouble after that."

"Like I said, I can't be part of this, Bryce. Facilitating a home invasion? What is it with you and breaking and entering? If you get arrested right now, you'll probably lose the election. And you know what that means."

"I don't care. I think my friend is in trouble and I'm going to do whatever it takes to check on him. I just told you I'm going to kick someone's door down, maybe you should be there to arrest me, once I do. But if we find evidence of a kidnapping, then you have to get involved, right?"

"Okay. I've trusted you this much and you sort of gave me an out. What's the address?"

Bryce shared Emily's address with the detective, who agreed to meet there in twenty minutes. He jumped in his car and drove off toward Emily's apartment, kicking himself for allowing Peter to put himself in this situation.

I'm sorry buddy, never again. You shouldn't be the one in trouble; you're new to the hospital with no family ties to Indianapolis. Your personality would get you hired anywhere you wanted to go.

Bryce waved his hand in apology as a blast from a horn signaled its driver's displeasure with Bryce's aggressive driving.

Hang on, man, I'll be there in a few.

"Come on, we need to get back. Bryce is going to figure it out soon enough and come looking for him. We need to be ready," said Tony.

Emily waved him off and continued walking through the aisles of Von Maur. Today was her day to pick out a new wardrobe before they left for a warmer climate. Peter wasn't going anywhere. And the way she had Tony enamored, neither was he. She pulled a light blue dress off the rack and held it against herself.

"What do you think? Would this be okay for Belize?"

Tony nodded quickly, glancing around the store. "Yeah, just grab it and let's go. I want to be in the apartment when Bryce comes by.

Emily huffed and put the dress in her cart. "You're no fun. I guess I'll just buy the rest when we get down there."

They walked to the register, and Emily laid her items on the counter. The cashier was polite and tried to strike up a conversation with them, but Emily was the only one to interact with her. Until it was time to pay.

"That will be $406.43. Will this be cash or charge?"

"Cash," said Tony, pulling out five hundred-dollar bills and laying them on the counter.

The cashier completed the transaction on the register and placed the large bills underneath the tray in the drawer. She looked up with a concerned face. "I'm sorry. It looks like I don't have enough change to break that hundred. Do you happen to have any smaller bills? If not, that's okay, I'll just have to make change at my manager's office."

Tony smashed his palm on the counter, rattling the cash register and sending the cashier back a few steps. "No, I don't have any smaller bills. You don't keep ninety dollars in cash in your drawer? What kind of place is this?"

His outburst turned heads through half the store. *Not here, not now.* Emily quickly grabbed her items and folded them over her arm. "Tony, it's OK. They can keep the change. Let's just get going." She looked at the cashier and tried her best to reassure her. "I'm sorry, he has a medical issue that causes decreased impulse control. He doesn't mean it. Please, keep the change as an apology. Have a nice day."

Emily placed her hand on Tony's back and pushed him ahead toward the exit. "Let's go. I'll give you a pill when we get in the car." *Or five.*

Once in the van, she reached into her purse and removed a prescription bottle of Alprazolam. She removed one of the two milligram pills and handed it to Tony, along with a bottle of water. "Take this. You can't cause a scene like that. It's going to attract attention that we don't need. Try your meditation exercises and try to calm down."

"Sorry, I just really wanted to get out of there. Then when she didn't have the correct change, I lost it. That isn't happening as often as it used to, but I'm still not back to normal. Peter's kick to my head set me back a bit, I think."

No kidding. Emily rubbed his shoulder for a moment while he took the pill. "We'll head back to the apartment. I'll stop and get gas so we can head out once we have Bryce."

"Are you sure we'll be able to let Peter go? I think he knows who I am, and he certainly knows who you are," said Tony.

"Trust me. I have enough dirt on Peter to keep him quiet even if we kidnap his buddy Bryce. He didn't know about the hidden camera I used when we were dating. I have videos of him doing all sorts of humiliating things. Plus, there are a few things he's done in the hospital that I could probably have his medical license revoked over." She grinned and grabbed Tony's thigh. "Can you imagine? Peter humiliated and unable to practice medicine. That would be amazing."

Tony smiled weakly and turned to look out the window while Emily drove back toward the apartment.

Bryce parked next to Detective Stephenson's empty cruiser. He jogged inside the apartment building, up a flight of stairs, and found the detective standing outside Emily's door.

"I knocked several times, but no one has answered. I keep thinking I hear something, but I can't be sure," said Gregory.

"Let me give it a shot," said Bryce. He kicked the bottom of the door with the sole of his shoe three times hard enough to rattle it on the hinges. He then cupped his hands to his lips and leaned toward the door. "Peter, it's Bryce!" he screamed.

Come on, say something. Make a noise.

A few faint thumping sounds penetrated the solid door, and both men leaned in closer to confirm the sound.

"That's all I need to hear. Stand back," said Bryce, sizing up the door in front of him. He rocked back on his heels, preparing to launch forward, when a hand on his shoulder broke his focus.

"Wait, have you ever kicked a door down before?" asked the detective.

"Nope. Good time as any to learn, though."

"It's not that hard. Aim just inside the handle with the ball of your foot. Don't kick the door, but aim a foot behind it so your momentum carries you through. This door has a wooden frame and should break the jamb easily."

Bryce picked his spot and checked his stance. *Just like kicking a field goal. Same cadence, strike through the target.* He lunged forward onto his planted left leg and kicked his right leg out toward the door. He struck it just inside the handle and followed through with his quad muscle and the entire weight of his body. A loud crack filled the hallway as the door jamb gave way and the door swung open. Bryce's momentum carried him through the entryway, and he found himself in an empty living room.

"No, stop," mumbled Greg as he stepped over the remnants of the doorjamb and entered the apartment, his palm resting on the grip of his handgun.

Bryce heard the thumping sound coming from a door to his right. He reached out to turn the knob, but it was locked. He stepped back to line up a second door breech when again a hand to the shoulder paused his effort. Bryce turned around, hands ready to fight whoever it was.

"Relax, cowboy. That was a nice entrance, but this one should be easier." The detective reached over the door frame and removed a small brass key. He inserted it in the doorknob and unlocked it with a simple twist of the wrist. Bryce turned the knob and pushed the door open. He saw Peter laying naked on the bed, a thin sheet draped over his lower half.

The two entered the room quickly with Bryce going to Peter's side and examining him. A plastic bite block held his mouth open, packed tight with a pair of women's underwear. A large bruise covered the swollen left side of his face, with his left eye swollen shut. *What the hell?*

He removed the bite block and the underwear while the detective checked the bathroom and the rest of the apartment.

"The place is empty," he said and then looked at Peter. "Are you okay?"

Peter opened and closed his mouth several times and moved his jaw back and forth. "I think so. I have a killer headache and I gotta take a monster dump. Been holding that in for a day."

Bryce grinned at his friend. "I think you're going to be okay. But let's get you out of here and evaluated at the hospital. You look like you got worked over pretty hard. Who did this to you?"

The detective examined the handcuffs and reached into his pocket. He pulled out a key and placed it in the hole, unlocking each in quick succession. "Glad the key fits. These cuffs are the real deal."

Peter rubbed his wrists and examined the superficial wounds on each of them. "I know, I bought them. Emily's boyfriend hit me in the face. Real cheap shot too. Listen, Emily and her boyfriend said they would be back in a few hours, and that was a while ago. They may be back at any minute."

"Okay, I'm going to call this in. It's time to report this to my department." The detective stepped out into the main room and left the other two alone.

"Peter, are you really fine? I am so sorry this happened. I knew she was a bit nuts, but didn't think it was this bad."

"Tell me about it. I think her new boyfriend has her brainwashed. It's like she's a completely different person. All she talks about is money and getting out of Indiana. She would sit in that chair and show me pictures on her iPad of where she's going to travel. The dude must be loaded."

Bryce found Peter's clothes and handed them to him. "I wonder if he knows she's nuts."

"Absolutely. I think this was actually his idea. I heard them talking about using me to get to you."

Bryce stopped and considered that. "Get to me? What do you mean?"

"I think she may be dating the guy who you saved in the Bahamas. His name is Tony, and he's a big dude. Dresses like he comes from money."

"I think you're right. A few hours ago, the neighbor showed me a picture of the two of them together. But how would that be possible? How did they even meet?" Bryce found Peter's clothes and handed them to him. "I'll give you some privacy. Come out when you're ready to get out of here."

Bryce joined the detective in the kitchen to give Peter some privacy and perhaps a shot at restoring his dignity.

"Hey, look in the freezer," said Peter from the other room.

Bryce opened the freezer and saw the cardboard box in the corner. He pulled it out and opened the lid.

"Oh, that's disgusting," said the detective. "Who keeps frozen rats in their kitchen?"

"Someone who is trying to get a hospital to fail its accreditation," said Bryce.

"You realize we came in here without a warrant and we can't use any of this as evidence, right?"

"Fortunately, the hospital doesn't need to bring a lawsuit to get rid of her. And we have Peter's testimony and face if they have any doubts whether I'm telling the truth."

Peter walked out of the room slowly. "I'm up. Let's get the hell out of here."

"I've got several officers on the way to secure this apartment and take a statement from you, Peter. Are you able to hang out for a bit?"

"Honestly, I'd rather get him checked at the hospital. Can you send someone over there to talk to him? If he has a fractured orbit or a head bleed, I'd like to know that sooner rather than later," said Bryce.

The detective agreed, and the trio exited the apartment, descended the stairs, and stood outside by the police cruiser.

"Peter, I will have a victim advocate reach out to you. They can help you with counseling and any other resources you might need."

"Thanks, but I'll be fine. I'd feel a lot better if you can arrest the two of them, though. The guy's name is Tony. I think Bryce can give you a lot more information about who he is. They met in the Bahamas earlier this year."

"Is that the guy you saved in that internet video?" asked the detective.

Bryce nodded. "Yep, some thanks I get, huh?"

"My department is looking into both of them, and we should have them soon enough. Why don't you two stay here with me until other officers arrive? Then one can escort you to the hospital, just in case."

"That would be great, thanks. Peter, do you want to sit in my car?" asked Bryce.

"Nah, I'm loving the feeling of the sun on my skin and the sounds of nature. Being stuck in bed for a day really sucked."

Bryce looked at a bulge in Peter's front right pants pocket. *That was empty when I handed them to him.* "Thrasher, what's that in your pocket?"

"What? What pocket?" said Peter, his face turning deep red.

"Tell me you didn't," said Bryce, laughing.

"Didn't do what?" asked the detective.

"Throw them away, Peter. I'm going to get you some help and introduce you to a wonderful lady at my church."

"Fine, you're probably right." He reached into his pocket and removed a pair of handcuffs. He stared at them briefly before throwing them into a garbage can outside the complex door.

Detective Stephenson shook his head. "Peter, I'm guessing it wasn't very hard for Emily to get the upper hand with you, was it? Listen to Chapman. Get some help before you really get taken advantage of." He looked at Peter's facial wounds and then added, "well, worse I guess."

Chapter Sixty-One

Emily drove in silence nearly all the way back. In less than twenty-four hours, they should be on their way to southern Florida with Bryce tied up in the back of the van. Tony had purchased a boat for cash in Ft. Lauderdale and hired a provisioning company to stock it with enough supplies for a month. *In less than a week, Bryce will be out of Tony's life forever and we can begin moving through the Caribbean without a care in the world. Screw medicine. It was going to be a long and difficult career path, anyway. The system has changed significantly in the last decade according to the doctors she's worked with. No one is happy. Everyone is burned out and looking for their next career. Might as well skip the career and marry straight into a comfortable retirement.*

"Are you sure we're good on funds?" she asked Tony.

"Yes. I've been investing heavily in crypto-currency for the last five years. My dad hasn't blinked an eye as I put over a hundred million of our family portfolio into the accounts. It's split between Bitcoin, Litecoin, Ethereum, and a few smaller coins. All of it is untraceable at this point, and he doesn't have the access codes to take it back. There are even ATMs where we can withdraw local currency from the crypto wallets."

A hundred million? Emily glanced sideways at Tony and imagined his body turned into solid gold. *How much does a hundred million in gold even weigh?* She looked at him with a combination of awe and pity. *Someone so rich, yet burdened by a cognitive impairment from his near drowning. He'll need someone by his side to help him through the rest of his life. Someone to help him make decisions and make sure he is safe. Someone to help him spend his money. Someone like me.*

"Baby, that's amazing. I'm so impressed. You'll have to teach me all about crypto. All I know is the one with the cute little dog. Doggy coin I think?"

Tony turned toward her. "It's Doge. Like saying doze with a lisp."

"Oh, okay. I think he's adorable. Hey, we're almost back. I'm going to park on the far side of the lot for now. I don't want to have this big van right by our door."

"Good idea. We can move it closer before we load Bryce in."

Emily pulled into the parking lot using the farthest entrance from her apartment. She parked the van and opened the side door to grab her new wardrobe items. She slammed the side door of the van closed and then turned around to walk toward her apartment. Her movement stopped when she ran into an arm held across her chest.

"Stop," whispered Tony. "There's a car in front of your apartment that looks like an unmarked police car. And who is that standing around it? They're looking in our direction."

No! It can't be! "Oh my God, that's Bryce and Peter," said Emily. "We're too late! We need to get out of here. If they see us, we're screwed." She turned around, opened the sliding door of the van, and tossed the bags back inside. They landed with a loud metallic crash.

The three men scanned the parking lot while they chatted and waited for the uniformed officers to arrive. They barely noticed a nondescript white panel van pulled in and park at the far end of the lot.

"Bryce, I think I'll take you up on that offer to meet someone from your church. But it may take me a while before I'm ready to date again," said Peter.

"I get it. You've been through a lot. Christmas is a few months away. That's always seemed like a romantic time to me," said Bryce. "In fact, I have an icebreaker you can use. When you're on the date, order a bottle of pinot. When the server brings it, smugly say, 'Most people think Christmas is a time for Noel, but I think it's a time for noir.'"

Detective Stephenson laughed only once at Bryce's joke. "Yeah, that will break the ice and you'll up frozen out of the date. Don't use that line."

"Thanks buddy, I've got my own system already," said Peter as he rubbed his wrists and flashed a broad smile to Bryce. "Tony hits hard, that's for sure. I owe him a few payback punches."

A loud thumping noise pulled their attention back to the panel van. The passenger side door was closed and a younger woman was walking away from the van.

"Hey, is that Emily?" asked Bryce. "And that big guy, is that Tony?"

Peter took a step toward the van. "I know that figure anywhere. I guarantee that's Emily. And that other guy is about to wish I was still handcuffed to a bed."

"Guys, let me take the lead on this," said Detective Stephenson as he ran past Bryce and Peter, his pistol in his right hand. His IMPD badge was clearly visible on his left hip. "Stop! Police!"

Detective Stephenson ran back toward his car, ripping the driver's door open with a quick pull. He looked at Bryce and Peter and said, "Take him to the hospital. I'll go after these two. I'll call you when I have them in custody." He slammed his door and pulled out of the parking space, the dash mounted lights making Bryce squint as he watched the car speed off in pursuit.

"Well, we sure timed that well. I think your day was about to get a lot worse, Peter," said Bryce.

"Not me, buddy. They were using me as bait to get to you. Tony had told Emily he planned to let me go once they captured you. I think they were planning to dump you in the Gulf of Mexico."

"Seriously? What did I ever do to her?"

"Man, I have no idea. I knew she bordered on the edge of crazy town, but it seems like she got elected mayor some time in the last few months. I think she's pissed off at the world and was more than happy to do whatever Tony wanted, as long as she'd have access to enough money to travel and never worry about working."

"What's Tony's beef? Is it still from when I kicked him into the wall at the Grotto?" asked Bryce.

"Seems to be. But something's off with him. He's not normal, Bryce. He has some impulse control issues and his temper is awful."

"I'm not sure what he was like before he drowned, but I wonder if those are a side effect of his anoxic brain injury. Either way, let's get you to the department and checked out. I'll feel a lot better when we get the call that they are in custody." Bryce opened the door for Peter and they headed to the hospital.

Emily and Tony heard a shouted command but could not make out the words over the sound of their doors opening. Emily jumped in the driver's side of the van and fired up the engine as Tony climbed into the passenger seat. She glanced back toward her apartment and saw the trio running toward them. *Does that third guy have a gun?* "Hang on." Emily pushed the accelerator and pulled out of the apartment parking lot, taking the turn fast enough to squeal the tires and throw Tony against the door.

"Hey, be careful," he said as he reached to lock his door and clicked his seat belt into place.

"Seriously?" She glared sideways at him. "We just kidnapped someone and you beat the hell out of him. Now it looks like the police are after us. We have no time for careful. Where did your hide your car? We need to get out of this van. It sticks out like a butterfly in a beehive."

"It's in a parking garage ten minutes away. I'll setup my phone to navigate to it."

"Hey, I think we need to get rid of the phones, too. If they know who we are, they're going to track us with them. And no more credit cards." She smashed her hand into the steering wheel. "Damn it, all we needed was a few more hours, or Bryce to show up without a cop."

Tony reached over and touched her shoulder. "It's okay, the money is still there. The only thing we missed out on was me getting even with Bryce. We'll just have to lie low and find another time to do it.

Let's get to my car, get out of town, find another car, and then get to Florida. The boat is ready to go."

Emily smiled nervously back at him. *Sure, it sounds good out loud. But there was a lot that needed to go right in order for that to happen. Once we have a clean vehicle, it should be easy enough to drive to Florida. No one can find us if they don't know what or where to look for.*

"Okay, I have it mapped out. Says we're six minutes away. I have a few thousand dollars in cash in my bag. We'll be fine. We just–," Tony's sentence was cut off by a ring tone coming from his phone. He looked at the caller ID and saw his father's name. He stared at the phone and didn't answer, choosing to allow it to go to voicemail. "I'm going to have to get in touch with my dad at some point. He won't say anything, but he'll want to know what's up."

Screw him. I am the family in your life now. "Okay babe, let's make the car swap, ditch the phones, and disappear," she said.

Chapter Sixty-Two

"Do you want the good news or the bad news?"

"Hit me with it Chapman; I can take it," said Peter.

"The CT scans were normal except for a broken nose. You have no other facial fractures and there's no bleeding in your brain."

"Which of that was the bad news? I actually think that's all pretty good news," said Peter.

"Well, with the broken nose, you'll need to avoid strenuous activity for the next few weeks. So, no weight lifting."

A soft knock interrupted their conversation, and they both turned toward the door as it swung inward. One of the newer nurses in the department poked her head in and looked at Peter. "Just checking to see how you are doing, Dr. Thrasher. I'm so sorry this happened. Is there anything I can get you?"

"Thank you, I'm fine. But I may need help choosing a restaurant for dinner later this week. Is that something you're certified in?"

She gave a soft laugh and turned to exit before looking back over her shoulder. "To be honest, I barely passed the restaurant selection course. I just couldn't finish the test on time. Too many options to choose from. But I received high honors for my work with the dessert menu." She let the words hang in the air, the door shutting punctuating the end of her sentence.

Peter gave a low whistle and turned to Bryce. "Exactly how strenuous of activity am I allowed to engage in?"

Bryce shook his head and buried his head in his hands. "What happened to that lady at church I was going to introduce you to?"

"I'll call her, I promise. But first we should call Diane Hopkins and let her know Emily sabotaged the site visits. We can have your detective friend attest to the presence of the same species of rat and the expired products in her apartment. I bet we can get those violations removed."

"Good idea. But let's worry about you for now. The department isn't going anywhere."

Bryce's phone buzzed in his pocket, interrupting the conversation.

He looked at the screen and answered immediately. "Hey Detective, it's Bryce. Did you get them? I'm here in the room with Peter; I'll put you on speaker."

"Hey guys, did Peter check out okay? Anything wrong on the scans?"

"Nothing major; I should be fine soon enough," said Peter.

"That's great news. I wish I could share some as well, but unfortunately, it looks like Emily and Tony slipped away. When I left the apartment, I wasn't able to find them right way. The other officers en route to the complex didn't see them either. We found the van in a parking garage, but of course it was empty. We're reviewing footage now to see if they left in another car or ran on foot. Don't worry, we'll keep looking for them until they are in custody. But you two should exercise extreme caution. We'll send an officer to watch your homes for a few days if that's okay."

"That would be great, thanks. Detective, I heard them talk about the Caribbean a lot. It sounded like they were planning to take a boat out from a Gulf state and head down," said Peter.

"Perfect, that helps a lot. I'll reach out to the FBI and get them flagged in all the databases. If they use a credit card or anything with their ID, we'll know immediately. I'll be in touch if I hear anything else. You guys do the same. Take care."

Bryce ended the call and looked at Peter. "I think what we all need is a vacation."

"Now that sounds like a great idea. Where are you thinking?"

"I still have that free week on a private island in the Bahamas. I'm going to call tomorrow and get it scheduled. It's time we had something positive to look forward to."

"We? Do I get to go?"

"I'm inviting everyone," said Bryce with a smile.

Epilogue

"Are you ready, sweetie?" asked Marybeth, holding her daughter's shoulders as they stood outside the courthouse.

"Yes, I'm ready to get past this and give closure to the Jenkins' family. Let's go."

"I'm proud of you for doing the right thing. The three months will be over before you know it. When you're out, we'll find a nice sunny place to celebrate."

Vincent Leoni led the way toward the courthouse entrance, followed by Mackenzie and Marybeth. He glanced down at a newspaper kiosk and smiled at the headline.

Dr. Bryce Chapman Wins Race for Coroner By Record Margin

"Hang on a minute, this old cowboy isn't as fast as the rest of you," said Charlie Hearst, hurrying to catch up to the group.

"Hi, Dad. You almost didn't make it in time."

"Sorry honey, I'm trying to wrap up the sale of the dealerships. This whole Jenkins thing has destroyed them, and I need to get some cash to pay off your mother's divorce settlement."

"Whatever. Let's just go," said Mackenzie.

Derek Chappelle met them just outside the courtroom. "Good morning, Mackenzie. We're just about ready to get started. Will you come with me for the administrative part? Your family can join for the formal plea proceedings. And Charlie, I wouldn't leave town if I were you. The two of us are going to have a chat about a car accident that happened the other day."

Marybeth sniffed loudly as a tear worked its way through her lacrimal duct and drained out of her nose. Vincent put his hand on her shoulder, which she quickly grasped and then leaned her head on.

Charlie huffed at the display of affection between his former spouse and his personal attorney. "You no-good, double crossin', son-of-a–" said Charlie before he was interrupted by his now ex-wife.

"Enough! You have no say in my life anymore, Charlie," said Marybeth.

He pursed his lips tightly and glared at the back of Vincent's head, but did not reply.

"Mr. Hearst, one last piece of business," said Vincent as he reached into his jacket with his free hand and held out an envelope toward Charlie.

"What in tarnation ya got for me now?"

"My resignation letter, sir."

THE END

Mailing List Signup

I hope you enjoyed reading *Deception*! Please take a moment to sign up for my mailing list to stay up-to-date on my new releases. As a free gift, you will receive a copy of *The Muddled Mind: An Eclectic Collection of Short Stories*. Seventeen individual short stories I have written across several genres. I hope you see you on the list!

Mailing List Signup

Acknowledgments

Deception would not have been possible without the ongoing support of my wife Cheryl and the frequent encouragement of my friends and family. Your comments, messages, and pictures you send while holding my book inspire me to keep going along this journey.

I'd like to thank my cover designer, Julia Duquette (https://www.intheblackwoods.com/), for creating such wonderful artwork. Julie Schrader (https://bookwormyogi.com/) is my proofreader, whose patience with my spelling, grammar, and punctuation is greatly appreciated.

To my beta readers, thank you for investing your time in my rough drafts and providing constructive feedback. Your advice helps make these stories come alive. Any errors in grammar or type setting are mine alone. Please reach out if you find errors, as I want my readers to experience the story without the distraction of grammatical issues.

Thank you for reading *Deception*! The next book in the series is titled *Vengeance,* an action-packed thriller set in the Bahamas. Scan the QR code to view *Vengeance* on Amazon in paperback or e-book.

Also By Brian Hartman

Bryce Chapman Medical Thriller Series:

Redemption (Book One)
Deception (Book Two)
Vengeance (Book Three)
Hanging By A String (Book Four, pre-order)

Psychological Thrillers:

Lake Sinclair
It Happened In The Loft

Short Story Anthology:

The Muddled Mind

About The Author

Dr. Brian Hartman is a practicing Emergency Medicine Physician in Indianapolis, Indiana. He is married to his wife Cheryl, a dentist with whom he has two boys, Evan and Andrew. They enjoy traveling to tropical locations, including several of the settings of Redemption. Brian began the formal pursuit of writing as a creative escape from the stress of the COVID-19 pandemic.

Redemption is the first novel in his medical thriller series starring Dr. Bryce Chapman. Brian has written dozens of short stories and has several independent novels in production. He transfers his experience as a practicing physician to the characters and events of the books, letting the reader see inside the mind and emotions of the team caring for patients. The lives of doctors and nurses do not stop when they leave the hospital and his books explore the events and back stories that make our lives interesting.

Brian enjoys interacting with his readers via email and social media. Find him online:

Website: https://www.brianhartman.me/
Email: brianhartmanme@gmail.com
Facebook: https://facebook.com/brianhartmanme.

Printed in Great Britain
by Amazon

33572721R00205